STONEHENGE

Harry Harrison
and
Leon Stover

CHARLES SCRIBNER'S SONS • NEW YORK

for
our wives
JOAN MARION HARRISON
and
TAKEKO KAWAI STOVER
who built Stonehenge
with us

CONTENTS

Nor is thy Stone-Heng a less wonder grown,
Though once a Temple thought, now prov'd a
Throne.
Since we, who are so bless'd with Monarchy,
Must gladly learn from thy Discovery,
That great Respects not only have been found
Where Gods were Worshipp'd, but where Kings
were Crown'd.

—John Dryden

Part One

1473 B.C.

I

In the grey dawn the city was as sharp-etched as a silhouette against the sky and the distant hills. Its presence commanded the valley all about it; the paths between the trees and fields led to it. The hill on which it sat was gently rounded at the base, but angled up steeply at the top to the city, thick-walled and impregnable. As the first light coloured the stone the great gate under the rampant, carved lions was swung open by invisible hands. Threads of smoke from the many cooking-fires within the walls rose straight up through the motionless air. A boy leading a goat came slowly along the rutted road between the fields; men and women with baskets of produce appeared down the lanes. They halted when they reached the road, stopped by the sound of sudden hoofbeats, staring with dumb curiosity at the two-horse chariot as it rumbled by them.

In the open gateway high above, the guards looked down with interest as the horses clattered on the stones of the ramp leading up to them. The charioteer was in a great hurry. One of the horses slipped and nearly fell; the rider lashed it forward. Since the sun was only newly risen the man must have been riding by night, a dangerous thing to do and one that evidenced a most unusual need for haste. The seasons came and went, the rain dampened the earth and crops sprang up, the animals were slaughtered and the young ones grew. This was the pace life moved at. There was no reason for unseemly haste by night that risked crippling and killing a sacred horse.

'I know him now,' a guard called out. He pointed his bronze-bladed spear. 'It is Phoros, cousin of the King.'

They drew aside, raising their weapons in salute to his rank as Phoros came up. His white cloak was black with blown spittle from the stumbling horses and he appeared no less tired himself. Looking to neither right nor left, he drove the exhausted animals through the tall opening of the gate, under the lions, and into the city of Mycenae.

Perimedes, War King of the Argolid and Master of the House of Perseus at Mycenae, was not at his very best. He had slept fitfully the night before—the wine perhaps, or the dull ache of old wounds, or, more surely, Atlantis.

'Oh, the bastards,' he muttered to no one and to everyone, slumping low in his great chair and reaching for the figs in the basket on the table before him. He chewed on one and even its rich sweetness could not sweeten his mood. Atlantis. The name alone stung like a thorn or even a scorpion's lance.

Around him the day's work of the great megaron was already beginning. With the king awake no one sleeps. There were occasional hushed voices; no one dared to speak too loud. On the elevated round hearth in the middle of the chamber the fire was being built higher to cook the meat, the fire he himself had kindled years before when the palace and this megaron had first been built. The thought did not warm him today, just as the figs could not sweeten him. Under a nearby canopy his two daughters and some house slaves were carding fleeces and spinning the wool into thread. They stopped talking when he glanced their way, turning their attention more closely to their work. Though his face was set in anger Perimedes was still a handsome man, heavy-browed, with a thin-edged nose above a wide mouth. He was well into middle age, yet his hair and beard were still as brown as in his youth and there was no thickening of his waist. The white scars of old wounds made patterns on the tanned skin of his arms, and when he reached out for an-

14

other fig it was obvious that the last two fingers were missing from his right hand. Kingship is something hard won in the Argolid.

The slave, Avull, entered at the far side of the megaron and hurried over to him, bowing low.

'Well?'

'Your cousin, the noble Phoros, son of . . .'

'Get him in here, you son of a chancred goat. This is the man I have been waiting for.' Perimedes almost smiled as the slave hurried away to usher in the ship's captain.

'We need you, Phoros. Come here, sit by me; they'll bring us wine. How was your voyage?'

Phoros sat on the edge of the bench and looked at the polished marble table-top. 'Uncle Poseidon in his might drove our ship quickly all the way.'

'I'm sure of that, but it is not details of the seafaring that I care about. You have returned with the ingots of tin?'

'Yes, but a small amount, less than a tenth of a ship-load.'

'Why is this?' Perimedes asked, quietly, a sudden pre-monition darkening his vision. 'Why so little?'

Phoros still stared at the table ignoring the wine in the gold cup that had been set before him.

'We arrived during a fog—you know there is much fog off the coast of the Island of the Yerni—then waited until it cleared and sailed along the coast to the mouth of the river we know. I beached the boat there and left men to guard it and followed the overgrown path to the mine. We came to the place where the tin is stored but there were no ingots there. We searched nearby and found some, but almost all were missing. The ingots are stored close to the mine.' Phoros looked up now, staring squarely at the king. 'This is not the word you wish to hear. The mine is destroyed, all there are dead.'

A wave of quick whispers died away as those nearest in the megaron passed the word backwards as to what had been said. Then there was silence and Perimedes was silent as well, his fists clenched, the only movement a heavy pulse that

15

beat beneath the skin of his forehead.

'My brother, Lycos, what of him?'

'I don't know. It was hard to tell. All of the bodies had been stripped of armour and clothing and had been there many months. The animals and birds had done their work. There was hard fighting there, a battle with the Yerni. All the heads gone, not a skull. The Yerni take heads, you know.'

'Then Lycos is dead. He would never surrender or be captured by savages like that.'

Anger burned a knot of pain in his midriff, and Perimedes kneaded it with his hand. His brother, the lost tin, the dead men, the Atlantean ships all coming together; these were dark, unhappy days. The pain did not go away.

'Is it true? My kinsman Mirisati is dead?'

Perimedes looked up at the angry man before him. Qurra, first among the chalceus, the workers in metal. There was the smell of smoke and sweat about him. He must have come directly from his furnace when he heard the news because he was wearing his leather apron, burned by many sparks, and soot was on his arms and smeared across his forehead. Forgotten, the stubby hammer was still clasped in his right hand.

'... dead, certainly,' Phoros was saying. 'Everyone at the mine must be dead. Mycenaeans do not become slaves.'

Had he been too ambitious? Perimedes thought. No, there had been no other course open to him. As long as the cities of the Argolid warred one with the other they remained weak. Lerna fought Epidaurus, Nemea sank the ships of Corinth. While at the same time the ships of Atlantis sailed freely where they would and grew rich. Only the united power of the cities of the Argolid could challenge that ancient power. The rocky plains of home had been tilled and bore fruit, but never enough. Across the sea were the tempting riches of many lands, and his people already had a taste for these riches. Bronze-armoured warriors with brazen weapons could take what they willed. Bronze made them. They ate bronze and drank it because they would be nothing without it. Soft golden copper was everywhere but that was not

16

enough. With the mysteries known only to them, the chalceus, the workers in metal, combined the copper in the burning throats of their forges with the grey tin, and the result was noble bronze. With this bronze Mycenae forged weapons to conquer, weapons as gifts for the other cities of the Argolid to bind them all together.

Mycenae no longer had bronze.

'The mine. We must reopen the mine.'

Perimedes spoke the words aloud before he saw that another had joined them, a short, brown man—Inteb the Egyptian, now wearing a robe of thin white flax instead of his usual rough working-clothes. Gold thread was set into the edge of the robe and there was a collar with precious stones about his neck; his black hair was oiled and glistening.

Then Perimedes remembered. 'You are leaving us.'

'Very soon. My work here is done.'

'It is a work well done, you must tell your Pharaoh that. Here, sit, you will eat with me before you go.'

The women quickly brought plates of small fish fried in oil, cakes drenched with honey, and salty white goats'-milk cheese. Inteb picked delicately at the fish with a gold fork taken from his pouch. A strange man, young for his work, though he knew it well. From a noble family, so in a sense he was the ambassador for Tuthmosis III as well as a builder. He knew things about the stars, could read and write, and had supervised the building of the new, massive outer wall of the city. As if this were not enough, through his craft he had erected the great gate and mounted above it the royal lions of Mycenae. It was well done indeed; nor had the price been high. Tuthmosis III, busy with his wars in the south, was no longer troubled by the Argolid raiders who sank his ships and burned his coastal towns. An arrangement between kings.

'You seem troubled?' Inteb asked, his voice bland, his face emotionless. He freed a fish-bone from between his teeth and dropped it to the floor.

Perimedes sipped at his wine. How much had the Egyptian heard about the tin-mine? There should be no stories going

17

back to Pharaoh of Mycenaean weakness.

'A king always has troubles, just as Pharaoh has troubles. That is the way of kings.'

If the comparison between the ruler of this brawling city state and the mighty ruler of all Egypt troubled Inteb he did not show it; he took a honey cake in his fingertips.

'I am troubled by the dung-flies of Atlantis,' Perimedes said. 'Not satisfied with their own shores, they come here and cause dissension among us. Their ships appear along the coast with weapons for sale, and our little squabbling princes are only too eager to buy. They know little of loyalty. Mycenae is the armoury of the Argolid. Some forget that. Now there is an Atlantean ship at Asine in the south, a floating bronze-smith's shop, doing business in our waters. But it will not be there long—nor will it be returning to Atlantis. My son Ason led our men against it as soon as we heard of its presence. You may tell Pharaoh of this. You have my gifts?'

'Safe aboard my ship. I am sure Pharaoh will be pleased.'

Perimedes was not so sure. He talked of equality among kings, but in his most innermost thoughts he knew the truth. He had seen Egypt, the cities of the dead and living, the teeming people and the soldiers. If that power were turned against Mycenae his city would cease to exist. Yet there was power and power—because Egypt was so great Mycenae did not become small. It was the first city of the Argolid and the mightiest, and that was something to be proud of.

'We will walk together before you leave,' Perimedes said, rising and buckling on the royal dagger of Mycenae, broad-bladed and set with jewels.

But before they could pass through the doorway there was a cry and they turned to see two men in armour half carrying a third man between them. He was coated with dust mixed with blood, and his mouth gaped in the agony of near exhaustion.

'We found him this way, crawling on the road,' one of the men said. 'He has word; he is one of those who marched with Ason.'

Once again the coldness possessed Perimedes. He could

18

almost hear the words the man would speak—and he did not wish to hear them. This was a day of evil. If there were a way to remove this day from his life he would. He seized the man by the hair and crashed him against the wall, and shook him until he gaped like a fish drawn from the water.

'Speak. What of the ship?'

The man could only gasp.

One of the slaves came running with a jar of wine and Perimedes tore it from his hands and dashed the contents into the exhausted man's face.

'Speak!' he ordered.

'We attacked the ship—the men of Asine, there ...' He licked at the wine that streamed down his face.

'Asine, what of them? They fought by your side, they are of the Argolid. The Atlanteans, tell me.'

'We fought—' he choked the words out one by one—'we fought them all ... Asine fought with Atlantis against us ... they were too many ...'

'My son Ason, in command—what of him?'

'He was wounded, I saw him fall—dead or captured ...'

'And you returned? To bring me this word?'

This time the king could not control the anger that flooded through him. With a single motion he drew his dagger and plunged it into the man's chest.

2

Inteb leaned against the rail, staring unseeingly at the bubble of foam and rush of water beneath the counter, equally unaware of the brawny form of the steersman a few paces away. It was spring and the storks would be crying in the reeds along the Nile and he would soon be home. Home after three years to the heart of the world and of civilization, away from the dirt and the petty squabbles of the barbarian Mycenaeans. He had done his duty, as distasteful as it had been at times. Some men were great generals and fought wars and served their Pharaoh in that fashion. Though violent death was the usual reward it was still an easy thing to do. Soldiers tended to be simple men because of this, and a little brutal, which was only natural considering that butchery was their trade. Tuthmosis III had need of these men. Yet he also had need of Inteb. Mycenae was the stronger for his having been there; but he felt that these years had been plucked from his life and lost to him.

But not completely. In all those months of bad wine, winter rains and burning summer sun he had found one thing, one memory that it would not be a distinct pleasure to forget, one man to call a friend. The friendship had been one-sided perhaps, since Ason knew him only as one of very many in the palace and gave him no pride of place. Strangely enough this did not bother Inteb; love did not have to be returned still to be love. He had been happy to sit at the feasting and wine-drinking, sipping his own while the others swilled, watching them grow nobly drunk. They were a rough unruly violent group of men, the nobles of Mycenae, and Ason could hold his own with any of them. Yet he was something more, a man destined to be a king, who had inherited his father's sharp turn of mind, who was more than just a loutish barbarian. Perhaps Inteb had imagined all this, and even that did not really matter. It had made the years bearable. Though he had not said so, he had been just as shocked by the news of Ason's death as Perimedes. The strength of Atlantis had brushed aside this great warrior and crushed him like an insect. It was faintly disturbing that he would soon be in the land of his friend's murderers.

The ship heeled over hard as they reached Spetse, and its wake cut a great white arc in the blue water. Perimedes must not know that he was on his way to the court of Atlantis, son-killing enemies of Mycenae. He would be angry if he discovered it, and the years of labour to effect the friendship with Egypt would be in danger. Therefore this navigational ruse. On the other hand Atlas, sea-king of Atlantis, might be slightly annoyed if he discovered that his Egyptian visitor had recently been dining with an enemy, but would probably be more astonished at the bad taste displayed. The tiny warring states were like fleabites on the thick hide of Atlantis; they could be either scratched or ignored. Singly or together, they did not pose any threat to the countless ships or the home islands of Atlantis. Atlantean vessels sailed where they wished in these seas and along the mainland shore, trading as far away as Egypt, and it was said that the glories of Atlas' court were on a par with those of Egypt. But Inteb would believe that after he had seen it for himself.

On the third morning the round bulk of the island of Thera lifted out of the sea. Inteb had dressed carefully in his best white flaxen robe, jewelled collar, and gold bracelets, then had sat quietly as the slave oiled and combed his hair. This was to be a state occasion. The captain was wearing a clean tunic as well and had made some attempt at a rough toilet; clots of blood spotted his face where he had shaved with a none-too-sharp blade.

The island was a green gem in the blue sea. Groves of olive trees marched in ordered rows right down to the shore, and there were freshly planted fields between them. The white buildings of villages could be seen among the trees, and a fishing village clustered around the red sand beaches of a cove where small boats were drawn up. For a moment, through a gap between the hills, Inteb glimpsed a city on a hill far inland, colourful buildings rising one above the other. Then the helm was put over as they headed west around the island.

Soon they turned a rocky headland, and a great cleft in the shore came into view. It was as though a god had struck it with a giant war-axe and cleaved the soil and stone. Its sides rose straight up, and it ran deep into the land. The captain stood by the steering-oar, guiding them around the headland and into the cleft itself.

The thin clear note of a horn sounded above the hissing of the waves against the stones of the channel wall. Inteb shaded his eyes with his hand and could make out the forms of helmeted soldiers on the cliff high above, dark against the sky. Lookouts certainly, to herald the approach of any ships. And more than that. It took very little imagination to see the rows of boulders that could be levered over to fall on any unwanted ships in the channel below. Or buckets of burning pitch. Atlantis could defend herself well here.

Another turn and the sharp cliffs fell away suddenly. It was as though they had passed a barrier; the channel became narrower and very straight. There were tilled fields close by on each side, and the peasants stopped work, leaning on their mattocks and shovels to gape at them as they glided slowly by.

'A canal?' Inteb asked. The captain nodded, looking ahead and resting one arm over the steering-oar.

'So I have heard said. They brag a lot these Atlanteans. But it could be true. That cleft through the hills, they couldn't

22

have done that, but this part would be easy enough to dig given time and enough men.'

Straight as an arrow's flight the channel ran, towards the rising hills inland. There was no sight of the city now, but another ship came into view in the canal ahead. Seeing it, the captain ordered in the oars and steered for the bank. The other ship approached swiftly, until they could clearly see the jutting horns above the bow and the glare of the yellow eyes painted beneath them. It was an Atlantean trireme a full forty paces long, its banks of white oars dipping and rising in perfect unison like a great bird's wings. Then it was upon them, sweeping alongside, towering over them. The drum could be heard, slow and steady as a heartbeat, the oars moving in unison with it. There must have been fifteen or more oars in each bank, too many to count as the ship slid by. A sailor in the prow looked at them curiously, as did two more on the mast, but otherwise they were ignored. The officers, magnificent in bronze armour, rich with enamels and gems, and with high plumes on their helmets, ignored them completely. As did the fat merchants sitting under an awning on the stern deck, laughing together, lifting golden cups with jewelled fingers. Wealth and strength on easy display. The high stern and great steering-sweep moved by, and a flurry of foam marked the ship's wake. It was past and gone and they rocked in the waves raised by its passage.

'Fend off that bank,' the captain shouted, and they were under way again. He pointed ahead. 'There, lord, you see now why we unstepped the mast.'

A black hole opened up in the hillside ahead and the canal ran into it and vanished. The rowers became aware of it too and looked over their shoulders and muttered together and missed the beat. The captain raised both fists over his head and swore at them in a harsh voice that could have been heard the length of the ship during the most savage storm.

'Sons of noseless whores, lice upon the stinking hide of beetles in a sun-blown corpse! Tend your rowing or I'll flay every one of you alive and make a sail of your poxy skins.

23

We are coming to a tunnel, no more. I have been through it and it runs straight, but is narrow. Watch your rowing or you'll be breaking oars or worse. We'll be through quickly enough if you don't fear the dark.'

The black mouth swallowed them up. It was most frightening for the men who were rowing because they saw the tunnel entrance fall behind them and grow smaller, all light vanishing with it. The earth could be engulfing them, the underworld consuming them. The beat of the drum echoed from the rock around them, rolling and fading with the sound of thunder.

From the rear deck the far entrance was clear once their eyes grew accustomed to the darkness; a bright beckoning disc. The captain steered for it, shouting encouragement to his men, but stopped when his voice echoed back like mad laughter.

The moment of entombment passed quickly enough and they slid out into the sunlight again, amused at their fears now that the tunnel was behind them. Inteb blinked in the light and all but gaped at this scene they had come upon so suddenly.

They had entered a circular lagoon, rimmed by low hills on all sides that ran down in gentle slopes to the water. Grapes grew richly in this sheltered bowl, and the green shoots of the spring-sown crops were already high. Porticoed villas as well as simpler dwellings were half shielded by the tall trees. In the lagoon was an island, connected by bridges to the shore, almost filling it so that the lagoon became a moat of surrounding water. Moored on this island were the ships of Atlantis, row after row of them, almost too many to count. Triremes and beaked warships, fat-bellied merchantmen and swift galleys. Behind the ships were the busy docks and warehouses, and beyond them rose the hill and the city that Inteb had only glimpsed for a moment from the sea.

This was Atlantis.

Atlantis was a riot of colour that almost hurt the eyes, of brilliant paintings on white plaster that made a jungle of

24

unreal birds and leaves. There were living creatures in this jungle as well, monkeys climbing on the rooftops and porches, along the beams. Inteb had seen these strangely human beasts before, but never in such numbers. Other animals too, donkeys bearing loads, cats watching everything from the open windows. Most curious of all were the elephants, which seemed to roam at will. They were totally unlike the great African war elephants that he knew; these were as small as horses and far lighter of skin. The people made way for them and occasionally would reach out to touch their thick hides for luck or for blessing.

Inteb stood on the summit of the acropolis and the soaring blue walls of the royal palace rose before him in a majesty that did indeed rival that of Egypt. Then the bronze-covered doors swung open and he was bowed through by servitors in royal blue robes.

Within was a hall, and then another hall that ended in a stairway, all dimly lit with soft light that filtered down from above. There was chanting in the distance and the smell of incense and a half silence broken by the shuffling footsteps of the slaves who followed him with the gifts. Men passed, slim-hipped and dressed in tight-fitting short garments, looking at him as curiously as he did at them. On the walls were frescoes of these same youths clutching the horns of charging bulls and dancing in the air above them. More paintings, of odd fish and many armed squid, waving underwater plants—then flowers and birds. Women passed, as strangely attractive as the men, wearing many-coloured skirts in tiers, tiny hats perched high on their elaborately curled and combed hair, their bare breasts full, and cupped out and supported, nipples tinted blue. There were other women who were dressed for the hunt; the royal hunting preserve was well known and they would be on their way there. They wore brightly painted calf-high leather boots, and short green skirts that ended above the knee and were held at the waist by a wide, bronze-studded leather belt. Supporting straps from each side of the belt crossed in the middle of their chests and passed over each shoulder. Since the women wore

25

no upper garments, these served to outline their bare breasts and draw attention to them—which Inteb thought slightly disgusting. Then there was sunlight again as he emerged into the roofless megaron at the heart of the palace.

Word of Inteb's arrival must just have reached King Atlas who appeared to be holding court, seated on a high-backed chair against the far wall beyond the hearth. Clerks with clay tablets were being hurried from his presence while a prisoner in wooden fetters was pushed out by the armoured guards. Inteb drew back into the shadows until the disorder ceased, to make a proper entrance as befitted his rank and mission. The prisoner, naked except for a breech-clout, was bruised and filthy with caked blood. One of his guards thumped him in the ribs with the pommel of his sword to move him faster and he stumbled, then looked back over his shoulder to curse the man.

Inteb stood stunned and unmoving.

It was Ason, son of Perimedes, prince of Mycenae.

This time the guard hit harder, Ason slumped and was half dragged from the chamber.

3

Ason awoke to darkness, not knowing if it were night or day in the black hole where he had been imprisoned, not caring. The various aches in his body had now merged into one gigantic whole, a pain of outrageous proportions that seemed to be centred about his head. When he started to sit up the pain leapt upon him like a waiting animal, dropping him back to the unyielding stone floor. The next time he tried he was more careful. He now knew the pain as an enemy he would defeat. He ran his hands over his body and could find no new wounds, or rather none of any importance. Then, with utmost care, he touched his fingers to the throbbing in his temple, to the contused swelling there.

It was night. It must be night if he were imprisoned in the same place he had been before. The acrid reek of dung was in his nose. The same place: the bull pens. The lion of Mycenae in the stables of the bull of Atlantis. But not dead yet. He dragged himself painfully across the floor to the trough of running water. It was cool and he buried his face in it, then his entire head, holding his breath as long as he could while it leeched away some of the pain. Then, a bit at a time, he managed to manoeuvre himself until he was sitting with his back against the cool stone wall.

He must have slept in this position because more time passed and when he opened his eyes again there was a ring of light about the great wooden door and he could hear the scraping of the bars being pulled back. There was time to close his eyes and shield them with his arm before the light lanced in as the door swung open. Leather-shod feet stamped up and he blinked at the dim forms that stood over him. There was no point in resisting now and he permitted himself to be hauled to his feet and dragged from the pen. Death was very close; he wondered vaguely why he was still alive after this length of time. But the pain in his head destroyed all capacity for thought and he went where he was led.

What happened next was most surprising. He had heard of the Atlantean baths; many stories were told of the wonders of this city, but this one at least proved to be true. Well guarded, with two armed men before and two after him and one on each arm, he was taken to a dim chamber where light filtered in through openings in the walls high above. A terra-cotta tub, higher at one end than the other, stood in an honoured place in the centre of the floor. An attendant came forward, bowing and waving him towards the tub, while the guards drew back to the entrance.

'Here, sir, if you please, use this step.' He stripped off Ason's loincloth with practised skill and held his arm while he climbed into the empty tub and sat down. The attendant clapped his hands sharply and a slave brought in an immense jar of water, freshly heated and steaming, and set it in the hole in the clay counter next to the tub. With a dipper the bath attendant poured water over Ason in soothing streams, his words coming as steadily as the water.

'Water, such perfect water. Atlantis is blessed with flowing springs that are guided close by through channels and pipes, a wonder to behold. Hot springs and cold, sir, which are blended here.'

There was a sponge in a niche in the wall which he used to scrub Ason with, ever so gently, removing the dirt and clotted blood, then pouring more water over him as a rinse. The water cleansed Ason's wounds and washed away his aches along with the filth. He stood when he was instructed and climbed out to lie upon a cool slab of stone where the attendant poured scented oil on to his skin and hair and worked it in with supple fingers. The soreness was kneaded

28

from his muscles and more oil applied to the still-open cuts. Under this treatment the worst of the pain had ebbed away by the time the man began to shave him with a sharp obsidian blade, and he was half asleep when someone else stamped into the chamber and stood over him. Ason opened his eyes to see a face of unsurpassed ugliness: the nose had been broken, apparently many times; one eye was almost closed by scar tissue; both ears had been torn away, and part of the lower lip so that the man's clamped teeth peeked through. His hair was grey and cropped short enough to reveal even more scars.

'Do you know about boxing?' the man asked in a harsh voice that exactly matched the face. Ason blinked then shook his head: he had no idea of what the man was talking about.

'No. I didn't think one of your kind would. Then you had better listen to old Aias and everything he says. Learn fast. If you don't make a good show out there and last awhile before you are killed, it will be my head as well. Do you hear me, stranger?'

Ason did not bother to answer this time but closed his eyes instead. A sudden agony of pain lanced through him and he sat up, pushing the attendant to the floor, clutching his side expecting to see a gaping wound there. Nothing was visible except a reddening area of skin. Aias smiled down at him— an ugly sight, with the hanging flap of lip—clenched one great fist and held it out.

'That is boxing. Your first lesson. In boxing the hands are closed to make fists, and with your fists you hit the other man. In the arena you will have the leathers around your fists to make them harder and to protect the knuckles which break easily.' His own were knobbed, scarred, and deformed. 'There are many good places to hit a man, but I have no time to show them all to you. For you it will be best to try for the middle of the body or the head. Now—stand and make a fist and hit me.'

'Give me a sword and I'll hit you.'

'No swords here, mountain man. This will be done the

Atlantean way and you will be killed with great style by someone who is a master of this sport.'

His fist lashed out suddenly and caught Ason a light but painful blow on the point of his jaw, rocking back his head and sending the agony surging through it again. Roaring with anger, Ason jumped for the man, swinging a powerful blow that the boxer easily ducked.

'No, not like that, you're not hacking with a sword. Throw your fist as if you were throwing a spear ... Better, better, but still not good enough. Don't leave yourself so exposed or I can do *this*. Hurt, didn't it? Themis will do worse. He will butcher you, mountain man.'

Ason backed off, his fists still before him, still wary.

'Is that the man who wishes to fight me? Isn't he a son of Atlas?'

'He is. But also a mighty boxer, which is more important to you at this time. Do you wish to die out there like a quaking slave or like a man?'

'I wish to kill Themis. Show me more.'

There was too much to learn—and no time to learn it in. The guards looked on and laughed while Ason pursued the squat form of the boxer about the chamber, flapping and swinging his arms like a crane's wings and getting little result for all his efforts other than an occasional lazy blow to his ribs. But the exercise had cleared his head, and when the boxer left he poured a jugful of water over his head, laughing when his guards cursed at the water slopping about their feet. He made no protests when he was once more dried and rubbed with oil. The attendant dressed him in a high-waisted, tight-fitting breech-clout of layered leather, then strapped on boots of the same hard leather that reached up to mid-calf. Lastly the heavy leathers were strapped about his fists. All the guards had their swords drawn when they led him out.

'Put up your swords,' he said to them. 'We have the same destination. I wish to meet your worm-infested prince in combat.'

He meant what he said. He would have preferred to fight with bronze dagger or sword, even the war-axe these Atlanteans favoured. But a weapon was just the means to the end; it was the battle he lusted after. There was no thought of defeat—or rather there was always the thought of death. It was not to be feared or welcomed but was eternally there. You killed the man who fought you. If you wounded him deeply he would die in any case so it was only right to finish the battle that had been started. When two men fought one died. Sometimes both died. The weapon was of no importance. The battle was.

For Ason the world was a simple place and his pleasures were few and equally simple. He seized the opportunities that life presented as they came, taking the same sharp pleasure from the hunt and spearing of a wild boar as from the possession and embrace of a woman. Both were over with quickly. He always had good friends to drink with who would fight beside him—and in battle he found the greatest pleasure of all. Nor was there any shortage of conflict in the Argolid. Ason's earliest memories were of screaming men beyond the walls, of wounded men, dead men and of blood-drenched bronze swords. His first toy had been a small sword —and it was not a toy. He had not had it a day when he had chased and killed a chicken and brought its bedraggled body to his father in triumph. Soon there was larger and more dangerous game to pursue, and finally, after he had come of age, the most dangerous game of all. He had a spear and he had poked it in under the lip of an Epidaurian helmet and through the man's eye. His only reaction had been surprise at how easily the man had died, far easier than some stag he had killed.

Women found him attractive, as did men—his blue eyes clear and his skin unwrinkled. His brown hair and beard, when trimmed and combed as they were now, were very much the colour of amber. If his nose was slightly large it was no more a deformity than the beak of a hawk which it did resemble. His teeth were white and sound; they could be little else on the simple Mycenaean diet. A jagged scar across his chin was one with its many fellows that lay a white tracery over his tanned body. In the past he had

31

walked—and run—for a day and night and had still been able to do battle at the end of that time. He had the muscles for it, smooth, tough muscles that moved easily under his skin and were not knotted and protuberant like those of men well past their prime. That he was intelligent could not be doubted, in that he was like his father Perimedes, but he used his wit to enable him to fight better and never to question at all why he was fighting. Some day he would have to, when Perimedes was dead and he was king of Mycenae, but as yet he had no reason to. Now there was another battle ahead and he walked to it as easily as he had walked to any other conflict during his twenty-one years of life.

It was at this moment that a far-off deep rumbling, as of some monstrous animal stirring in the earth, shook the ground beneath his feet.

The courtyard was immense. The palace surrounded it on three sides, while the fourth was cut off by a low wall with a drop of some kind beyond. A large stairway broke the central wall, flanked by bright red wooden pillars that were wider at the top than at the bottom. More pillars framed the balconies and openings above, many of them adorned with the gleaming golden double-axe of Atlantis. A colourful crowd, both women and men, were at all the balcony and window openings, but Ason was only distantly aware of them. What he saw were the sword- and axe-men around the wall of the courtyard and within every doorway, and the man who stood alone on the sand.

Themis. Dressed just as Ason was and shining with oil—with his fists hanging at his side like swollen clubs. He started towards Ason, pacing slowly, and Ason went to meet him.

'I shall not talk to you, just kill you,' Themis said and swung his fist.

Ason jumped backwards, lessening the force of the blow so that it bounced from his shoulder. He swung his own fist in return, a mighty blow that would have killed a bull had it connected. But it whistled harmless in the air as Themis dodged it.

32

Then bright pain shot through Ason's side and he sprawled helplessly back on to the sand. There was the distant roar of voices.

'Stand up,' Themis said. 'That was only the beginning.'

Ason rose shakily and the slow butchery began.

Blow after terrible blow struck him, bruised him, shattered him. He could not hit the wavering form of Themis, nor could he reach him. Just once he fell forward and managed to clutch the other man, to strike a single heavy blow in his side, then he was hurled away and the hammering attack to head, arms, body, chest, went on. Ason had no way of measuring the time; it was long, just long, and still he swung ineffectually and the club-like blows struck in return. Blood ran from his brow into his eyes and was salty in his mouth; blood covered most of his body, and the yellow sand stuck to it when he fell. Then a blow even harder than the others landed in the middle of his body, striking him down, almost paralysing him so he could only lie there like a fish on the shore, gasping for air. Themis turned to the king and the watching crowd above.

'This is the sport,' he shouted. 'Every blow struck where it was intended and in the manner desired. But that is over. Now it is the time of the bone-breaker. I shall snap his bones as I wish, his arms and his ribs, and then I shall blind him and destroy his face and only then, when he knows what has been done to him, shall I kill him.'

His final words were drowned in the sea of hoarse voices. Yes, they wanted to see this, see this skill and sport to remember it and talk about it in years to come. This was a very good day for them all.

All except one. Painfully Ason rolled over and pulled his knees under him, fighting the pain and shaking the blood from his face and rubbing his eyes with his forearm so he could see. No way out. No way to bring this man down with him. This was not how he preferred to die and this thought hurt more than all the blows.

Under his knees the ground shook and he dropped forward on to his hands to steady himself. The voices roared even

33

louder in his ears. Had he weakened that much?

When he saw a section of the great building tear loose and slide to the ground he realized that the great sound was outside of him and that the world was shaking beneath them all.

This was no tremor. This was an earthquake of the kind that rocked cities and levelled them.

Still not comprehending completely, Ason blinked up at the shaking wall and crumbling columns. People were screaming in panic, some dropping into the courtyard, some falling heavily from the upper windows. Brass sheathing ripped and tore away, while pieces of the stone cornice broke free and a massive length crashed into the sand near Ason, broken fragments stinging his skin.

It *was* happening. All hesitation vanished in that instant and he sprang forward, getting his clumsy fists under a carved length of stone as long as his forearm. With all his strength he heaved at it, muscles hard as the rock itself, lifting it into the air and over his head. Themis was coming towards him again, arm back to strike a killing blow.

But Ason struck first. Even the raised, padded fists could not stop the falling stone. Down it came on Themis' head, felling him in that instant, stretching him out silent and unmoving, the jagged end of rock buried deep in his skull.

But even as Ason turned to flee he heard his name bellowed above the thunder and screams. Atlas was leaning from the balcony above. 'Kill him for me! Kill that Mycenaean!' he shouted, and a young noble in bronze armour sprang from the box, falling heavily to the sand with the weight of all his metal. He stood, drawing his sword, starting towards Ason. Two of the warriors in the arena were also running towards him—the others were lost in the mob—and Ason did the only thing he could do. He turned and fled.

The dark opening of a doorway was before him and Ason ran through it. Clouds of dust made it hard to see and he stumbled over the fallen debris on the floor. Around him the palace groaned like a living thing, and sharp cracks opened in the walls as the heavy beams built into the stone structure bent and snapped. Rubble filled the stairwell ahead; he turned and, with his clubbed hands, followed a wall that led to a larger room, tumbled full of wreckage but clearly lit by the sunlight that poured in through the fallen ceiling above. He circled the mound, climbing the wreckage, looking for an exit. There was none. He was trapped in the room. There was a harsh cry as the first of his pursuers appeared in the doorway, blocking his escape.

Bronze helm with high, blue, horsehair plume. Bronze shoulder-guards and breastplate over heavy leather, a leather kirtle and bronze greaves on his lower legs. And a heavy, glinting, sharpened and deadly bronze sword raised high to cut him down.

Bloodstained, near naked, Ason ran to attack.

The warrior stood waiting, coldly, then brought the sword down in a sharp cut to catch Ason at the base of the neck, half decapitate him, kill him.

Ason raised his bare arm, as though to ward off this unstoppable blow that had all the other's weight behind it.

And the sword struck his fist.

At the same instant Ason's right fist swung around in a hammer blow that caught the man on the side of his head below the helm, felling him like an ox. He moved, tried to stand, and Ason stuck again and again with his single hand—his left arm was hanging limp and dead—striking the same spot on the helm, bending and denting the solid bronze until the man lay still.

He scrabbled to reach the fallen sword with his gloved hand but could not pick it up. He was tearing at the leather and laces with his teeth when the other two men appeared in the doorway. Ason backed away slowly as they came after him, one slightly behind the other. There would be no escape this time. With a sword he would have fought them, but not fist against swords. They came on.

Suddenly the second man shouted aloud in pain; he writhed and fell, and Ason saw that someone was bent over him, pulling a dagger from the man's back. At this the first Atlantean turned, uncertain, and Ason hurled himself upon him, driving him down with the weight of his body, beating at him with his good fist. The man roared and struggled to pull away, to free his sword, and managed to squirm clear. But he raised his sword arm just enough; the already reddened dagger slipped up through his side between his ribs and into his heart. Ason rolled over, still ready to fight, to look up at the Egyptian.

'Inteb! What are you—'

'There is no time for explanations now. We have to get out before all Atlantis collapses about our heads.'

'This room has already fallen in. Cut these accursed things from my hands first so I won't have to bear them to the grave with me.'

Inteb did not pause to argue. His dagger was well tempered and razor-edged and slipped through the bindings on Ason's right hand. The leather fell away and Ason stretched his numbed fingers before reaching over and seizing the wrist of his dangling left arm. While he had been fighting for his life he had forgotten this arm; it felt as though it had been split down to his wrist. Which it might have been. The sword had hacked through the leather and Inteb cut the few remaining strands and pulled them away.

The hand was swollen and inflamed—but uncut. Inteb held out the lead plate that was deeply scored but not chopped through. This and the thick leather had stopped the sword before it reached Ason's hand. He worked the fingers back and forth, ignoring the pain this produced, but could find no broken bones.

A greater tremor shook the building. There was the rumble of falling masonry and thin screams in the distance. More of the ceiling fell on the far side of the room. Inteb quickly wiped his hand and the bloody dagger on the tunic of a dead Atlantean and pointed to the mound of rubble.

'We might be safer climbing out this way instead of trying to get out through the building the way we came.'

'Help me to get this armour off first,' Ason said, pulling at the thongs that held the dead man's greaves in place.

'We don't have the time ...'

'This is full armour, the best. No one will stop us when I am wearing it.'

There was truth in this—and Inteb knew that arguments would avail him nothing. So there, in the centre of the toppling palace, they stripped the corpse and Ason put on his armour.

They climbed the mound of stone and plaster at its highest spot. Inteb succeeded in bracing himself against a fallen beam while Ason clambered on his shoulders and clumsily, one-handed, pulled himself through the opening. With his good hand he easily pulled Inteb up after him. Around them was the ruined palace, still falling as the quakes continued. A hot wind blew through the skeletal walls, and pieces of ash fell from the sky, burning their bare skins.

'I have an Egyptian ship here,' Inteb said. 'If we can reach it we are safe.'

They were the only living things in the ruins. The Atlanteans had fled, though an arm sticking from the rubble and the occasional crushed body were evidence that not all had escaped. They scrambled through the broken remains of the palace, avoiding the gaping holes that dropped to lower storeys, and finally reached the now-deserted courtyard. Steps led down from it to a lower garden where red columns and stylized bull-horns lay fallen among the flowers and trees. From this terraced garden, atop the hill of the acropolis, all of the island of Thera could be seen below them. Stretching down the hill were the ornate buildings and temples, now mostly fallen in a jumble of ruins, with smaller buildings below. Then the ring of water of the inner harbour where ships were pulling from the shore, coming together in the mouth of the canal that led through the ringlike island to the wider outer harbour. At this distance little damage could be seen there, though vessels were jamming into the canal that led to the open sea.

From the far northern slopes of the island beyond the hills there rose up a white cloud, a climbing mountain of smoke that was already drifting overhead and dimming the sun. It billowed and rose, higher and wider all the time, shot sud-

37

denly through with quick flashes of lightning. Thicker, evil-looking black smoke boiled around the base, bursting into sudden explosions that sent arcing streamers of white out in all directions. One of these smoke trails shot towards the acropolis at an unbelievable speed, the black dot at its tip now revealed as a rock that grew to incredible size in an instant before crashing with a grinding tremorous explosion into the already ruined buildings below. Horrified and speechless, Ason and Inteb ran down the hillside towards the harbour.

When they reached it, the mooring was empty. The Egyptian ship had gone.

4

Inteb raised his fists in impotent fury as the stern of his ship vanished into the covered canal, then turned to follow Ason. They kept to the shore which was relatively clear of rubble, lowering their heads and shielding their faces against a sudden fall of hot ash particles. The wind was blowing more strongly now and they leaned into it. There were moans of pain and shrill cries for help from a dock they passed, but they ignored these as they had all the others they had heard since leaving the palace. But one of the voices rose above the others and Ason stopped suddenly.

'Mycenaean—I call to another Mycenaean!'

Ason stumbled out on to the wooden dock towards the wreckage of a long, narrow galley. It was half underwater and had been abandoned. The galley slaves, clamped to their benches, had been left to die. It was one of these who had called to Ason, who now stood on the dock above looking down at the man.

'You are Tydeus, son of Agelaos. We have fought together.'

Tydeus looked up, filthy and naked, the water almost to his waist. He had to shout to be heard above the other slaves howling at Ason in a half-dozen tongues.

'I was taken at Asine, as you were, and imprisoned here since. A wooden clamp is upon my right ankle; your sword can cut it.'

Ason drew his sword and stopped, angry, when Inteb pulled him by the arm. He could not leave a Mycenaean here to die. But Inteb was interested in more than a single life.

'This galley is only half foundered. If it can be bailed out we have a ship.'

'Little chance of that,' Tydeus said. 'We were loaded, heavy, ready to leave, when great boulders fell from the sky. The biggest struck near the stern there, right through the bottom. Everyone panicked and fled. Left us here.' He laughed humourlessly. 'The overseer was the last one off, tried to get by me. I grabbed his leg, pulled him back. We choked him and passed him along to stuff into the hole. Not much of a man alive, not a very good plug dead.'

Inteb looked at the body that was submerged up to its shoulders. The man's head bobbed as small waves rocked the galley, mouth wide open and eyes still staring with horror.

'He appears to be a fat man,' Inteb said.

'A pig,' the nearest rower said.

'Then he will close the hole well, even better when he starts swelling up. And we can push cloth in around him for a better seal.

Word had passed in quick whispers and now all the slaves were silent, staring at Inteb, awaiting his word.

'They seem to have stopped the sinking. I'll tend to the plugging, these others can start bailing. Then we'll have a ship that can get us away from here, at least to Anafi or Ios, they're the nearest islands. Shall we, Ason?'

'Of course. There'll be no other ships for us.' He jumped into the galley and Tydeus guided his sword to the shackle that held his ankle.

No time was wasted now in freeing the other rowers. They bailed with their hands where they sat, and Tydeus ran to the ruins of the nearest buildings and returned with buckets, clay pots, anything that would hold water. He brought flaxen sailcloth as well from a looted ship-chandler's, and Inteb cut it into lengths with his dagger. He wadded these rags and pushed them into place around the corpse, which bobbed and gaped sightlessly at the hurried activity until finally it fell over as the galley was bailed out. Some of the galley slaves were dead; those in the prow had been drowned when it had

40

gone under, and one in the waist had been decapitated by a falling stone. The surviving slaves ignored them and bailed frantically, hunched over beneath the fury that exploded in the sky above. The air was thick with dust and almost unbreathable. With painful slowness the galley rose in the water while the hot wind sent it banging into the dock.

'Enough,' Inteb finally said. 'Some can keep bailing. All the others must row now while we are still in smooth water.'

Ason hacked the bow-line with his sword, then ran back the length of the ship, between the slaves who were unshipping their oars, to cut the one at the stern. The figure of a man loomed suddenly above him and Ason raised his sword until he saw the other was unarmed, his face and head caked with dried blood. Ason slashed at the line.

'There is room for one more aboard your ship, mountain man.'

It was Aias, the boxer. Ason slashed with his sword but the man jumped nimbly back.

'Stay and die, Atlantean, we have no need of you.'

'No Atlantean, but a slave from Byblos. Used as a punching sack by the nobility. I see dead men aboard. Let me take one's place and row with you.'

The line fell free and the galley began to move out.

As Ason turned away and the oars dug in, Aias leaped and fell sprawling on the foredeck. He grinned up out of the red mask of his face as Ason spun about.

'Kill me if you wish. I would be just as dead if I stayed on shore.'

'Take an oar,' Ason said, dropping his sword into its slings. Aias laughed hoarsely, seized the nearest corpse and hurled it from the rowing bench to the deck, using it as a footrest as he slid the oar into its socket.

They were the last ship to leave. The sky was dark as dusk now. The hot wind sending waves before it across the water so that the rowers had to bend all their strength to the oars to move the galley against it. Only when they reached the canal was the force of the tempest cut off. The galley moved quickly through its dark length while falling rock crashed and rumbled on the wooden covering above their heads. Then they were through, into the choppy waves of the outer harbour.

There were no longer any ships blocking the tunnel. Wreckage and half-foundered ships bobbed and scraped against the rock wall. A single ship, low in the water, limped into the tunnel and was gone. The galley went after it, pushing through the wreckage. All around were heard the cries of drowning men. One of them swam to the galley and clung to an oar, reaching up to the gunwale, holding on. The rower, still clamped in his foot stock, brought a pail down on the fingers and they vanished. Then they were into the tunnel and darkness closed around them.

'The tunnel's blocked, fallen in!' a man shouted and Ason called out even more loudly above the panic-stricken voices.

'No—I can see the other end. It's the sky that is dark, but the tunnel is still there.'

They went even slower, feeling their way when the oartips brushed the rock walls. Then a gust of mephitic air, laden with ash, blew over them and they knew they were almost through. Finally the canal opened out ahead and beyond that the safety of the open sea.

One man was lost overboard when they raised the sail; a single wail as the wind caught him and hurled him into the ocean, then nothing more. That is how close the end was for all of them, just the strength of their arms and the thin wooden hull of the ship keeping them from the hungry sea. A single reef was all that could be let out of the sail, but it helped. This and the rowers kept them off the unseen shore.

The night was endless. The men rowed to the point of complete exhaustion, then rowed still more. When there was no strength left in their arms to pull the heavy oars they bailed until they were able to row again.

Dawn came upon them unawares. Because of the layers of clouds there was no colouring in the sky, just a sudden awareness that forms could be dimly seen. Then, in shades of grey, the waterlogged galley appeared to view with the

42

men slumped over their oars. Far fewer than had been there at sunset the night before. Tydeus stood solidly at the steering-sweep where he had been all night. Aias looked up from his oar and grinned his hideous gap-lipped smile at Ason. For all of his years he was one of the few men still rowing, slowly but steadily.

Off to port, no more than twenty stadia away, the dark bulk of Crete rose out of the sea.

5

Once more, from the depths of their strained bodies, they
had to find the energy to seize the bloodstained handles of
the oars and row again. The wind was driving them towards
the rocks. Mast and sail had borne the increasing pressure of
the wind all night until finally it had been too much. There
had been a splintering crash as the mast broke like a dead
stick and fell over the side of the ship, crushing one rower
as it went. Now the dead weight of the mast and sail in the
water slowed their progress—but also made it more difficult
for the wind to drive them ashore. They left the sail there,
hanging clumsily over the side, and bent to their oars.

They rowed. Heads down, pulling, not stopping, rowing for
survival. They were moving slowly along the shore—yet it
was getting closer at the same time. Details could be seen,
rocks standing out in the surging surf, trees overhanging the
edge high above. They rowed. One, then another, falling
from exhaustion, unconscious, only to awake and seize the
hated oar again. The headland reached far out into the sea,
a grey arm waiting to seize them, and the last few minutes
were the worst. They were actually in the surge of breakers
from the rocks, white foam all about, when they passed them
by.

They ate on the rear deck, mixing the wine with water and
drinking it greedily. Someone had brought up a pithos of
olives which they dipped into and ate by the handful, and

there was a wheel of hard cheese that they broke chunks from and chewed. Basic fare, no more or less than they had at home, and they ate hungrily. Even Inteb had his share, his hunger masking for the moment the pain of his flayed palms. Tydeus was relieved at the steering-sweep and he dropped down beside them on the deck, sprawling as exhaustedly as the others.

'You are the seaman, Tydeus,' Ason said. 'Your father Agelaos had a great ship—you must have sailed it?' Tydeus nodded, his mouth filled with cheese. 'What is our course—and what do we do next?'

Tydeus squinted at the sky and the receding shore.

'We don't return to Mycenae this way,' he said.

'That I was sure of. What lies in this direction?'

'Deep water, monsters that eat ships, nothing.'

'There is always something. We can't even row to Crete to surrender—if we should want to—we are well past the island. What other islands lie in this direction?'

'None.'

The word was coldly said and drew a responsive shiver from the circle of listening men. To sail a ship meant to sail along a coast or, as in the closely spaced Cyclades, to sail from island to island. One island was always in sight ahead before the last one dropped astern. At night, or in case of storms, the ship could be pulled ashore on some beach. What else could be done? The ocean was a vast waste, more empty of landmarks than the emptiest desert. If you sailed out upon it how could you return? A man could tell directions from the sun—but what happened on cloudy days? To leave the security of a shoreline was a form of madness. And now they were leaving Crete behind, the undying wind forcing them away from its shores. If a man were to look ahead he would see nothing except heaving water, nothing at all.

'Then we are lost,' a rower said. 'And will die out here.'

'The wind will die first and we can return.'

'And if it does not?'

'A moment,' Inteb said, and their voices stilled. He took out his dagger and knelt, drawing on the wooden deck with

45

its point. 'I am no ship's captain, but I do know something of the parts of this world, as well as mathematics and geography and other matters I have studied. I am also an Egyptian and I sailed from Egypt and here is how it was done. We sailed along this shore here in a line like this. Past cities and islands until we reached the Argolid and the port of Tiryns here.' He had scribed a half-loop upon the deck, a half-circle, and now he pricked the boards at the centre of the loop.

'From Tiryns we sailed to Thera, and now we have passed Crete and are going in this direction, into the emptiness of the sea.' They watched in silence as he slid the blade further on until it touched the spot where he had started.

'There you see it, Egypt and the Nile, Thebes. Somewhere on the far side of the water there, in that direction.' They followed the direction of his pointing knife, saw nothing, and turned back to him with widened eyes.

'But—how far?' someone asked. Inteb shrugged.

'Forty skēne, eighty skēne. I don't know. But if we continue south far enough we shall come to that shore. And it seems we have very little choice in the matter. We cannot return, even to Crete and the Atlanteans, against this wind. Crete will soon be out of sight—and then what do we do? Sail before the storm, that is all, and instead of praying for the wind to die pray that it blows until we reach the African shore.'

There was nothing else they could do.

Inteb sat in the open doorway of the cabin for the light and scratched marks on to a fragment of broken pottery, recording his inventory of the ship's supplies. Sitting here, he could also keep track of the galley's course, recording the shadows as they lengthened across the deck outside and told him both the time of day and the direction of their sailing. When they ventured too far to the east or west he would call out instructions to the steersman to point them south again. Ason had slept and now sat inside with his bronze sword and a whetstone, working out the nicks and putting a

46

better edge to it. A cup of wine mixed with honey sat near-by, as well as some raisins.

'Raisins,' Inteb said, ticking off his list. 'Barley meal and cheese, olives, olive oil, and some dried fish with the worm in it. We won't starve. Wine and water, though some of the water is beginning to stink already. There are ship's supplies, thread, cloth and needles to mend the sail we no longer have. Tar for caulking and wood for repairs, but there is nothing we can do with them until we reach a shore. The overseer has swollen nicely and is still making a fair plug though he is beginning to smell more than the water and no one will sit near him when they row. Some chests that belonged to the bronzesmiths who had deserted, and to the captain.'

'What's in them?'

'The chalceus' tools for working bronze, the usual thing. Some jewellery, a lot of clothes, then a chest with a seal that I broke. It has three swords and four daggers in it, part of their stock in trade. Nothing else of real importance.'

Ason looked into his cup. 'How much wine and water?' he asked.

'We won't be thirsty for a while yet.'

'How long?'

'If we are careful ten, maybe twelve days. But the fish will have eaten away the overseer and we'll have sunk by then.'

'You are in a cheerful mood today, Inteb. Will we reach land before that happens?'

'Hawk-billed Horus may know, or your gods who watch from Olympus—but how can I tell? The sea may be too wide to cross, we may go in circles forever, a storm may come and swamp us. Could I have some of that wine? I feel a need for it.'

Ason handed over a silver cupful and Inteb buried his nose in it, drinking deeply, hoping the strong fumes would burn the thoughts of death from his brain. He stared into its depths, seeking some omen there, then drank again. Ason looked up at him, aware of the sudden sadness.

'Do you feel the end so close? Yet you were the one who told us how we could go on.'

'To speak of a decision in the abstract is one thing, to do it is another matter. When I am asked to build a wall or a tomb I draw a plan. I do not have to build the thing myself, I may even turn my design over to another builder and go away and he will see that it is built. I do not have personally to be involved with what I design. So to design a voyage that has never been done before is one thing, I am very good at that. To take the voyage is something completely different.'

'That is a new way of looking at things.'

'Different from yours, strong-thewed Ason. To you, I imagine, the thought and the deed are one; the thought of the battle comes with the battle.'

'You begin to sound like my father.'

'Perimedes leads the Argolid, as well as Mycenae, because he thinks of more than just the battle. He thinks of alliances and high walls and bronze for the swords men must fight with.' Sudden memory struck Inteb, and he looked up. 'Your father's brother, Lycos, I heard of him before I left the city. He is dead.'

'How could you know? He was far away—I cannot tell you where.'

Inteb glanced out at the deck, then shouted a course change to the steersman before he answered, wondering how much of the truth he should tell.

'You have known me for three years, Ason. Do you call me friend and think of me as a friend of Mycenae?'

'Yes, I suppose I do. But you were in Atlantis ...'

'Sent by Pharaoh, on his mission. I told them nothing of my work in your city.'

'I believe you. My belief strengthened by the two men you killed to aid me. But why are you asking this now?'

'Because I know far more about your city than you may realize I do. The megaron of your father covers all Mycenae. People gossip and talk, nothing is secret long. I know there is a mine on a distant island in the cold sea and that all of your tin comes from there. Your uncle Lycos was killed there and the mine destroyed. Perimedes did not take the loss lightly.'

'No, he would not. My father is a maker of mighty plans

and his holy bronze is a big part of it. Poor Lycos, what a cold and wet place to die. I sailed with him, when he went back there, but I returned on the ship with the tin. He stayed on, swearing no one could root the tin from the earth as he could, but it looked simple enough. There were others to do the work. Did many die with him?'

'All. Your cousin Phoros returned with the word.'

The overseer lasted two days more before his obvious state of decay became too intolerable. And he was beginning to leak around the edges. A thin and broad-shouldered young man named Pylor, from the island of Kea, said that he had much diving experience after the sponges that grew off-shore there, and he volunteered to look under the galley. A line was tied under his arms and he dived and came up quite soon after.

'Lots of fishes,' he reported. 'And not much of that whoreson left below the waist except for hanging bones. He's been used up.'

Tydeus, who had experience in patching ships at sea when they could not be properly careened on a beach, showed them how to make a mat that could be slung outside the hull. They took the largest piece of sailcloth they had and sewed rope-ends and rags torn from good clothing to one side of it. Lines were attached to the four corners of this and, with much shouting and pulling and a number of dives by Pylor, it was passed under the galley and over the hole and the truncated corpse of the overseer. The rags and rope-ends faced the hull and would mat together to form a temporary patch. Once this was in place all that remained was to pluck the corpse from the hole and put a wooden cover inside the ship. Boards were cut and shaped for this and held together with bronze pins, but there were few volunteers to remove the noisome plug.

'I'll take one arm—who'll have the other?' Ason asked. Some of the men actually leaned away when he looked around at them and Inteb had managed to be out of sight in the cabin.

Aias laughed at their squeamishness and pushed them aside and went to stand beside Ason. 'I've hugged women and boys and sheep to my body, mountain man,' he said. 'This will be the first time for a stinking corpse but I have a mind to try it to see what it is like.'

A single strong heave did it and the overseer bobbed astern in a flurry of fish, while Ason and Aias washed their arms over the side. Very little water came in around the patch and the wooden cover was quickly secured in place and sealed with pitch. After that only a slight amount of water leaked in, though no one wanted to think what would happen to these makeshift repairs in a storm.

One day was very much like another after this and Inteb recorded their passing on the inner wall of the cabin. He measured out the water and food himself while Ason stood close by, or slept in the doorway so no other could enter. The water began to run low and tasted increasingly foul, and with it Inteb mixed more and more wine, of which they had a greater supply. Most of the men were unused to this and with the heat of the sun many babbled and others fell down and had to be propped over the benches with their faces out of the bilges so they did not drown.

It was on the twelfth day that they sighted the dark line of what might be clouds low on the horizon before them. They rowed then, all of them, without being told, and the line grew darker and larger and was not clouds at all.

'The coast, it must be,' Inteb said and the galley rocked wildly as the men stood to see themselves. There was a shore ahead, land, any land, it did not matter. The endless voyage was over and the boldest were already bragging about it to each other. They were already remembering it as being twice as long as it had been, and their memories would improve with age.

It was Tydeus, at his accustomed post at the steering-sweep, who first saw the sail. A dot to begin with, perhaps a rock, but as it grew clearer he called to the others. They crowded up to look until Ason ordered them back to the oars. But Aias remained on the deck, staring at the sail as though

50

it were a face he remembered, even tugging away the drooping scarred flesh over his eye so he could see better.

'That dark sail, the way it is set. I know them. They are the men of Sidon.'

6

The ship moved swiftly towards them, swooping down like a dark bird of prey. They threatened attack and combat— and this was something that Ason felt he could take care of. No armoured fists here or sinking ships to deal with, but the straightforward threat of arms that could be met in the same way.

'Inteb, open the bronzesmith's chest and give weapons to those who know how to use them. The rest of you, quickly now, bail water into this ship.'

They did not stop to ask why but did as they were told; the orders were definite, and as the dark ship came closer the galley sank deeper in the water. The men with the swords bent low and hurried to conceal themselves in the stern cabin and under the narrow foredeck, while those who had the daggers sat on the rowing-benches and concealed the weapons beneath them. Aias refused the offer of a weapon and held up a clenched fist.

'Mine are with me always,' he said dropping on to the bench nearest the cabin. 'What will you have us do?'

'Take them by surprise,' Ason said. 'Put your ankles back into the stocks and close them, as though you were locked in. Take in most of the oars. Look sick, that should be easy enough; look dead if you are afraid to play-act. The mast and sail are gone, the ship waterlogged, you are slaves who have been deserted. Let the men of Sidon see a ripe fruit easy for the plucking so they will be unprepared. When I call to you we will all attack at once and we will not stop until they are dead. One ship will leave here, one crew alive. It will be ours.'

Aias, perhaps from his many battles in the arena before the crowds, gave a fine performance. He had boxed with nobles whom he could have slain in moments, yet had managed to lose to them and in doing so proved their superior skill. Now he collapsed on the bench, calling hoarsely to the approaching ship, while whispering at the same time to the men in the cabin.

'They're coming on steadily, using oars with the sail furled. Men hanging over the sides, pointing and shouting. Helms on some of them, but no armour that I can see, swords and spears. They're taking in the oars now, drifting close.'

There were guttural shouts from the dark ship that loomed above them, drifting down upon them. High stem-posts rose fore and aft, darkly painted, and just as dark was the sail now furled, angling across the mast in the high lateen rig. There was more shouting and laughter and then the galley shuddered as the ship bumped against them. Feet thudded on the cabin roof, while another Sidonioi jumped down to the foredeck with a line, bending to tie it securely. Others boarded once the two ships were lashed together, tall dark men with black hair and beards, their hair held back by a circlet about the head. And Ason still waited. Until now they had ignored the galley slaves and he wanted as many of them aboard as possible before he made any move. Then a man appeared in the doorway, one of their leaders, with his robe dyed purple unlike the plain white of the others, and he held a richly decorated sword in his hand.

Ason plunged his own sword into the man's middle, kicking the body out of the way as it fell, seizing the sword from the limp fingers, roaring the lion roar of Mycenae.

The rowers rose up and killed the men nearest them. Aias lashed out a fist as a dark-bearded man turned towards him, hitting him so hard that he crashed into the next man toppling them over; before they could recover Aias hurled them both into the sea.

53

After the first surprise attack the men of Sidon rallied and stood back to back with their weapons drawn. They were bold fighters and did not retreat, but shouted instead for help from their ship. More men climbed over the sides to join them and the fighting became fierce and deadly.

Ason's sweeping sword cleared the rear deck and then, instead of joining the battle in the ship below, he mounted the rail and clambered up the side of the black ship. A spear stabbed down but he lowered his head and it glanced from his helm. Before it could be drawn back for a second blow he stabbed upwards with his sword, impaling the man, then pushed his body aside to climb to the deck above. Seizing the spear to use in place of a shield, he shouted aloud so everyone could hear him, then, like a farmer cutting grain, began to scythe his way slowly down the deck.

A warrior in full armour cannot be stopped. Another armoured man may fight him, and the better will win, but no one else. Spears rebound from his chest, swords from his helmet, the solid bronze of his greaves keeps his legs from being cut from under him. He is made for killing, as methodical and unstoppable as waves crashing on a shore, looking from under the rim of his helm and putting his sword into the soft and unprotected bodies of those who stand before him.

Ason thrust and cut and advanced steadily. The men who had attacked the galley tried to return to save their own ship, but were cut down from behind when they did. A wail of despair went up from the survivors but they did not stop fighting. Powerful men and good swordsmen, they fought on, singly and together, fewer and fewer of them, the last fighting as ably as the first, dying with guttural curses on his lips.

It was finally done: the last drop of blood shed, the last corpse stripped and heaved over the side. The men of the galley had suffered, but not heavily. The simpler cuts were washed with oil and sea water until they closed. But a heavily bearded, silent man from Salamis had been cut deeply in the stomach and he held the lips of the wound together to keep his insides from falling through. He made no attempt to stop the blood. Bleeding to death was the least painful way to die and they all knew it. They brought him wine, although he could only touch it to his lips, and sat and talked and joked with him until his eyes finally closed and he slumped down.

Ason mixed some wine and saw to it that they all had some. Then, while they were still laughing and cursing and filled with victory, he called to them from the high rear deck. His own mind had been made up ever since they had first sighted this ship and he had waited only for this moment to tell them.

'I know this shore,' he called out. 'I sailed here once. In that direction, some days' sail, not too long, is Egypt. You can go there if you want to; you can have your share of what we find aboard this ship and the galley.'

There were excited shouts at this because looters had already plunged into the holds and come up with cloth and flasks of oil, even ivory carvings which were highly valued everywhere. Ason could feel the rise of their emotions and at its peak he called out again and pointed his dripping sword in the opposite direction, west along the shore.

'You can do as you will—but I am going that way, to the west, and I ask the best of you to come with me. Past the Pillars of Heracles to the island of the Yerni, to avenge my uncle and my kinsman who were killed there. We will bring back tin, enough to fill a ship, tin that is more valuable than gold or silver—and you will have your share. So now I ask you, men who sailed the ocean where no one has ever been before, who battled and killed the men of Sidon, are you afraid of anything? Will you sail with me to the lands few men have ever seen—to return home rich? Who is with me?'

There could be only one answer, a roared cheer, again and again. How could they refuse? They could do anything, they knew it, anything! Ason dropped his sword to the deck and threw the spear into the air with his other hand, catching it as it dropped in his right, drawing it back farther and farther. Then he threw with all his strength, hurling the spear west towards the low afternoon sun. Up it arched, thrumming as it flew, the sun driving golden light from its bronze head, as though it would reach the sun itself. It was only a speck when it hit the water and vanished, and the men were still cheering.

Part Two

7

Inteb awoke coughing, over and over again without being able to stop, until his throat was raw and his eyes closed with the pain of it. He rolled on to his side and spewed out salt sea water until he was empty, drained. After this he was too weak even to open his eyes, although he remained conscious, feeling the hard ground under him and aware that he was shivering with cold and exhaustion. His eyes were grainy with sand, with the lids so stuck together that he had to rub to open them.

A grey sky low overhead, with blowing clouds. He lay on rough ground tufted with clumps of grass, in a small hollow. His last memories had been of the sea, the storm, the water closing over him. How had he come here? Certainly not by himself. Ason?

'Ason,' he called aloud, struggling to his knees. And then in near panic, '*Ason!*'

Could he be dead? Inteb stood swaying, then climbed the low ridge. From here he could see a stretch of beach with the waves still rushing strongly up it and bubbling back. Not far offshore the black wet backs of a bank of jagged rocks broke the surface of the sea, and he knew what had happened the night before. But how had he come here? He shouted again and heard an answering hail from down the beach. Ason appeared, dragging something long and dark, and waved to him. They met on the damp sands. Ason threw down the broken piece of driftwood and seized him by both arms.

'It was a bad night, Inteb, but we are alive and that is something to be glad of.'

'Others ... ?'

'None. The ship hit those rocks out there and flew apart at the blow. We went into the water together and the steering-sweep almost took our heads off coming down on top of us. But I used it to save us in the end. Held us up until we washed ashore. I called, there was no one else. I pulled you up there out of the wind and searched, out in the water as far as I dared go. Nothing. They must have all gone down with the wreck. Not many could swim, I suppose.'

He dropped heavily to the sand, leaning his head forward on to his knees. He had not slept and was very tired. He had been the leader and captain and responsible for the crew. And now they were all dead. His muscles ached and the sword was a cold weight across his back.

'Do you know where we are?' Inteb asked

'On the coast somewhere, I'm not sure. We sailed along it last time I came and one place looks very much like another. It's unsettled here as well, no sign of people, villages. Or food. Nothing came ashore from the ship. Just broken wood. We had better start walking.' He climbed to his feet.

'Which way?'

'A good question. Until the storm it seemed we had a good following wind, but it could have veered after dark. Walk east, that must be right.'

Ason gave one long look around at the deserted beach and fang-tipped rocks that had destroyed the ship, then led the way down the shore. The sand was soft and easy on their bare feet: their sandals had been torn off by the sea. Inteb followed, down the beaches of the featureless coast. They had walked only a short time when they came to an inlet that was too deep to cross. Turning inland, they followed it away from the ocean. Inteb had a sudden thought and bent and filled his palm and tasted the water.

'Just brackish,' he said. 'This must be the mouth of a stream. If we follow it some more it should be fresh water.'

The stream twisted and narrowed until it was clear water

running over moss-covered stones. They lay on their stomachs at its side and drank their fill. Ason sat up, wiping his mouth on his arm—and was suddenly still. Inteb saw him draw his sword.

'What is it?' he asked. Ason pointed.

Low, wooded hills rose up from the downland and through the branches could be seen a bare hilltop beyond. On the summit of the hill was a rounded construction of some kind. There was no one in sight and, after a moment, Ason led the way there, sword ready. They passed through the grove on an overgrown path and emerged on the hillside below the raised hummock of the structure. It was made of heaped earth, and stone slabs were visible at one side where the dirt had washed away.

'It looks very much like a tomb,' Inteb said.

Ason nodded agreement but kept his sword in his hand as they mounted the hill, only slipping it back into its slings when they realized that they were the first visitors here in a very long time.

'It is a tomb,' Ason said. 'I've seen this kind before.' He pulled at the heavy stone.

'Very much like Mycenae, in a far cruder way. Must you open it?'

'No, no reason to. We must return to the beach.'

The sun burned through the clouds and felt warm on their backs, and they walked in this manner until it was near midday. It was Inteb who called a halt, pointing to the curved beach ahead of them. He drove a stick into the sand and peered at its shadow quizzically.

'We seem to have turned north,' he said, 'and if this beach keeps on as it does we shall soon be walking west, back in the direction we came from. Could we be on a peninsula or a neck of land?'

'Possibly, but I don't remember any shaped like this. But there is a lot of coast, it's a big island. It goes north no one knows how far. This could be a part of the land I haven't seen. Or, and I hope it is not, an island off the coast.'

'I'm going to see what lies ahead,' Inteb said, scrambling

up a grass-tufted dune, tired of walking and only too aware of the rumbling emptiness of his stomach. He reached the top, looked around—then bent over and slid quickly back to the beach.

'Someone coming along the shore. I dropped as soon as I saw him—I don't think he saw me.'

'Just one?' Ason asked, slipping his sword from the slings.

'Absolutely. I could see all along the beach. He's alone.'

'There is nothing to fear from one man.'

Sword swinging easily, Ason strode down the sand. Inteb, feeling none of this same self-assurance, lagged behind. He caught up with him as they came to a rocky spur that ran out into the sea and Ason stopped there. There was splashing as someone moved out into the water and grumbled curses as a high wave surged up and broke against the rock. Inteb stepped back as the splashing grew near and the tendons in Ason's hand stood out as he closed his grip on the pommel of the sword. A man waded around the end of the rock and faced them—as startled as they were. A familiar, scarred and battered man.

'Aias!' Ason shouted and plunged his sword into the sand.

8

Aias walked, head bowed, so that the streaming rain ran from his hair and beard and dripped into his already soggy clothing. He trudged along at the water's edge dragging the driftwood after him, a length of splintered branch that he had found on the shore. The waves broke hissing up the sand and around his ankles and there was the rumble of unseen breakers on the rocks offshore. Aias walked on, turning inland from the beach on the path his feet had made during the many journeys back and forth here. The path wound up through the rocks to a larger jutting slab of stone with a natural shelter underneath it. Stuffed in here were the pieces of driftwood Aias had found; limbs and logs, branches and a single length of carved thwart from the wrecked ship itself. This and the steering-oar were the only reminders that the ship and the drowned crew had ever existed. Aias pushed the pieces of wood aside and made room for himself out of the rain.

After some time the rain stopped falling and Aias' legs had become stiff. He climbed out and stretched, hearing his joints snap, his muscles sore from the damp. Water dripped from the bushes, the grey sea was the same leaden colour as the sky. He turned his back on it and retraced his steps through the low, rounded hills to their tomb. A fit dwelling-place for men who would soon be dead—but, not of an introspective turn of mind, he never thought of it that way.

This was the first tomb they had found, the biggest on the

island and high enough to stand in, with the opening un-
covered by soil and sealed only by large slabs of stone. They
had levered aside the stones and hesitantly entered this home
of the dead. There were bones everywhere, some of the more
recent ones still with bits of leathery flesh attached, the
oldest ones in the rear already turning to powder. They had
cleaned house by kicking all of the bones to the far, dark
end of the tunnel-like grave. Mixed with the bones were
golden grave goods, collars and pins, useless decorations
that meant nothing on this island though they would have
been well received anywhere else. At first they had kept
them close by, but they were in the way in the cramped
quarters and had soon been thrown in with the rest of the
rubbish. Aias still wore a gold armlet, but only because it
offered some cheer in the greyness of the island. The others
were already there when he crawled through the entrance,
bent over something.

'Look!' Ason called out, holding up a brown bird whose
legs had been caught in their snare. It fluttered helplessly,
terror in its large round eyes.

'How shall you divide it?' Aias asked squatting down, as
eager now as the others.

'We are the wrong number,' Inteb said as Ason drew his
sword and whetted the edge against his thumb. 'Remember
the trouble with the last bird. If we were two we could half
it, quarter it for four.'

'And a feather each for four hundred,' Ason laughed.

Three grown men, on the edge of starvation, bent over a
mite of a struggling life that could provide only the tiniest
amount of nourishment. But their bellies growled for it.

The sound must have been in the air for some time before
they became aware of it, drowned out by their voices. It was
Ason, the hunter, who cocked his head suddenly to one side,
then held his finger to his lips. The others froze, motionless
and silent, and the distant moaning could be clearly heard.

If it had been night they would have been sure that the
spirits of the dead they had expelled from the tomb were
returning to claim it. There was a dirge of death to the sound,

64

the wailing of the dead; like dogs they felt the hairs on their necks and down their backs rise and Inteb shivered, not from cold.

'Voices,' he whispered. 'It must be people, chanting.'

Voices, getting closer, louder, and soon words could be heard. Ason strained to make them out, then nodded his head.

'Listen. You can understand the words. It is almost the same language; you can make out what they are singing.'

The same phrases, over and over again, a ritual chant. Clear now, louder and closer, coming towards them up the side of the hill.

> Back, back to the womb of the mother
> Inside, inside, the earth and the hill
> Dead, dead, sleeping inside you
> Born, born again out of the tomb.

Ason had his sword in his hand, crouching, ready to defend himself against any attacker, human or inhuman. Aias closed his hands and his simpler yet equally deadly weapons were ready. Inteb, never the man of action, huddled where he was.

The bird fluttered wildly on the sandy floor and before anyone could reach it freed its wings from the snare. Peeping loudly, it flew by them, the woven grass strands dangling, and out of the tomb.

There was a sudden silence as it burst from the opening and the chanting stopped. For a long, long instant Ason endured this threatening silence, then scrambled forward bellowing like a bull. Whatever was out there was better faced in the open. He swung his sword in short arcs before him and jumped to his feet outside with Aias just behind him.

Screams and cries, thudding feet, the sudden sight of people running, brown backs vanishing from sight. In a moment all except two of them were gone—and the long bundle dropped at their feet. A man, old, grey-haired, brown-garbed from head to toe, with the hood of his cape down over half his face. He was shouting distractedly, resisting the young girl who pulled at his arms. She leaned away in panic yet would not desert the old man.

'A funeral procession,' Inteb said, peering from the tomb's mouth, pointing to the dropped litter with the corpse that was sewn into uncured hides.

'And more frightened of us.' Ason lowered his sword. 'Not a warrior among them.' He stalked down to stand before the old man. The girl stopped tugging and stood helplessly beside him now. Her hood had fallen back in her struggles and her rich black hair hung to her shoulders. Her eyes were as dark, her skin olive, her lips full and trembling. Ason reached out and lifted the man's hood that concealed his face, and the old man cried out.

'Who is it? Who is there? Naikeri—what has happened?'

Ason took one look and let the concealing hood fall back into place. Something sharp and heavy had crashed into the old man's face. It had crushed the bridge of his nose and his eyes, blinding him, leaving only an inflamed scar the width of his face. When Ason did not speak the girl whispered, hoarse with fright, into the old man's ear.

'One man, three men, coming from the tomb. They are armed with bronze swords ...'

'Who are you?' Ason broke in.

The old man, who might have been a warrior in his time because he was well-muscled though slight of build, straightened up.

'I am Ler of the Albi. If you are a bronze-sword man you may know of me.'

'I know the name of Ler of the Albi. It was told to me by my uncle Lycos who said your people aided him at the mine.'

Ason kept his sword ready and looked about. He knew nothing about these strange people and they might be the very ones who had destroyed the mine.

Ler wailed in sudden agony. 'Oh, dead, all of them dead, slaughtered like animals, rivers of blood.' He shook his fists at the sky and writhed in torment, tearing at his clothing.

Ason turned to the girl, Naikeri, who was standing quietly now that they had been revealed as men, not spirits.

'What is he raving about?'

66

'The Yerni. They attacked us, killed all the men; my brother on the ground there was the last, and he was many months dying. My father was blinded. They killed your people too, everyone at the mine.'

Ason dropped his sword into its slings; they appeared to share a common enemy. Now that the sudden emergency had ended, the significance of the funeral procession was driven home to him.

These people had come to this island from some other place. The survivors of the shipwreck would not die on the barren island.

'Where do you come from?' Ason asked. Naikeri pointed back over her shoulder.

'From home. We always come here to bury our dead, at least our dead of rank. We must come a long way yet we still come. The distance does not matter since this island is sacred to us, because one time long ago our people lived here. Are still buried here in these tombs.' She grew angry with sudden memory. 'You have torn this tomb open and gone into it to steal the offerings—like that!' She pointed to the gold armlet Aias wore.

'You have a ship?' Ason asked.

Naikeri began to shout. 'Thieves and tomb robbers ...' She gasped and was silent as Ason reached out and seized her jaw in one hand, his corded fingers biting deep.

'Do you have a ship?'

9

From the first moment that the coracles put to sea Inteb was sick. They bobbed up and down on the surface of the water, spun in circles, and leaked. Loaded with a small amount of cargo, each coracle held two people, three at the very most. Ason and Aias soon managed to learn to control the stubborn craft, though at first they simply spun about in one place while they chopped at the water with the stubby paddles, laughing at their own efforts. Inteb never even touched a paddle; as soon as the bobbing craft left shore his insides heaved and he hung over the side voiding his stomach. After that he was carried as cargo, slumped in the bottom and awash with water, with the rowers' feet sometimes resting on him when they moved. Not that he cared. Pain, even death, would have been a relief from this rocking sickness. The sky spun and moved overhead and he closed his eyes to keep it from sight.

The journey to the mainland from the island took the better part of a day, even though they left at dawn. They crossed to land's end, the westernmost tip of the Island of the Yerni, and after that they slowly worked their way east along the coast, rowing most of every day and pulling into shore at dusk to eat and sleep. Guided by the old men, they stopped at a series of campsites that must have been in use for generations, mostly isolated beaches cut off from the land beyond by high cliffs and accessible only by sea. The Albi were secretive by nature, not particularly afraid of other people but preferring to go their own way.

One day blurred into another—strenuous work by day, exhausted sleep at night—and even Inteb lost track of how long the voyage was. It was only slightly past noon one day when they put into shore at the mouth of a wide stream.

'What is wrong?' Ason called to Ler who was being helped from his beached coracle by his daughter.

'This is the landing-place. We are close to home now.'

The coracles were quickly unloaded and inverted, their cargoes divided up among the younger girls and children. Once the others had been loaded with their burdens the stronger women and the old men lifted the coracles themselves, holding them on their backs and almost vanishing inside their rounded forms. Aias wanted to carry one as well but his offer was turned away; their habit of keeping to themselves was not easily broken. In single file they started up a barely discernible path alongside the stream, towards the dark curtain of the forest.

Rain had been threatening since early morning and the sky was low, pressing against the treetops until the tallest of them vanished in the mist. Dark, alien trees with flat and pointed leaves. Thick oak for the most part, broken by stands of beech and the occasional white arrows of birch trees. The ground beneath them was almost impassable, a tangle of undergrowth and hedge thick with thorn spikes. The track they were following wound along the grassy bank above the stream, rising and falling, first to avoid the marshy land at the water's edge, then the impenetrable forest. They walked on without stopping, silently, bent under their burdens, while the land itself rose steadily. At one point the stream gushed over a rock ledge in a small waterfall and broke on the rocks of a rapid. There was a stiff climb here and the coracles were passed up from hand to hand. The land above changed suddenly, giving way from unending forest to cleared downs and meadows. The path was more clearly seen and there was the smell of woodsmoke in the air. Very little could be seen after that because the mist turned to rain and they plodded on, soon soaked and chill.

It was nearing dusk when the first of the great mounds loomed up out of the rain, rising like a small mountain from the flatness of the moor. A buried tomb, but much larger than the ones on the island where they had been wrecked. The line of marchers wound around it, then past another mound, and the houses came into view. Their gabled, thatched roofs reached almost to the ground, to the raised earth-bank that surrounded them. Smoke seeped out from openings under the gables. The walls were of wattle-and-daub held up by logs still with their bark upon them. Small tilled fields were behind the houses, divided by piled stone walls. As the party approached, someone whistled, high and clear, with a peculiar warble on the last note. At this signal people appeared in the doorways and moved down towards them. Without goodbyes, the file broke up as they went their separate ways. Ason stopped and waited until Naikeri and Ler had reached him.

'How far is the mine from here?' he asked.

'The mine of Lycos? Not far,' Naikeri said. 'You can walk there and back in half a day.'

'You will go there in the morning,' Ler said. 'It was once our mine but Lycos gave us many gifts and we let him use it. We will use it again now for the copper there.'

'No,' Ason said without hesitation. 'It is a Mycenaean mine, you told me that.'

'You have no need now for the rich metal there. Nor do you have any boys to work the mine for you. They are all gone now, most of them dead, and it will be hard to find others to go back there.'

'If Lycos did it—then so can I.'

Ler smiled wickedly, forgetful in his own blindness that the others could see.

'Then you do not know. It was I who found the boys for Lycos, children of the Donbaksho out there who come to us for axes—none are as good as ours. Lycos gave me a gold cup and many other things to get the boys. Do you have a gold cup?'

70

'You will have a gold cup, even more if you can find the boys.'

'I would like to hold that gold cup now. I cannot see it but I could touch it with my fingers and feel its weight. When can I hold this cup?'

'Soon.'

The rain rustled on to the thatch roof in a continual hushed roar and trickled in through the doorway, making a puddle on the stamped dirt floor. Ason only sipped at his fermented milk, trying to see the future through a haze of fatigue and heat, memories and hatreds. One man against an entire land?

Ler's voice dwindled and vanished as he slumped and fell off the stool. An old woman hobbled over and dragged him to a lockbed built into one wall, then rolled him into it with Naikeri's aid. She had sat silently in the shadows all evening, listening but not speaking so they were scarcely aware of her presence. Aias leaned back against the rough wall, singing to himself with his eyes closed, drunk to extinction but unaware of it. Inteb swayed when he sipped at his mug and looked at Ason over the rim of it.

'We are here, Ason, after a journey none will believe.'

'There is no one to tell it to in this lost place.'

'Perimedes will send a ship and you will have men to aid you in reopening the mine.'

'How can I be sure of that? My father will send a ship—but when will it be here? Will it come at all through the dangers of the seas we crossed? Must I simply sit and eat pap and drink soured milk until it does arrive? These questions are tearing at me, Inteb, and I see no answers. I am a prince of Mycenae, a warrior of the Argolid, ready to fight and win or die. But how can I fight without warriors and with one badly nicked sword? How can I get aid without treasure for gifts? You are the wise man, my friend, can you answer these questions for me?'

Inteb's head bobbed loosely and his speech was thick. 'Count upon me, I'll help you, always help you, Ason. Love you. I could be in Egypt now at Pharaoh's right hand watching the lovely Nile rise—but look where my destiny has led me. Yet I am not sorry, not sorry.' He began to weep, and, weeping, fell asleep.

The fire burned low and the air was thick with the smell of fermented milk and smoke; Ason could not bear it. There was a pressure inside him, a knot of desire to fight someone—but whom? There was no one he could fight. Seizing the stone axe he rose and pushed out through the door, jarring his head cruelly on the low doorway as he went. Outside the rain was still falling and there was the rumble of thunder in the distance. He stood there in the rain, facing up into it blindly, not knowing whether to curse his fate or pray for aid.

Ason was suddenly aware of a motion nearby, of someone standing close to him; he jumped away and crouched, raising the axe. Lightning crashed not too far away and in the sudden light he saw that it was Naikeri. He smiled to himself as the darkness descended again. Was he now afraid of women?

'I can help you,' she said, coming close.

'You, a woman? What can a woman do?'

'Very much. Among our people women are like men in many ways, not as with other people. Since my father's blindness I do more and more in his name.'

'Why would you want to help me? There must be a reason.'

'There is!' He was surprised at the open hatred in her voice. 'My father is old and blind and it makes him weak. All of my people are weak. They want to keep to themselves and live as they have always lived and not be bothered by others. We have traded with the Donbaksho and the Yerni since time began and there never used to be trouble. They needed what we had, so they did not bother us. The Yerni used to do their murdering and killing only among themselves. Until, for no reason, they brought death here and killed our people and all our men, all my brothers, and did that to my father. Now our people want to move farther away from this trouble. I don't want to move. I want to

72

stay and kill all of them who did this thing.'

'I will kill them for you when I kill them for myself.'

A part of Ason was surprised at his own reaction. To be carried away by a girl's fury was madness. Yet it fitted his own madness exactly.

'You will get the boys for the mine?'

'Yes, whatever you need. You will have warriors?'

'Many are on their way here now, men who do killing of the kind you have never seen.'

'Do it then!'

Her shouted words were drowned in the closer roll of thunder as lightning blazed through the rain. Darkness fell again instantly but her image was burned into his brain, head back and wild-eyed with the rain streaming from her glossy hair and soaking her clothing until it clung tight to her body. A woman's body, still clear in his vision, with full rounded breasts and swelling flanks. He reached out and found that wet flesh under his fingers, and she came to him even as he pulled her. Her clothing came away and he felt the rain-cooled dampness of her skin and at the same time a mounting surge of lust that overcame him.

Down in the mud, on the ground, just as they did it in the spring, falling violently on top of her, pressing his body hard against hers until he penetrated her deeply and she screamed with pain and something greater.

Thrusting deep as he would thrust a sword into a man's vitals.

Taking her as he would take this Island of the Yerni. He could not be stopped.

Laughing into the roar of the falling rain, not hearing her moans or feeling her nails on his back or her teeth closed in his flesh.

Zeus hurled his lightning across the sky and the thunder boomed and rolled loud enough to stop the ears of anyone not already deaf.

IO

When they reached the valley floor they could hear a sharp thudding from ahead, as regular as a heartbeat. It stopped and the silence was broken a moment later by the crackling descent of a falling tree. They went on, along a well-marked trail now, until they reached a clearing in the endless forest. On the hillside was a low, rush-roofed, square building with mud-daubed woven walls. It was surrounded by small fields where knee-high, green-tasselled grain nodded in the breeze. Three women, bare to the waist in the warm sunshine, wearing only leathern skirts, were bent double tilling between the rows with sharp deer-antler picks, their pendulous breasts swinging as they worked. They looked up and gaped at the newcomers and one of them shouted in a high-pitched voice.

'Wait here,' Naikeri said. 'I can talk to them better if you are not close by.'

Ason and Aias dropped to the ground in the shade and looked on as children tumbled from the house and stood sucking at their fingers in the dooryard. There were a number of them, of all ages, alike only in their lack of clothes and the smears of dirt on their white skins. On the slope, high above, there was a sudden motion as two men burst into view, running heavily and carrying their stone-headed axes in both hands. Their shoulder-length hair blew free, and like the women they were naked to the waist and drenched with sweat. When they saw there was no danger they slowed to a plodding walk, looking constantly at the strangers as they

74

came up to Naikeri whom they knew. The women watched from the distance as the two men and the girl squatted and talked. She was being forceful and they grunted in response, shaking their heads and scratching deep under their hair with their thick fingers. In the end one of them stood and went to the house and pushed the children aside to grab a boy. He did not want to come but the man cuffed him, then dragged him by the ear back down the slope. There was more talk until they all stood and Naikeri left them, the men looking stolidly after her as she walked away.

'They are hard to talk to. Some of the boys came back but others were killed at the mine.'

'I didn't notice any shortage of replacements in that house,' Ason said.

'There are enough boys, here and in other places. But the cost will be high. They have broken one axe this year and want a new one. That will take months of grinding. This one even wants a copper axe-head if he is to get the boys for us. We have the mould and I think there is enough copper, but my father will not like it.'

'But you will still do it?'

'Of course. You know that.'

Ason believed her. He looked at the solid width of her thighs and flanks as she led the way out of the valley again, her muscles working steadily under the brown strands of her skirt. With her hair and skin she looked like one of the peasants at home, shorter perhaps, a worker in the fields. But here she was something else, a person of rank among her own people and able to talk to the Donbaksho men and make them listen. Just as he had listened and been convinced. Things were very different in this country, so far from the Argolid, and he had to learn the new ways. He would have preferred to lead his armoured men into battle and take what was needed. No men, no armour. A way would still be found.

It was nearly noon and filled with the heat of the day when they came out of the forest again at the mouth of a small valley. Small shrubs were growing here, but the tree-stumps and high grass showed that this area had been cleared

75

once, not too long ago. A dirt palisade sealed the mouth of the valley. Though it had been six years and he had been only a boy, Ason recognized the place at once. The mine.

Now he pushed the others aside and climbed the slope that he remembered as raw earth, where he and the others had laboured and sweated, digging and carrying dirt to heighten this defence. From the top he could see the end of the small valley where Lycos had worked so hard and torn so much wealth from the ground.

Ruin. The buildings burnt shells with fallen-in roofs, weed-grown and already sinking back into the earth. The raw cut in the ground was still there, and the heaps of useless stone and dirt, but even these were already sprouting with grass and weeds and would soon vanish from sight. The hollow logs that took the water from the stream under the palisade had jammed with leaves and dirt, and the water, no longer able to escape, had formed a marshy pond reaching back almost to the diggings. A pair of ducks, frightened by his sudden appearance, flapped heavily up from the water and flew away.

Ason did not notice them. He was seeing this place as he had known it before, busy with activity, trying to remember everything. His uncle, proud of what he had built, had taken him around and explained it all to him. He remembered being bored by it and wishing he could go hunting instead with the men who went out for deer. But he had learned despite himself, watching what the boys were doing, working alongside his uncle when he charged the furnaces, the final vital step that he would allow none of the others to do.

Here was the tin-stream, like a captured rocky rivulet in the soil. Lycos had thought much about this and had taken him up to the hillside above, chipped off a chunk of the reddish rock, and pointed to the black granules it contained. There was tin in the rock, but it was easier to find in the dry stream, where it had been washed out of the softer weathered rock by the rains of untold years. It was close to the surface, even on the surface at the narrow top of the stream, but this area had been picked clean years before.

76

Now they had to dig beneath the soil where the hidden stream of black stones and sand fanned out. The wooden tye was still there, though badly rotted and in need of repair, still with heavy granules of tin in it where the dirt had been dumped and the water of the brook had washed the lighter soil away. Not that all the tin was this easy to find. Most of it was sealed in larger chunks of rock and had to be broken with hammers to free it; the grooves and holes in the outcropping of rock where it had been pounded were clearly visible.

And the furnaces were still there, that was the important thing, the secret of their construction unknown to Ason. They looked simple enough, a cone-shaped hole in the ground with a smaller hole for the bellows cut in from the side to meet its base. But Ason had no idea of how they had been made, or what was the secret design that had shaped them. But they were there and he knew the art of charging them. The tin could be mined and smelted; it could be done. Perimedes must send a ship, sooner or later, to reopen the mine. They would find it in full working order again, with a rich harvest for Mycenae.

'Killed them all,' Aias said, and Ason realized for the first time how many bones there were in the camp.

Human bones, skeletons, most of them with the skulls missing. No armour or weapons, though sun-bleached scraps of leather and cloth fluttered here and there.

'Some of these are Mycenaeans,' he said aloud. 'We will avenge them.' In sudden anger at the reality of the death of his kinsmen, so far from high-walled Mycenae, he tore his sword from the slings on his back and whirled it brightly over his head.

'Vengeance!' he shouted, over and over. 'Vengeance!' and his lips curled back with the hatred that filled him and he clenched his teeth until they grated together. Men would die, many, many.

On the hilltop, high above, the man squatted in the shade of the stand of beech-trees. His body was concealed by the undergrowth and only his head was visible through an opening in their solid mat. But he did not move so he could not be seen; his face appeared part of the light and shade of the forest.

Silent as a painted statue. White-painted, with chalk rubbed into his light blond hair until it was whiter still. Although his cheeks and chin had been plucked smooth, the hair on his upper lip had been allowed to grow long, into a great drooping moustache. It had been combed out on both sides and worked with clay and chalk until it was stiff and hard and white as an animal's horns. Or a boar's tusks. Under the solid moustache his lips parted in a grin and he licked at them greedily. He had come a long way and waited a long time, until he had almost given up all hope of the treasure he had been promised. Now it would be his.

A tall, well-muscled man clad only in a short leather kirtle that stopped above his knees, decorated in front with a pelt of fox fur. He wore a bow on his back, a clutch of arrows tied in with it, and held a hunting-spear in his hand.

He laughed deep in his throat as he dropped slowly from sight and turned and made his way back through the undergrowth, then began running east at a steady, ground-eating pace.

His name was Ar Apa and he belonged to the teuta of Der Dak on the high downs.

II

Tired and out of sorts—even the strongest warrior does not enjoy walking and running day after day—Ar Apa came within sight of the walls of his dun late in the afternoon. Two half-grown boys were close by, driving home the cattle after a day's grazing on the down, and the sight of those great eyes, smooth muscles and sleek hides quieted him and made him forget his fatigue. He walked among them calling the ones he recognized by name, rubbing his hands on their warm flanks and feeling the hard strength of their short, sharp horns. They were sleek and fat now after the near-death of their winter leanness and he smiled at the beauty of them. One of the boys, running to head off a straying calf, got in his way and Ar Apa slapped him so hard on the side of his head that he fell and rolled, stumbling to his feet and sobbing as he ran on. Ar Apa waved to the other boy who came forward hesitantly, his eyes frightened and suspicious behind the mat of long blond hair that fell to his shoulders and half covered his face.

'Water,' Ar Apa shouted. 'Or you'll get twice what I gave the other one.'

The water was hot and foul after a day in the leather bag, but he only sipped a little to wet his throat, then poured more into the palm of his hand to mix with the chalk he had pulverized there. His moustaches were bedraggled and broken and he had to work the fresh paste into them to smooth them back to their original firmness. He sat on the

79

ground and grunted while he worked at them, then rubbed the remaining white water through the already stiffened mat of his hair. The cattle had gone on to the enclosure of the dun walls, their steaming dung the only mark of their passing. He broke a nearby clod with his toe, well-formed, solid; they were eating well. Very good. Wiping his hands on his kirtle, he took up the spear and the bow and arrows that had fed him during his long vigil and followed the cattle. He broke into a fast trot as he came within hailing distance of the wattled walls, shouting so they could hear him: 'Ar Apa comes, what a man, what a runner, what a hunter! He has run a hundred nights without stopping and killed a hundred deer without stopping and drunk only their blood and eaten their raw flesh without stopping. What a man. Ar Apa, Ar Apa!'

He smiled happily, almost believing himself so well did he shout, trotting down into the ditch that fell below the chalk embankment and surrounded and defended the dun, taking a short cut directly to the entrance to his own apartment. If anyone had heard his boasts they made no sign, but since they had been mostly for his own benefit he did not mind. It was doubtful if even the loudest war screamer could have been heard over the evening bedlam inside Dun Der Dak.

Walking through the doorway in the back of his apartment into his mother's, he looked out from the women's second-storey balcony on to the scene below. Cattle milled about, the cows lowing to be milked, while the sheep, their red wool whitened by chalk dust, moved bleating between their legs. Women were milking the cows and ewes into baggy-shaped clay pots, screaming at the younger children who ran among the animals seeking out lumps of dung to use as missiles to hurl at each other.

Ar Apa admired the rich scene, the bursting life, and only turned reluctantly away when he remembered the urgency of his message. He put on his hair-belt and slipped the handle of his stone-headed battle-axe into it. Then he slowly made his way along the high chalk bank that encircled the dun, that gave entrance to all the men's quarters on the outside of the ring of apartment dwellings, an unbroken ring except for the main entrance. Der Dak's rooms were here, spanning the entranceway, first in pride of place, where he could look down and talk to all those who came and went. But he was not here now. Ar Apa peered into the darkness and called but there was no answer. He went even slower as he retraced his steps back along the top of the bank, around the outside of the wicker-work of the apartment walls and past the openings of the other men's quarters. There were voices inside many of them and outside the next doorway, lying on a wolf-skin and just waking up, was a man named Cethern, getting old now for a warrior, ready for marriage, but still a great fighter. Cradled under his right knee was a man's severed head, yellowish and shrivelled beneath the film of cedar oil it had been soaking in, stinking a good deal despite this embalming treatment. Cethern opened his eyes which were red and inflamed, and smacked his lips many times as though trying to get rid of a taste he did not enjoy. He had been drinking mead all day—his breath declared it, if not the discarded pot and his squat little knobbly drinking-cup. Ar Apa sat down on his heels by him.

'Ar Apa has been away many nights,' he said. 'Running all the time, killing boar and hunting deer.'

'Cethern killed a champion from Dun Moweg,' the other called out hoarsely. 'Chopped him down after battling fifteen nights without a stop in the middle of the Stour river, cut off his head. Here is his head—have you ever seen a head like that? Moweg's champion.'

Ar Apa had seen it too many times and he let Cethern talk on while he pulled over the pot and saw that there was still some mead in the bottom. He drained it. 'Der Dak is not here,' he said.

Cethern shook his head and grunted no, lying back down.

'And the other, the one, who is there ...' Ar Apa did not speak the name but shrugged his shoulder in the right direction.

'He is there.' Cethern showed no desire to talk too much about him either and closed his eyes again.

There were things that had to be done. Ar Apa breathed out heavily and stood again, brushing his hard moustaches with his knuckles, clutching his axe. Even more slowly now he followed the walkway in almost a complete circle around to the first door on the other side of the entrance, the place of honour next to Der Dak's, and looked inside. The interior was invisible now with the sun gone and night upon them.

'Come inside, strong Ar Apa,' a voice said from the darkness, speaking with a strange accent and a wet lisp to all the words. 'You have come with something to tell me, something *important* to tell me?'

Ar Apa held even more tightly to the haft of his axe and blinked in the darkened chamber. There were hangings of cloth here and chests, as well as a sweet smell that he had never known before. And an even darker movement in the rear, a person, a man, the one they called the Dark Man whenever someone, drunk enough, dared to speak his name aloud.

'The gift . . .' Ar Apa said, the words not coming easily.

'I have many gifts, rich gifts, gifts never seen before by anyone. And I have a gift for you if it pleases me. But you must please me, Ar Apa. Do you please me? You took a gift from me, an amber disc rimmed with gold, made by the wonderful craftsmen that serve in great Dun Uala. And you told me you would go to the west to the place where all the men with swords were killed, to wait there and see if anyone came back. Have you done this? Have you seen anything?'

'I have done this! I have run a hundred nights and slain a hundred boar and eaten a hundred deer, all this I have done. I have gone to the valley.' Emboldened by the sound of his voice, he told all the things he had done or wished that he had done or heard that others had done or even imagined might be done. The Dark Man listened in silence. In the end Ar Apa even told him about the two men and the girl who had come to the burnt-out settlement and how one man had waved his bronze sword and sworn so loudly that, on the hill above, Ar Apa had heard him clearly. Then his voice ran down and he was silent, only coughing and spitting on to

82

the floor. He looked back over his shoulder through the door-way where the first stars were now appearing.

'You have done very, very well,' the Dark Man finally said. 'You have told me that which I wanted to hear and you have told me what a great hunter and warrior Ar Apa is, which I wanted to hear as well since I am honoured to be among such great warriors. Now—here is your gift.'

There was a rattle of bolts in the darkness and the squeak of hinges. Ar Apa walked forward with his hand out, every-thing else forgotten in his greed, and felt a cool hand, soft as a child's, touching his, pressing something cooler into it.

'It is gold, all gold,' the Dark Man said, and Ar Apa hurried out and looked at the wonder in his palm, clear and shining in the moonlight. Solid gold, heavy and precious. Already fixed to a necklace. A haft and an axe in gold, big enough to cover his palm. A double-headed axe, a wonder beyond belief, something never seen before.

Filled with the joy of it, Ar Apa went down to the great hearth in the centre of the dun where there was the sound of much shouting and talk, and the flames of the high leaping fire cast moving light upon the ring of pillar stones embracing the scene. As he stepped into the circle Ar Apa brushed his hand against his own red-tipped pillar stone, higher than he was by several heads, gaining strength by the touch. An ox had been killed and had roasted most of the day until now the skin was black and crackling and gave off a mouth-watering odour that hung in the air, heavier than smoke. Urged on by much shouted instruction, some of the newly initiated warriors lifted the ends of the green pole that had been thrust down the steer's throat and out the other end, and moved the steaming carcass so that the pole rested on two wooden hurdles. The older warriors were already calling out and boasting as to who should have the honour of cutting the meat and taking the choicest piece. Cethern would cut it as he always did, but not before the others had their say.

'I am a champion,' Nair said, jumping to his feet and beating his axe against his shield. There were sharp cries which he ignored, shouting even louder to drown them out. '*I* claim the right to carve the roast. In the raid against Finmog's teuta I called in the night outside the dun and when the warriors ran out I killed the first ten with my axe, killed the next ten with my axe and took their heads, and another ten and another ten ...' His voice rose with each repetition and he jumped and stamped on the ground until Cethern himself began to howl and beat on his own shield. He was hungry and out of sorts this evening and wanted to eat without the extended ritual of boasting that would last until the meat was cold.

'I am Cethern, I am the best, I am the killer of men, the stealer of cows, the dealer of death, with death in my hand, and death in my axe and death where I go.' Carried away, he spun in a circle, swinging his axe so that the men in the front had to fall back shouting angrily, and Nair growled in his throat and went to sit down at the back.

'Cethern the killer, a hundred men dead in an eyeblink and all their heads at my belt, a hundred times a hundred dead in a night and all their heads making a pile as high as my pillar stone and all their cows my cows and all their bulls my bulls and all their deaths my deaths. The best, Cethern, the killer, Cethern, the murderer, the bloodletter, the terrible ...'

'The great empty skin of air,' Ar Apa shouted.

There were appreciative cries at this and some laughter and Cethern howled with rage and looked about for the man who had insulted him. Ar Apa pulled a shield away from the man next to him and pushed through the crowd. He had listened to Cethern boast before and had been as angry as the other men, but like them had kept his silence because he knew that Cethern was as good as his boast. But not tonight. The glow of the golden axe still burned in his eyes and any man who could win an axe like that was as good a man as this bragging fool.

'Boasting fool!' he shouted aloud and the men roared with answering shouts. This was going to be a battle. 'I'll cut the meat. *I* am the champion. I ran a hundred nights and killed

84

a hundred deer and beheaded a hundred boar all in a single night.' He circled about Cethern who was growling and spitting as foam collected on his lips.

'Ar Apa's father was witless, he had no mother, he is no man, he has no balls ...' He choked on his own sputum and Ar Apa shouted back:

'I am the killer. I have an amber disc bound with gold, I have a two-headed gold axe, I talked with the Dark Man, I cannot be stopped!'

He swung his axe around in a swirling blow but Cethern jumped back and raised his shield so that the axe bounced from it. Everyone was shouting now; speaking the Dark Man's name aloud was very bold and they appreciated it and so did Cethern who moved away again to dodge a blow. The women and children were running up to stand behind the seated men and watch, their eyes round, silent figures in the darkness.

'Ar Apa is a liar,' was the best Cethern could say, swinging a blow himself that the other dodged.

'Look, look!' Ar Apa shouted, seizing his axe-haft in his teeth as he backed away, reaching for his belt and the small bundle pressed against his skin there. He unwrapped the necklace from around the golden axe and held it high, glowing redly in the firelight, then plunged it away again at the appreciative shouts. Cethern rushed at him and caught the blow on his shield and spat his own axe into his palm.

After that the serious fighting began. If Cethern was the better axeman he was past his prime and had drunk a lot that day. Ar Apa was strong and angry, pushed into ferocious attack by the golden axe and how the others had cheered at the sight of it. He rained down blows upon his opponent, pushing at his body and trying to tangle his legs while at the same time hammering with his axe as if he were chopping a tree. It was all Cethern could do to keep his shield up to catch the blows that crashed upon it, not able to free his own axe from the pressure of Ar Apa's shield. They went around the fire like this, thundering and straining, shouting wordless curses at each other. Almost in desperation, feeling the flames at his back, Cethern pulled his axe away and swung a sharp quick blow up under the other's guard that caught Ar Apa on the thigh, drawing blood. Ar Apa sprang back and the men shouted even louder.

Still possessed by anger, Ar Apa was not bothered by the wound and it infuriated him even more. He felt the numbness in his leg muscles and saw his own red blood and shrieked with fury, an ear-splitting blast that silenced all the others. Even Cethern hesitated a moment and peered over the top of his shield.

Ar Apa threw his arms wide, hurling his shield away from him so hard that it flew over the men and fell among the squealing women. Then he seized his axe in both hands, raising it above his head, leaping in at Cethern. He did it all in an instant, unthinking, possessed by fury that overwhelmed him. Cethern crouched and raised his shield and drew his own axe back for a counterblow that he knew the other could not avoid.

The axe came down with such force that Ar Apa's feet left the ground. Striking the hide-covered wooden shield, splitting it, driving through with such force that it caught Cethern on the forehead and he fell. He was half stunned, and rolled about trying to get back to his feet.

He never did. Ar Apa raised the axe high again and brought the polished sharp weight of the stone down on Cethern's forehead, through the bone and into his brain, killing him instantly.

All the warriors were shouting again, pummelling each other with enthusiasm while Ar Apa strutted before them, waving his battle-axe around and around his head with joy, so that bits of gore flew from it and spattered them. Then he threw his axe aside and stood over Cethern, straddling him, and pulled the man's bronze dagger from his necklace. A rich object this, one of the very few owned by any warrior in the whole teuta, and sharper than anything else was sharp. Clutching it in both hands, pressing and sawing through the dead man's neck until he had severed his head and the body and the ground beneath was soaked with blood.

86

Then he stood and tucked the long hair into his belt so that the severed head hung there and the last blood drained down his leg.

Numbed by success, he walked stiff-legged over to the roasted ox and with the dagger, still dripping with gore, cut from it the champion's portion for himself.

12

'I'm sure it's ready now,' Ason said. 'See, there's no more ore on top of the coals.' He bent over to peer into the glowing mound where a shimmer of rising heat was clearly visible in the warm sunlight.

'Patience,' Inteb advised, brushing at the charcoal smudges on his arms and hands. 'The walls of Mycenae were not raised in a day, nor is tin drawn from stone in a few brief moments. That was the fault the first time we tried this. Don't you remember that the coals were still glowing when we raked them aside?'

'How can we be sure?'

'We cannot. But it does no harm to wait.'

Ason did not have the patience to stand and watch while the smelting continued, being of completely different temperament than the builder Inteb, who waited quietly while stone was worked to his design and buildings and walls raised. Leaving the Egyptian by the furnace, Ason walked over to the tin-stream where Aias lolled on the grass nearby, apparently asleep. That he was not was proven when the two boys fell to whispering and stopped their digging. Aias had a small pile of rocks to hand and a good aim; the boys shrieked as the missiles hit them and fell to shovelling again with deer shoulder-blades. They scooped the gravel to one side, then filled their basket with the deeper soil that contained the grey-black nuggets. When the basket was filled they pushed and dragged it to the sloping wooden sluice of the tye and dumped it in. The water from the spring ran over the muddy mixture and they stirred it with their hands so the lighter particles would be washed away. There were still not enough boys. These should have returned to their digging while others picked out the black pebbles for still others to pound into fragments. The boys worked faster under Ason's gaze, putting the wet ore into other baskets, then hurrying back. They would break up the walnut-sized lumps later.

Everything about the operation was makeshift, but was the best they could do with the limited labour available. If they had had treasure, bronze, gold, they could have bought more boys. Only Naikeri's hatred for the raiders had carried them this far. There were rough lean-tos for sleeping, just slanted roofs of boughs and branches. They cooked over an open fire; they drank plain water. And they were mining ore. The earth-covered mounds of the charcoal-making fires were burning well, and if they had charged the furnace correctly this time they would have their first tin. Ason resisted the temptation to return to the first furnace and went instead to help Inteb with the dirty work of charging the other furnace that they had prepared. It was just a round depression in the clay, sloping towards a hole in the centre the size of two cupped hands. A mound of charcoal was heaped in there, topped with pulverized ore, then ignited. The bellows boy was called over to pump air into it, leaving the other furnace to burn itself out. Lycos had smelted tin this way and Ason remembered the steps. So far all they had produced was an evil mixture of charcoal and slag. And tin was what they needed, tin. Through his harsh thoughts Ason was aware of someone calling his name, and looked up to see Naikeri standing on top of the granite-studded wall of earth that sealed the valley.

She was wet with sweat, her hair matted and moist, her mouth gaping as she tried to catch her breath.

'The Yerni have been seen near my father's home and he is frightened. He will not stay any more but is taking everything and going to our people in the west. He is very afraid that this time he will be killed and all of us destroyed. He thinks the Yerni have gone mad as rutting deer and he will not stay where they can reach him. You must come with me and stop him.'

'Let him go. It means nothing to us here.'

'Nothing!' She spat the word and clenched her fists with anger. 'How is this mine open, why are you digging for tin? It is all my father's wealth that did this, his gifts to the Donbaksho that brought the boys here, that provide your food. Even a copper adze-head. I made him cast it in his blindness to get what you needed. And now you scorn him. Where are the Yerni warriors you were to kill in vengeance, where are their heads? You take everything and give nothing and then say my father is nothing.'

Ason turned away from her and folded his arms and looked at the mine-workings, not hearing her. If she were not so important he would have silenced her, but he could not. Neither could he lower himself to trade angry words with a woman. He waited until her voice had stopped then turned back.

'What can I say to Ler that would make him stay?'

'Say that you will protect him, that you will kill Yerni, talk to him of vengeance for his dead sons and murdered people. Perhaps you can anger him, I cannot. He wants only to run.'

Ason did not like it. He was needed here at the mine. There would be long arguments with Ler and promises made that he might not be able to keep, endless talk and no action; he hated this. Yet he had to do it. If talk could take the place of warriors he would have to talk—because he had none to stand behind him.

'I'll come,' he said reluctantly. 'I must tell Inteb what is happening.'

There was no other course open. With a long last look at the dying furnace he led the way out of the camp and along the ill-defined path. He went at his fastest pace and could hear Naikeri behind him panting to keep up—which made him smile.

Well away from the mine the trail dipped downwards

from the open heathland to pass by the edge of a thicketed marsh. As Ason worked his way down the slope he felt, with a hunter's instinct, that there were eyes upon him. There was game in the fenland, deer and boar to be sure, but mainly water-fowl and small game. This was different. He looked ahead and stopped, pulling his sword from the slings as he did so. Naikeri nearly ran into him.

'Why do you stop?' She had to gasp out the words. Ason pointed down the slope with his sword.

At the bottom, at the very edge of the boggy thicket in the sedge grass, stood a man and a hulking wolf-like dog, both as unmoving as stone. The man was short and dumpy, with a pasty white skin that was rounded with fat over the muscles below. He wore only a breech-clout of red fox fur, and his legs were encased up over the knees in waterproof boots made from the skin off the hocks of a wild horse. Gripped in one hand were a thin spear tipped with a toothy bone point and a long pole snare. At his waist, hanging in a net, were a gutted hare and a brace of dark-feathered duck.

'Who are you?' Ason shouted, brandishing his sword, and at the sound of his voice the man splashed back into the overgrown bog. Naikeri shouted a harsh, strange-sounding word and pulled at Ason's arm.

'Put away your sword,' she said. 'It is one of the people from the deep fens, the Hunters they are called. They trade with us, they do not make war like the Yerni. He is here for a reason. Let me go first and talk to him.'

Ason lowered his sword—but did not return it to its slings —as Naikeri went ahead. The dog growled deeply and showed its fangs as she came close, but the Hunter hit it in the ribs with the haft of his spear and pushed it behind him. Naikeri sat down on her knees and the short man, after looking up at Ason, stepped up on the grass and sat down on his heels. They talked for a long time and Ason was getting restless before Naikeri called out to him.

'Put your sword away and come down, slowly. He has much to tell us.'

The Hunter and his dog looked at Ason with identical suspicion as he approached and sat down cross-legged on the ground three paces away.

'This man is Chaskil,' she explained. 'I have met him before many times and he speaks our tongue as well as his own.'

Chaskil seemed reluctant to speak any language. He stared at Ason, dark eyes peering from beneath fatty eyelids. His face was flat and his nose was depressed, without a bridge; his hair black and lank. After a long while he turned away from Ason and looked into the distance. When he finally spoke his words were heavily accented but understandable.

'I am Chaskil and she is Naikeri and you are Ason or so she has told me. I am Chaskil of the Hunters who have hunted here forever and we talk about it. We hunted here when it was cold in all seasons and we talk about it. The Albi came and we talk about it. They came to the moors and they do what they must do and we do what we must do and we talk about it. Then the Donbaksho came to the forest with their tree-killing axes and we talk about it. Then the Yerni came to the downs with their cows and man-killing axes and we talk about it. We talk about a tree-killing axe.' He fell silent and fingered his hunting-knife, a row of tiny, delicately flaked chips of flint set in a wooden handle. Naikeri had experience with these solitary, hidden people and knew how to speak with them. Ason was baffled and thought the man mad.

'We talk about it,' she said. 'We talk about the Yerni and we talk about the axe. Do we talk about your axe?'

Chaskil stirred at her words and shifted his weight so he could lift his left foot. Under the sole of his horseskin boot was a broken piece of polished greenstone, the type of lorg stone the Albi ground and polished for the making of woodworking axes and adzes.

'That's a piece of broken axe-head,' Naikeri said. 'An Albi axe-head. Is it your axe-head?' She went on and he nodded. 'The Albi are friends of the Hunters. We give them axe-heads so they can make dugout canoes. So they can go fishing along

92

the coast. They give us help. They guide us in our trading travels. They tell us things they have seen. Have you seen something?'

'We talk about the Yerni. We talk about my axe-head.'

'You will have a new axe-head as soon as one can be made. You will come to my father's house as you always do and we will talk of it there. But you do not go to my father's house but instead meet us here. Why is that?'

'We talk of Yerni.'

Ason had a sudden thought. 'Are there any nearby?' he asked. Chaskil turned to look squarely at Ason.

'We talk about Yerni who killed a Hunter. Who watch the place where you dig in the ground and make smoke. We talk about Yerni who hide and watch ...'

'Waiting for me to leave!' Ason shouted, springing to his feet. 'They have been watching, they know my sword, they waited for me to leave ...' Then he was pounding up the hill and over it back towards the mine. Naikeri talked to Chaskil, then hurried after him.

After the first burst of anger Ason slowed down and forced himself to go at a steady run that would take him back to the mine without stopping and without exhausting himself. As he jogged through the shadows of the high trees he found himself smiling with anticipation. If the Hunter were right this was his chance for revenge. Yerni—it was something to look forward to and he hastened to the meeting with all his heart.

When he neared the mine he slowed down and went more carefully. If they were hiding nearby he did not want to disturb them. As he approached the base of the hillock that sealed the valley, one of the boys burst over the top of it, running as if death were at his heels, and at the same moment Ason heard a high shrieking.

'They are here!' Ason shouted in return and ran as hard as he could, sword ready. The valley and the mine opened before him, changed drastically in the short time since he had left.

The rain-shelters over the furnaces were knocked down

93

and burning. The boys were gone. And Inteb's body lay on the ground, half in the water running from the tye. Near him was the body of a stranger; farther up the valley was another.

Howling with anger, Aias stood halfway up the valley wall where he had climbed, hurling stones down at three Yerni who were trying to climb up after him. They were shouting even louder at this unnatural way to fight and were trying to get up high enough to reach him with their stone-headed battle-axes. One of them climbed ahead of the others and instantly regretted it when Aias leaped down beside him. Long before he could swing his axe around, the boxer's fist lashed out against the side of his head and he fell and tumbled down the hillside. Then Aias had scrambled higher again, calling back insults. He had not gone unscathed himself—his chest and arms were wet with blood.

Ason ran quietly and was almost upon them before they were aware of him. The last man Aias had knocked down the hill was stumbling to his feet and groping for his axe. He saw Ason coming and shouted a warning. He raised the axe but died a moment later when the point of the bronze sword tore out his throat. The other two turned to attack Ason, and he smiled and let them come.

He could have killed them quickly but he wanted them to die knowing who he was and why he was doing this. The sweat started out from their faces and they swung wildly as he cursed them. One tried to rush him and Ason slashed his legs so badly that he could do no more than rise to his knees.

When he had told them what he wanted them to know, Ason attacked and killed each of them quickly and then went back to make sure that the other two Yerni were also dead. Both had fallen victim to Aias' fists. The nearest one lay with his eyes open, a great bruise on the side of his head, which was twisted around at an odd angle. His neck had been broken and he appeared to have died at once. The other lay on his back, rolling from side to side and clutching at his head. Aias must have hit him squarely on the nose, breaking it all over his face, and he was just regaining consciousness. He shook all over and his bloodshot, blackened eyes opened

94

when Ason pushed his sword against the base of the man's throat.

'Who are you?' Ason said.

The Yerni looked wildly about him and reached for the sword, but dropped his arms back when Ason pressed harder.

'Nair,' he gasped, choking under the sharp pressure.

'Where are you from?'

'I am—of the teuta of Der Dak.'

It meant nothing to Ason. He shook the sword angrily and kicked the man in the stomach. 'What are you doing here? Why are you raiding this place?'

'The man—Dark Man—gifts—the Dark Man.'

He rolled sideways suddenly, slapping at the blade at the same time. Ason lunged but his sword only stabbed into the ground. Before he could lift it again Nair was upon him, grappling with him and pulling a bronze dagger from his necklace. Ason grabbed his wrist before the thrust could go home and had his own sword-arm pinioned the same way. They strained, face to face, Ason smelling the man's foul breath and the reek of his unwashed body. Over his shoulder he saw Aias running up, his fist drawn back for a decapitating sweep.

'No,' Ason called out. 'He is mine.'

Aias stopped, but stood ready. Ason did not try to bring his sword around for a cut—it was a clumsy weapon at these close quarters—but instead bent all his strength to turn the dagger aside. Slowly, shaking with the effort of the struggle, the point was turned away from his own skin and forced back towards the midriff of its owner. Nair looked at the approach of the blade, his eyes starting from his head, put all of his strength against it and still it turned and turned until the point was touching his skin. He never thought to release the dagger but instead held it in his own fist as Ason fought against him and, with a single convulsive effort, plunged the weapon home deep up under Nair's breastbone. He held it there for a long moment as the man writhed and died.

95

13

Inteb's head was bruised and raw where an axe had struck him down, but he was still breathing. Naikeri had arrived in time to see the last man slain, looking on with pleasure at this first payment of vengeance she had worked so hard for. She now sang softly to herself as she tended Inteb, dampening his head with cool water from the stream.

Ason sat down heavily next to the corpse, stretching the strained muscles of his hand.

'They came after you left,' Aias said. 'They must have been watching. They came yelping and howling up the valley, sure of themselves. They knew who was here. Inteb was unarmed, tried to run. Chopped him down. I broke that man's neck before the Egyptian could be killed. All the boys ran. I threw my club at this one, then hit him in the nose. Another one hit me. I ran too. Up the cliff there. Then you came back.' He grinned through the blood and bent for a handful of water to wipe his face.

'Round up the boys and get them back to work,' Ason said. 'Put up new shelters.' He went over to look at Inteb who now had his eyes open and was blinking dazedly.

'Yerni ...' he said weakly, then tried to look around.

'All dead. But one of them talked to me before he died.' Naikeri looked up when he said this. 'What is the teuta of Der Dak? That is what he said.'

'Der Dak is a bull-chief of one of the tribes of the Yerni. One of five tribes; five teuta that fight against each other all the time. If the Yerni have any allegiance at all it is to their bull-chief. Der Dak's teuta is the one closest to us. These men must have come from there; Dun Der Dak is four days' walk to the east. Why did they come? Did Der Dak send them?'

'He talked about someone called a Dark Man. Is that one of their chiefs?'

'I have never heard of him, or anyone by that name. Perhaps it is one of their gods.'

Inteb groaned and sat up. 'You came back in time, praise Horus,' he said weakly. 'Are they dead?'

'All of them, and no thanks to Horus. A man stopped us, some kind of hunter from the forests around here. He saw the Yerni watching us.' He turned to Naikeri. 'And why weren't your people watching out for raiders? You seem to know when your own places are threatened, but not the mine.'

'My people have other things to do than spy for you. We work hard and must defend ourselves. And what about my father—you said you would see him?'

'Your father! Your people! I cannot defend him and them and this mine, and smelt tin, not one man by myself. I am needed here.'

'If you do not help my father you will have no more food or boys—or mine. What do you choose?'

What could he choose? He had to have the help of the Albi. But how could he guard them all from the murderous Yerni raiders?

'Why don't you stop the raids?' Inteb asked, answering his unspoken question. Ason turned to listen. 'The girl told you that the Yerni have never acted like this before. Apparently the different tribes of the Yerni make war on each other and trade with the Albi. A sensible arrangement. But someone has stopped being sensible and is sending out these raiding parties. Find him, kill him, the trouble will stop.'

'But who is it?'

'Der Dak!' Naikeri said. 'Who else could it be? The men of his teuta do not make war without his orders. They fight alone, that they do any time, but would not come this far, all together, unless he told them to do so. Go and kill him and the trouble will be over.'

'And his entire following of loyal warriors? I can fight one man but not all of his men.'

'Perhaps you won't have to,' Inteb said, touching the side of his head and wincing. 'This arrangement of the teuta with its bull-chief and warriors sounds much like one of your cities of the Argolid—'

'You dare compare noble Mycenae or Tiryns to these stinking savages!'

'Patience, kind Ason, I compare only the lines of authority. I have dwelt in many places and I find that people are very much the same everywhere. They have rulers and gods, and among the people there are those who kill and those who are killed. Those who lead and those who follow. Let us profit from this experience.'

'I could call this Der Dak out and kill him and that would stop the raids. Do they speak as your people do? Would they know what I was saying? The one I killed seemed to understand me.' He looked at Naikeri.

'Their talk is a little different, some words are different, but they will understand you. I can tell you some words so they will understand you better.'

'What is it that they are most proud of?' Inteb asked.

Naikeri thought for a moment. 'Their fighting ability, they always brag about that, and how bold they are and how fast they can run and how many beasts they have killed. Oh yes, and how many cows they own. And have stolen. They love their cattle more than their women, I have heard. And their jewellery—the gold torques and bronze daggers they get in trade. They are very vain.'

'If I leave in the morning will you show me the way?' Ason asked.

'With all my heart. If Der Dak's men killed my people, I want to be there when you slay him.'

Aias came up and called to them. He had two battle-axes in each hand, three twisted gold bars around his neck and a bronze dagger hanging there as well.

'From the bodies,' he said.

'For the mine,' Ason said. 'We will not have to depend upon Ler's bounty now.'

'I will take the axes,' Naikeri said. 'They are Albi made. You take the torques and the dagger. Wear all of it. Only that much jewellery will give a warrior high enough standing among the Yerni to challenge a bull-chief.'

'The furnace,' Inteb said, climbing slowly to his feet. 'We have forgotten and it should be finished by now.'

They hurried to it and watched closely as Inteb raked the ashes away from the little pit underneath. He pried into it but could see nothing but the crumpled ash. Ason grabbed up a singed length of fur that was sopping with water and wrapped it around his hand. He groped about in the bottom, drawing something out with a great hissing, dropping it as it burned his fingers.

A disc of silvery crackling metal, convex on the bottom and flat on top, thick and heavy.

'Tin,' Ason said. 'At last. It can be nothing else.'

Naikeri and Ason left Ler's house at dawn the next morning. At first the old man had not heard them and was intent upon moving his own belongings at once. Naikeri shouted and pleaded with him and after a time he listened. In his blindness he would really prefer to stay in the place he knew and in the end they prevailed. If Ason defeated Der Dak the raids would cease and Ler could live in peace. He wanted to believe that and they convinced him. There were a number of wooden chests that had been dug up from under the dirt floor and he rooted through one of these, pushing aside a small boulder carved all over with shapes for the open-casting of various types of copper axes and adzes. He came up with a bronze skullcap, its plume-socket empty, that was lined with padded leather, profit of a trade of years previous. It was not the helmet of a nobleman, but it would do. Ason also had a thick hide tunic that might help turn a blow and carried one of the round Yerni shields. And he had his sword.

That alone was more important than all the rest together.

Their path took them across the high moors, along a trail marked by generations of trudging feet. It had rained during the night and the air was filled with the pungent smell of loam, damp earth and heather. A hawk moved in silent circles over a copse, then folded its wings and dropped like a rock, soaring high again with some small animal in its talons. The sun was warm but the air cool, a day for doing things. Ason hummed to himself. Naikeri led the way carrying a back-pack filled with the food they had brought. She walked at a steady, tireless pace, her legs moving smoothly, the thrust of her buttocks visibly working between the open spaces of her wool skirt, strands of brown yarn opening and closing between her narrow waist and the tight bands that gathered them on her upper legs. Ason looked at this and felt desire returning, a desire unsatisfied since that night in the rain and storm. He had love—Inteb satisfied him and cared for him—but he missed the soft embrace that only a woman could supply.

When the sun was overhead they turned off the well-marked path and went down the bank of a small stream, to a quiet spot where they could drink and eat. Wordlessly, she took a piece of sun-dried meat from her pack and gave it to Ason. He chewed it and cupped water from the stream with his hand to wash it down. They were silent for there was nothing to say. Neither of them knew anything about conversation for conversation's sake alone, so they were not disturbed by long silences. Yet Ason had his eyes upon her while he ate; there are languages that do not have words. Naikeri finished eating and brushed the crumbs from her hands.

Then she removed the copper pin that held her upper garments together and slid down her short skirt of open stranded wool. She took off her clothes and lay back on the grass of the slope, her eyes half closed. The sun was warm on her olive skin, the air still and silent here except for the distant drone of a bee among the flowers.

Ason laid his sword aside, opened his tunic, standing above

her. Her breasts were full and round, lying to each side and resting against her arms, the nipples dark eyes staring silently into his. He put his hand down and moved her legs apart; she lifted her knees and made a small sound. Then he was on top of her, his full weight upon her, penetrating deep with a single thrust that made her cry out in pain. She cried again, a different sharper sound and her legs locked about his back sealing him to her. When he plunged deeper, filling her, she sank her teeth into his shoulder, drawing blood: he was not aware of it. Only later did he feel the pain and he slapped her so she opened her mouth and fell away, crying.

When Ason went away to wash in the stream Naikeri pulled her clothing to her and put it on, slowly, shaking.

Ason was soon ready to leave but she did not rise, still sitting in the same place where the tall grass had been pressed flat.

'Do you have a wife in this far-off place you come from?' she asked.

'It is time to leave.'

'Tell me.'

'No, no wife. This is not a time to talk—'

'This is the time. You are the first man who has ever had me. If you want me—'

'I want you when I want you, nothing more. When the tin is mined I will leave this place and return home. When I marry I will marry there. A queen for a king. Get to your feet.'

She was angry and did not stand, pulling away from his hand when he reached for her.

'My line is the oldest of the Albi; you saw our tomb. If we had queens I would be one.'

'You are nothing.' Ason dragged her to her feet. She showed no emotion now when she spoke.

'Then I will never be your queen. But you can take me as a woman, you have taken me twice. Let me be your woman. There are many things I can do to help at the mine, you know I am strong. And I will be there to warm your bed at night.'

'If you wish,' Ason said, already moving off towards the track they had left. Naikeri shouldered her pack and followed him. Smiling to herself where he could not see.

The first days were the easiest. They would rise before day-break, and as soon as it was light enough to see the path they would set out, stopping only with darkness. But on the third day Naikeri led them off the trail and up through a stand of silver birch trees to the top of the hill. They had to force their way through the thick undergrowth and at the top they crawled the last distance to peer out from under the hedges there. Just below them the open downs began again, a vast plain, covered with grass for the most part. A herd of dark cattle grazed here, watched by some boys. A man lay sleeping nearby with an axe and shield close to hand. Beyond them was the rounded form of a circular building.

'Yerni,' Naikeri said. 'They must be of Der Dak's teuta because his dun is the closest, out there. His people are on the plain on all sides of the dun where he has his warriors and cattle. If we are seen he will know about it quickly enough and you will have to fight all of them at once if you are not here for trade. They do not like strangers on their lands.'

'We must get close to the dun without being seen, so that I can call out their bull-chief. How will we do that?'

'Move only by night.'

As long as they avoided the widely scattered boolies and circular cow-pens there was little chance of being discovered. A dog barked when they passed one isolated homestead, but dogs bark at a lot of things and they were not seen. The waning crescent moon rose later and by its light they moved faster along the cow-paths. Naikeri had been this way before, by daylight, and seemed to have no difficulty in finding her way by night. Well before dawn she pointed to a curving shadow on the plain ahead.

'Dun Der Dak,' she said.

14

When the first grey light pushed at the darkness, Ason took out the jewellery removed from the slain Yerni and dressed himself with it—all three torques in place and the bronze dagger suspended from his neck, Yerni style. Naikeri handed him the cup-shaped helmet she had rubbed with sand during the night so that it shone and reflected the gold of the rising sun. He took the shield in his left hand and the sword in his right and rose. 'Stay here where they cannot see you,' he ordered. 'If I am killed, return and tell the others. If I win and it is safe I will send someone out for you. In any case do not let yourself be seen. A hero with a single woman for a following is something to be laughed at, not feared.'

Ason then rose from their resting-place, turned around to face the dun, and did not look back again. He waited, silent and still, until the sun had cleared the horizon and sounds of morning bustle arose from inside the walls before him. He could see people moving about. With a steady pace, the naked sword in his hand, he went forward alone against the dun and all the fighting-men inside it.

No one noticed him until he was a few paces away from the entrance. A woman and some of the older boys were there, tugging at the bars to let the cattle out for the day. She looked up and squealed and Ason stopped.

'Der Dak!' he bellowed at the top of his lungs. Then 'Der Dak' again.

The boys and the woman ran away, and shouted voices

raised questions inside the dun. Warriors were coming out of the doors on the mound above, like ground squirrels from their holes. A dog, a great dark animal with matted fur, caught Ason's smell and ran at him barking and showing its long fangs. A single slash of the sword killed it and it fell in a silent dirty heap. Ason raised his voice again.

'Come out Der Dak so I can kill you as I have killed your dog. You will be easier to kill than your dog. You are a coward made of dung, a woman wearing a stolen goat's pizzle on a string tied to your loins. Come out and face Ason, the man who will kill you.'

There was a roar of anger from the first doorway that drowned all the other voices. Der Dak sprang out, clutching the sides of the opening in his hands as he peered down. His hair rose high in a stiff white-chalked mane, like boar bristles, and his moustaches were just as long and white, reaching down to his shoulders and curling outward. He had just awakened, naked, boiling with rage.

'Who is it that invites a quick death like this?'

'I am Ason of Mycenae, first son of King Perimedes my father. Come out, murderer of my kinsmen, and face the man who has come to kill you. Come out coward—to your death.'

Der Dak was chomping his jaw with rage now at the insults, and a froth of saliva wet his lips. He saw the bronze sword and heard the words Ason spoke and knew who he was. Plunging back into his quarters, he prepared for battle.

Ason had forgotten the others, but Naikeri had not. From her hiding-place she watched the warriors emerge one by one. Most of them carried weapons but did not appear ready to use them. They gathered on the top of the mound, shouting loudly to one another and pushing for a good position to watch the coming battle. None thought to interfere. They looked forward to it happily and shouted for the women to bring them mead. They called out when Der Dak emerged ready for battle, his shield on his arm, a great stone-headed axe in his hand. He jumped to the ground and when he came forward Ason saw what he wore on his head.

A Mycenaean helmet. Dented and badly cared for with

most of the high-arched plume of horsehair missing, but a Mycenaean helmet nevertheless. It could have come from only one place.

The bull-chief was a powerful man and they were evenly matched. He had fought and killed many men and their heads now sat above his doorway. His axe-head was twice the size of any other and he had the strength to wield it. Wearing armour, Ason would have been immune to any attack and would simply have cut the man down when he came close. But now it was the Yerni who wore the bronze helm and had his shield before him as impenetrable as any bronze. Ason thrust, but the shield pushed his sword aside. Then he had to spring back and raise his own shield to catch the axe and deflect it. It struck with a boom like thunder and he felt his arm shiver and ache with the blow.

They circled each other, spitting curses, swinging their weapons in ruthless attempts to batter through the other's defences. It was a wild battle with no quarter given and no quarter asked. Soon they had no breath for cursing; they could only gasp, and their bodies ran with sweat. And blood.

Der Dak drew first blood with a backhand swing of the great axe that glanced from Ason's shield and struck him in the upper arm, grazing the skin. It did not hurt much and was no hindrance, but the blood ran freely and the watchers shouted happily at the sight. Der Dak grinned and intensified his attack. Ason gave ground and looked at the blood and gaped, lowering the shield as though the arm were weakened. Der Dak saw this and pushed even harder, sweeping his axe down with a force that would strike through the lowered shield.

Ason had been waiting for this blow and was ready. Instead of trying to avoid it or raising his shield, he brought his sword up so that the point rested on his shield, thrusting the sword above him to catch the blow.

It did, just below the axe-head. Before the axe could touch the shield or drive past it to the man that held it, the axe-handle struck hard on the edge of the sword.

Bronze cuts wood.

The handle was severed, the axe-head thudding to the ground, and Der Dak was left with the useless length of wood in his hand. Then Ason's sword-point whirled round and up like a swooping bird and found its nest in the pit of the bull-chief's stomach. Deep. Sliding in easily until the point rested against the man's backbone.

Der Dak threw his arms wide, his shield bouncing and rolling away, and gave a single last hoarse shout of pain before he folded forward and died.

Ason stood over the slumped body and hurled his shield away as well. Naikeri had told him about the customs of these people. They took heads. Severed them with a bronze dagger kept only for that purpose. Sawed off slowly : a man's neck is a very strong thing. He would show them a better way to do their butchery. In a screaming arc the sword came down, driven by the strength of both his arms. Der Dak's head rolled away from his body.

The cold anger still possessed Ason. He bent and took the Mycenaean helmet from the severed head and put it on in place of his own bronze skullcap, letting the cap drop to the ground. The stiff moustache made a ready handle and he seized Der Dak's head by it and strode towards the warriors on the mound. Those who were armed made no move to raise their weapons as he sprang up and stood before them.

'Der Dak is dead!' he shouted. 'Who is next in line? Who becomes the new bull-chief?'

One of the warriors came and stood before him.

'I am Ar Apa.' As soon as he said it he sat down on his heels. He was silent a long time. Finally, when Ason did not speak he struck himself on the chest. 'I am a killer, I am a hunter, I ran for a hundred nights and killed a hundred deer, I killed Cethern after a battle that lasted ten nights and his head is above my door.'

'Did you kill my people at the mine?' Ason asked, coldly, tired of the bragging. Ar Apa spread his empty hands.

'Der Dak did that. And others. Many from Dun Uala. They had rich gifts and went all together to the mine. Many did not return.'

'Did Uala lead them?'

'Uala led them, but that was not why they went.' He looked uncomfortable. '*He* gave them gifts, even before they went.' For all his bragging Ar Apa was loath to speak the name and only pointed his head over one shoulder.

'The Dark Man, is that who you mean?'

'Yes, he is called that.'

'Take me to him at once.'

'He is gone. He fled while you battled.'

Ason was silent then and Ar Apa, emboldened, began boasting again. Ason did not listen, the words were repeated after a while in any case. But he did hear Naikeri's whisper from behind him and he nodded agreement. He repeated her words aloud.

'You wish to be bull-chief?'

Ar Apa did not answer the question directly; if he did so he might appear to be challenging Ason and he had already seen more than once what the bronze sword could do.

'There must be a bull-chief,' he said.

Part Three

15

It was the time of samain, time for the choosing of a new bull-chief. Ason wore his sword and freshly painted leather armour, the round shield with its polished bronze bolts on his left arm. His bronze dagger hung about his neck in the Yerni manner. The dents had been hammered from the recaptured Mycenaean helmet, but the missing tufts of horsehair could not be replaced in this land where the only horses were stunted, soft-maned ponies that were hunted for food whenever they were found. But Ason had killed wild boar with his spear, fast dark brutes even more deadly than the boar of the Argolid, and their hair was thick enough to fill the gaps in the helmet's crest. Nor was there any shame attached— the wild boar was as respected here as the noble horses of home. The Yerni warriors stiffened and whitened their long moustaches with clay to resemble the boar's tusks, stiffened their hair for the same reason. There was much honour in bearing that boar's crest.

Aias was impressive enough in his leather armour and bronze skullcap that Ason had first worn to battle against Der Dak. His half-armour resembled Ason's, though of course was not as elaborately decorated. Among the effects belonging to the slain leader had been a bronze-headed axe of the type used for chopping down trees. But it could be used for chopping men as well and was carried with that intent.

Inteb, the least warlike, wore simple leather and carried a plain wooden shield covered with heavy hide. But his stone axe was well made and as good as any the Yerni boasted. He carried a small pack with food while Aias bore the larger bundle with gifts for the new bull-chief.

By midafternoon of the fourth day they saw the chalk mound and the wattled walls of the dun rising from the flat down ahead of them. Twice that day they had passed herds of cattle being driven in that direction; the herd-boys and cattle both rolling worried eyes in their direction and keeping out of the path of the armed men, the Yerni warriors scowling and fingering their battle-axes as they passed. Now more cattle were visible ahead, in temporary pens that had been thrown up around the dun, raising clouds of dust that rose in great billows.

The path they followed was well worn by many feet and thick with cow droppings as it wound between the low She-mounds that surrounded the dun. Here were buried warriors from the entire teuta, returned to the Earth Mother, awaiting She of the Mounds to escort them to the Land of Promise. This was the life centre of the tribe, where the annual assemblies were held and all other great events: the planning of cattle raids, the initiation of new warriors, and the raising up of bull-chiefs.

When they had passed the last cattle pen they saw that a large crowd had gathered outside the walls of the dun and some sort of ceremony was in progress. A high-pitched wailing that hurt the ears sliced the air and set the teeth on edge, and a man's voice could be heard shouting above this sound.

It was a burial, that much was clear when they drew closer. The death-house had been built, a wall-less structure that was no more than a pitched roof made of small logs supported by four corner posts, just high enough and long enough to hold a single body. Women and boys had been labouring for days to loosen the earth around the death-house, hammering in deer antlers to pry the hard chalk up in lumps. Now their work was finished and the warriors, already drunk, listened in appreciation to the tall man, impressive in a white tunic that fell almost to the ground, who was chanting in a loud clear voice. His hair was grey and shoulder-length, his beard

112

full although the hair had been plucked from his upper lip so he had no moustache; only the Yerni warriors had these. At his feet was the decapitated corpse, the head carefully tucked beneath the right arm, glistening with oil and draped with a boar's skin, while next to him a man sat squat-legged blowing strongly into a wooden mouthpiece that was fitted to an inflated skin. He puffed energetically until his face grew red, blowing the skin up like a bellows that helped to smelt the tin. But the stream of air, instead of serving some useful purpose, was blown through a hollow length of bone that had been pierced with a row of holes. This produced a continuous squealing noise that rose and fell in pitch—but never ceased—as the sweating man opened or closed the holes with his fingers. Supported by this sound the shouted chanting could be clearly heard.

He led the warrior's life, the good life that never ends. Died he in battle, shouting he died, battling he died, died as Lug made man to die. Dying this way he cannot know death but instead has put his foot along the warrior's path that leads to Moi Mell. Now we send him to Moi Mell and She of the Mounds will make his path easy. Now he goes to the place of youth forever, where there is no pain and there is no death, where there is no sadness, where there is no jealousy, where there is no pride, where there is no fear. It is a place of plenty he goes to, with flocks and herds as far as can be seen and to them there is no end. There is a pig roasting there so big that forty men cannot lift it, and he will have the first cut from this pig. There are pots to drink from that are never empty. This is where he goes and this is where we send him.

The bone and bellows squealed louder; the warriors shouted until they were hoarse as the corpse was slid into the death-house. As soon as the last logs had been put into place to seal it they began to shovel the loose chalk with the flat shoulder-blades of deer, each trying to outwork the others. The mound of chalk rose until the house was covered

113

and the warriors reeled with exhaustion and drink. Ason found it wonderful to watch and turned reluctantly away only when Ar Apa appeared beside him.

'You are here,' the Yerni warrior said, and there was more than a trace of relief in his voice. Apparently the succession to bull-chief was not as straightforward as he had believed and Ason's presence might assure that station for himself.

'Who are they burying?' Ason asked, his attention still on the ceremony.

'Der Dak. Samain is the time when a bull-chief is buried.'

Ason looked at the growing mound with renewed interest. 'It was summer when I killed him. I thought he must have rotted by now.'

'Our druids know many things. They know what has been and what will be, and they heal the sick. They painted the body every day with cedar oil so it is as you just saw it. You must come and drink.'

Ason would have stayed to listen but Aias smacked his lips together loudly and Inteb turned away as well: this crude embalming bore little resemblance to the sophisticated Egyptian techniques he was familiar with, by which a body was rendered as impervious to corruption as a block of wood. They went past a long rack of flayed sheep-carcases and through the entrance into the dun.

Noise, confusion, colour; complaining animals, shouting people. The inside of the great, spacious dun was a riot of activity as tumultuous as any feast-day in Egypt or funeral game in Mycenae. The Yerni warriors were here, strutting through the crowd with their axes and shields, touching their knuckles to the proud white stiffness of their moustaches. Their women were here as well as numerous children, the smallest of them naked, all of them dirty, playing underfoot, rolling cylinders of carved chalk. But there were strangers too, dark Albi with their packs and trade goods, Donbaksho staring about with wide eyes, bearing poles on their shoulders hung with plump hares and fowl. And others as well, tall blond men of a kind Ason had never seen before. They were warriors, that was clear from their cow-horned bronze helmets and the long daggers that slapped against their legs, with heavy gold bracelets on their wrists and huge gold link-fasteners to close their cloaks. Yet they carried great baskets on their backs like slaves, and their women bore even larger packs. They were setting these down but none had been opened as yet, and Ason wondered with interest what goods they might contain. Then a pinch-wasted beaker was put into his hand and he lowered his head thirstily to the ale.

Later Ar Apa led them to the fire-pits where the smoking carcases of sheep and cattle gave off rich odours of fat and meat. With their flint knives the women were hacking off strips and chunks of meat that were seized instantly by the many grasping hands. Ar Apa pushed and cuffed the crowd aside, and directed the slicing of the best cuts from the flanks for Ason and his followers. When they had the meat he dug into his wallet and produced a handful of white crystals, mixed with crumbs of dirt, and held it out to them.

'Salt,' he said proudly and sprinkled some on to their meat. Ason felt the saliva flow in his mouth as he chewed. Some of the visitors must have brought the salt for trade; he had to get some before he returned. The salt meat brought back his thirst and then there was more ale. He was beginning to find out why samain was the event of the year.

Angry barking and fierce growls now drew their attention, and they clutched their cups and followed the others to a crowd on the far side of the dun, pushing through to stand in the front rank.

'Are those dogs?' Inteb asked, keeping a firm grip on his axe.

They were fierce and unruly beasts, pelted with curly dark fur and large as bears. Ason had heard of them but never seen them before, Yerni wolfhounds bred to hunt wolves and wild boar, brought here for dog-racing in the funeral games. Now the two hounds wanted each other, pulling at their collars so that it took all their masters' strength to restrain them, lips drawn back to reveal bright red gums and the polished ivory fangs of their teeth; spittle flew as they howled with rage. The two owners were shouting wagers and curses over the growling roar of the animals and finally agreement was reached. The watching circle pushed back and the great beasts were released. They flew at each other.

They were evenly matched and savage in their rage and passion. They locked in a growling tangle, then fell apart, snapping and darting at each other. Then they joined again, muzzles buried in thick fur, worrying through to the flesh below. This went on until one of them managed to slash the other's leg open with its great fangs. Blood spattered the dust now and the fight would only have resulted in the wounded beast's death if the owners had not rushed in and called for help to separate the animals. Axe-butts and spear-hafts finally drove them apart and the wagers were paid. Sharp yipes of pain resounded as the loser beat his animal mercilessly for the defeat.

There was almost too much to see, too much to do. Albi traders had come across the narrow sea from the green island of Domnann to the north to bring their worked gold and bronze. The Yerni warriors crowded about offering all that they had for the pieces they valued the most. The horned men, Geramani they were called, from across the sea to the east, had more things of value than the precious salt. Warm brown lumps of amber, some with miraculous insects buried in their depths and visible when held up to the sun. They also had well-worked bronze daggers—Ason turned one over and over in his hands beneath the watchful eyes of its owner, and wished he had something to barter with. In their packs they had brought Egyptian beads as well, and Inteb laughed when they were pointed out to him.

'They and I are a long way from home,' he said, holding one of them in the palm of his hand and squinting at it. He handed it back without saying any more until they were out of earshot of the Geramani. 'Inferior work, badly glazed, not fit for sale in Egypt but certainly adequate for this part of the world.'

There were good things to eat, fresh apples and plums, sweet pieces of honey still in the comb. Yerni sausage that they had never tasted before, as delicious as any in the Argolid with its rich lumps of fat and meat, sharp with salt and some kind of seeds, smoked over the fire until it had grown hard and nourishing. And to drink, mead that had been flavoured with hazel nuts, fermented from honey, fermented heather-berry juice and more ale and more and more. Before the sun touched the horizon their stomachs were replete, their eyes full of strange sights, their ears deafened by sound.

Nor did samain stop at sunset. The fires burned higher and the wavering light washed the walls of the apartments and the milling crowd within the circular enclosure of the dun. From the darker corners there came muffled squeals and laughter as women, visitors and Yerni alike, with no trade goods other than those they were born with worked to earn small tokens and gifts. Torches of burning reeds lit up the displays of gold and jewellery, stone axes and fine flint knives, bronze daggers and amber discs—as well as simpler offerings of game and fowl, salt and sweet fruits. There was something for everyone.

More important events were in preparation. A fire had been laid in the largest pit in the centre of the dun, and the women brushed the ground around it until it was fairly free of animal droppings, then scattered oak and laurel leaves all about the pit. Two post-holes next to the fire were cleared of a year's accumulation of debris, and a pair of upright logs, each as tall as a man, were inserted in them under the first druid's instruction. They had been hollowed into a semicircle at the top to support a shorter log that was placed across them to form a horizontal lintel. When this free-standing archway had been completed the druid himself applied a thick wash of chalk water until the wooden structure was as white as bone. While he was doing this the Yerni warriors began to arrive, dressed in Albi cloth and all their finery, and fully armed, to seat themselves around the fire. Even before they had all arrived one of them, goaded by impatience, was on his feet and declaiming in a loud voice what a fearless and dangerous fighter he was. The choosing of the new bull-chief had begun.

By the time all the warriors were there the fire had leapt up higher and hotter so that they sweated under its golden light, shouting for ale and swaggering about to display their golden torques, bracelets and rings. The noise was loud and continuous, many times drowning out the one who was speaking, but no one seemed to care. The act of speaking before the assembly was the important thing, not the empty content of the familiar and repetitious brags and lies. They shouted loud insults at one another and, one after another, sprang to their feet to strut about the fire and bang their axes on their shields, boasting of their exploits at the top of their lungs. This went on all night, without a break, with some warriors dozing where they sat, waking often to shout again and reach for the ale. Ason pushed through to the inner circles of warriors and called out insults as loudly as the rest at the most outrageous lies and no one thought to question his presence there. Inteb watched from outside, sipping the sweet mead, which was very much to his liking, until he fell asleep. Aias, his wallet bulging with the profits of the day's exploits, wagers won as well as some adroit thievery, went seeking greater physical success among the women. He had been admiring the tall, full-breasted and blonde Geramani women all day, and now he managed to lure one away from the firelight with his rich gifts. He would give her some solid memories to take back with her to her northern forests.

By dawn most of the Yerni warriors were sprawled out asleep in the dust, or nodding dazedly while Ar Apa strutted up and down before them calling out the glories of his strength of arm in a loud hoarse voice. He had husbanded his energies and had given only short speeches during the night, saving himself for this final effort that would impress his dazed and half-drunk warriors. It was succeeding. In the small hours of the morning he had risen and begun his harangue, shouting·down anyone who tried to interrupt him, even knocking back with his shield one drunken warrior who tried to speak at the same time. His powers of

118

oratory were no better or worse than the others, but he did have an enviable staying power that made them nod their heads with respect before they fell asleep. When the sun had burned off the morning mists and risen clear of the eastern horizon, he was still being enthusiastic about the strength of his arm and all his other inimitable talents. He stopped for a deep breath then shouted his war-cry over their silent heads.

'Ar Apa abu! It is time for the fire passage and the purification of the cattle.'

The Yerni warriors stirred and called back happily at this. They downed the last dregs of ale in their cups and went to relieve themselves against the wooden animal-pens until the reek of urine was strong in the air. When Ason awoke, Inteb and Aias were both at his side and they went to join the others outside the walls of the dun, looking on with interest as the Yerni women and children joined the men in dragging out the two great wicker-work structures that had been completed the day before.

Lying on their sides they resembled open-ended baskets twice as tall as a man, sagging and of irregular shape. They were thrown down outside, on each side of the entrance to the dun, and ignored while five wretched men were dragged from some place of imprisonment in the animal-pens that lined the walls below the second-storey apartments. Their legs must have been bound because they staggered and fell until goaded to their feet at spear-point, doing this with difficulty since their hands were still tied behind their backs. They were Yerni warriors—that was obvious from their garb and whitened moustaches and hair—though none whom Ason had ever seen before. He called out to a nearby warrior who was shouting threats at the prisoners and had to spin him around before he could get an answer.

'Them? Thieves, creeping thieves. Came to steal our cattle at night, but we saw them. From Dun Finmog—but they won't be going back there!' He laughed aloud at his own wit and turned away to throw lumps of cow-dung at the men just as the others were doing.

They were led outside the walls and, guarded closely by spear- and axe-men, had their hands cut free. Then they were pushed into the wicker structures, three into one and the remaining two into the other. Once they were inside, the shouting Yerni fought for places to grab at the upper edge of the open end until their weight was enough to pull the basket-like structures upright. With the open ends flat on the ground it was obvious what they were.

Heads. Bulls' heads. The nostril openings were painted red with ochre and the eyes were black circles with red centres. Great, naturally curved boughs formed the horns. Pronged stakes pinned the structures immovably to the ground, and armloads of wood were heaped around their bases. All of this was supervised by the druid who had presided at the funeral of the day before, aided by two younger men in the same long robes. The captives clutched at the branches that penned them and looked out wild-eyed at the druid when he screeched at them. The crowd grew quiet.

'Silent snakes on your bellies you came here. Creeping stoats in the water you came here. Spirits of the night you came here from Dun Finmog—and we know why. The cattle of Dun Finmog are scrawny and fall down sick and die, and your teeth chatter in your head with fear. You know that the finest cattle are here, the fattest cattle are here, the sweetest fleshed cattle are here. So you came to steal our cattle—but our warriors are here too!' A loud cry went up at this and there was a great clashing of clubs on shields and a rain of oaths. The druid went on without pause.

'A hundred and a hundred of you came and a hundred and a hundred of you were killed and your heads made a pile higher than the dun. But five were taken because it was right to capture some because it was almost the time of samain and the purification of the cattle. That is why you are here.'

There were more shouts that ceased instantly as the druid drew himself up and slowly lifted his right foot from the ground until he stood balanced on one leg.

'One foot,' he called out and then raised his arm even more slowly.

'One hand,' he said, much louder, as he pointed at the penned men.

'One eye!' he cried at the top of his voice and cocked his head as he closed his left eye. 'Die, burn, die, die, die!'

That was the end of the ritual and the pleasurable part began. Warriors ran with burning brands from the fires and thrust them into the dry wood around the two great wicker figures. The men inside coughed as the smoke rose, then began to scream as the first flames burned their legs. They climbed up inside the heads to escape the heat and the watchers shrieked with laughter until tears ran from their eyes at the sight. The women and boys were then driven away from this enthusiastic scene and formed a double row to the nearest cow-pen. The gates to this were opened and, lowing with fear, the cattle were driven down this road and through the gap between the wicker figures that were now burning rapidly. The men inside were just charred lumps and no longer complaining. By the time the last of the chosen cattle had been driven through the purifying passage and into the dun the fires had burned low and the excitement was over.

One by one the Yerni warriors swaggered back to the circle about the ashes of the council fire, picking shards of meat from between their teeth and already calling loudly for ale. Ar Apa was there before all the others, standing in front of the whitened arch—and this was no chance location. When one of the warriors came too close he raised his axe threateningly until the man changed his mind and went to sit with the others. But when Ason came up Ar Apa waved him over.

'Will you sit by me?' he asked.

'What does that mean?'

'That you are sitting, you do not wish to be bull-chief yourself. That you are sitting by me, that you will support me.'

Ason thought a moment before he spoke.

'I will support you now and you will become bull-chief. You will not forget this?'

'Never!' Ar Apa's eyes were wide with excitement and he crashed his axe against his shield. 'My memory is the longest, my arm is the strongest—I will not forget.'

There were none opposed to Ar Apa's selection as bull-chief—at least none who spoke up before that union of axe and sword. The word was quickly passed as to what was happening and the crowd grew larger and larger. Ar Apa sat before the henge drinking, nodding in agreement while the druid paced back and forth before him extolling his virtues and repeating all the feats of strength and skill that he had ever done. This appeared to be very much of a ritual, including the recital of a great list of ancestors going back into the remoteness of time. There were more nods of agreement—and even a few cheers—when events came more up to date with veiled references to Ar Apa's handling of mysterious black forces, perhaps a reference to the Dark Man. There was a pause after the druid had described Ar Apa's mighty companions of bronze and at this point Ar Apa slowly rose to face the druid.

'Tell us,' Ar Apa shouted, 'is there a special purpose for this day? How can this day be more favourable than others? What can it be favourable for?'

There was hushed silence as the druid closed one eye and squinted up at the clouds, spinning in a circle on his heel while he did so, looking for some omens in their shape. He must have seen something because he stopped suddenly and clapped his hand over his open eye as though the sight had been a terribly strong one. Some of the braver warriors squinted up at the clouds themselves, though most did not, and the silence was absolute.

'There is a shape,' the druid said, touching the upright of the henge lightly as though to gather strength from it, not looking at Ar Apa while he did so. 'A shape. A shape not unlike a double-axe, perhaps a double-axe of gold. With darkness behind it. If this day a warrior of a double-axe were to stand as protector of his people he would surpass all others in battle-valour. But his life would be short, very short if he did this.'

All eyes were on Ar Apa as he shouted the ritual answer.

'What care I? I have a double-axe. What care I if I live only one night and one day? All will remember me because the memory of the deeds done will always endure.'

With slow and careful motions the druid reached inside his loose clothing and withdrew a short length of branch still with the golden leaves upon it. Oak leaves. He reached up to brush the leaves against the crosspiece of the wooden lintel, intoning the words in a deep voice at the same time.

'I touch the Queen of Battle, the Destroyer, I touch her.'

Then he turned about and let the leaves touch Ar Apa's forehead, calling out at the same time, 'Ar Apa Uercinquitrix!'

The crowd of spectators roared the words in response.

'Ar Apa Uercinquitrix!'

Now the left-hand upright was brushed by the leaves while the druid called out, 'I touch the Earth Mother, she is our Creator—Ar Apa Uercinquitrix.' Once again the spectators echoed his words in response as he turned back to Ar Apa and touched the branch to his left shoulder. Ar Apa's head was back, his fists clenched, possessed by the power of his elevation.

'I touch her, She of the Mounds, the Restorer,' the druid intoned as he touched the right-hand upright, then Ar Apa's right shoulder.

'Ar Apa Uercinquitrix!' they all shouted, over and over, their new leader, the new bull-chief, carried away by their enthusiasm as he stood before them bathed in the welcome wave of sound.

The hand pulled at Ason's arm and he shook it away. When it clutched him again he turned angrily, ready to strike. Naikeri was standing there. She had to shout to be heard over the roar of Yerni voices.

'One of my people, just came and told me. A boatload of large men with horns, they must be Geramani, came to the mine two days ago. They left at once and are gone now.'

'What are you saying? What does it mean?' Ason had a sudden cold premonition.

'The mine... ?'

'They destroyed nothing, it is just as you left it. But they did take all of the metal discs that you had left there.'

The tin.

Gone.

16

The days grew shorter and shorter until they were shorter than any days had ever been in the Argolid and the nights seemed endless. Some days there seemed no day at all when the clouds piled thicker and thicker in the sky and wept a chill dampness on to the sodden forest below. Part mist, part rain, from dawn to dusk, so that the day seemed only a grey period in an endless night. The small store of tin that had been smelted to replace the stolen ingots grew with painful slowness. In the continual damp the boys became rebellious and ran away when they were not watched. The charcoal fires grew wet and went out, and there was no dry wood to fire them with.

Since the return from Dun Ar Apa, Ason had changed in many ways. He would not admit defeat, at least not aloud, and kept the work of mining and smelting going with a cold ruthlessness. Before dawn he was out in the forest with their heaviest bronze axe, cutting wood for the ceaseless appetite of the charcoal kilns. He slept little and, many nights, spent the entire night tending the smelting fires, almost drawing the tin from the ore by the strength of his own hands. He did all the physical things needed to keep the mine in operation, but he never talked about Mycenae or the ship they had been expecting. With winter here they could no longer expect the ship—no one would face the cold storms of the ocean at this time of year—and without a ship their mining was a useless labour. Did Mycenae still exist even? Had the union of Atlantis and the other cities of the Argolid pulled down the remaining warriors of Perimedes and levelled the city? It was possible. Anything was possible. They could stay here smelting their few miserable discs of worthless tin at world's end until they grew old and died, and that was all there was to it. Ason would not talk about these things, nor would he even answer when others mentioned them. Aias seemed happy enough with this new existence, but Inteb could never forget where he was and worried at the fact as at a sore tooth, hurting himself and wincing but not stopping for all of that.

'I have talked with Naikeri's father, old Ler,' he said once, hating the silence of the forest and willing to talk to himself if no one else would. 'He may be blind now but he has travelled. Knows all about this island and the other one to the north, Domnann, where more of his people live. And he even knows where the Geramani come from and says that they are the ones who trade with Atlantis—and I believe him. That's where they get those Egyptian beads and the other things. They cross the water from here in their boats to a great river to the south-east, some outlandish name I can't remember. That is where they come from, up the river. Far up. He says if you go up this river far enough you come to another river that runs down to another sea. If he is not lying, which he might very well be, or making up the entire story, that would be the Danube running into the Eastern Sea. We know the Atlanteans are all along that river; they mine their tin there, and the Geramani know about tin. Why else would they steal it if they did not? They have traded our tin to the Atlanteans without a doubt. If they could do that—so could we. And thus make our way home.'

As usual, Ason's only answer was the ringing blow of bronze against wood as he turned to the next tree. Sighing unhappily, Inteb shrugged his shoulders and turned to lopping off the branches from the newly fallen trunk.

One evening, after another day spent chopping wood, Inteb and Aias joined Ason around the fire at the hearth. Ason dipped a bowl into the stew and blew upon it before raising it

126

to his mouth. The others did the same. It was hot and good, dried meat and grain with gobbets of fat floating on the surface. The wind moaned outside and blew a white tracery of snow under the badly fitting door. The last grey filming of daylight was gone, and now outside there was just darkness and the endless forest that stretched out into the blackness on all sides. There was warmth and light only here and, without thinking why, they leaned closer to the fire when the wind blew hard.

Something rustled outside, barely heard above the wind, and Ason lifted his head with a sure hunter's instinct. He half rose but even as he did so the door burst open, crashing aside, half falling from its torn hinges.

An armoured man stood in the opening, poised to leap, full-bearded and bronze-helmed with a long naked blade ready in his hand.

The men around the fire ran for their weapons as other armed warriors pushed behind the man in the door, swords ready—but all halted as Ason shouted a single word.

'Atroclus!'

The first swordsman gaped, lowering his weapon slowly, blinking in the dim light of the fire until the realization slowly dawned.

'Ason—my kinsman—but you are dead!' He half raised the sword again and Ason laughed aloud.

'Harder to kill than you realize, Atroclus my cousin. It is a tale long in the telling how I came here. But first—what of Mycenae and of my father? Sit and speak to me.'

Atroclus came closer to the fire, shaking the snow from his white wool cloak. Five other men followed him in until the room was crowded, putting their swords into their slings and calling out to Ason who greeted them all by name. Naikeri silently gave them ale and withdrew to the shadowed alcove where she slept.

'You know of Thera?' Atroclus asked. 'It was told that you died there.'

'I escaped as you see. Was the island destroyed—and Atlas with it?'

'We would all be happier had it been. There were many deaths on the island and some ships were sunk, but Atlas and his court escaped to Crete. For eight days the ground roared and blew out flame and ash until the island was covered with it, but no more than that. People have returned there and life goes on again, though we have heard that the ground still rumbles with some hidden complaint. All of this has enraged Atlas who, it is said, feels the explosion was directed against his person. He wages war all along the shores of the Argolid, and already his men have sacked Lerna and Nauplia. Perhaps he seeks treasure or captives to appease his gods, we don't know. We know he battles with us, and Mycenae is sore-pressed. When he heard of your death your father mourned and grew older. But when war came he put aside his mourning and led us in the fighting. There has been much blood shed, and there are many friends and warriors you will never meet again. It was late in the year before a ship and men could be spared to come here, and we were a long time on the ocean road with the winds and weather against us. Twice we had to careen and repair the vessel, and four men died in the passage. But we have come. Now—tell us of yourself and your presence here.'

'Told simply enough, but a question first. You have more men in the ship and chalceus among them to work the mine?'

'Seventeen men more and three of them chalceus.'

'They will find the mine open, some tin, the smelters burning and charcoal ready. We have not been idle.'

They talked late into the night and all of the ale was gone before the Mycenaeans rolled themselves into their cloaks and slept on the dirt floor. Ason pulled the coverings from Naikeri and took her, brutally and suddenly so that she made a small scream of pain. He laughed and did not stop, and Inteb, awake and hearing everything, pulled his own blanket over his head to try and cut out this sound he loathed.

Ason was up before dawn, and as soon as it was light he roused Atroclus and together they went down along the stream to the sea where the great ship was beached. Here there were more greetings and, wonder of wonders in this

128

cold place, warm sweet wine from Mycenae, from amphorae lashed in the cabin. The ship had been hauled up far above the highest tides, and now they took what supplies and food they would need and left two men to guard her while all of the others went to the mine.

'Things will be different now,' Ason said, leading the way along the familiar path. 'There will be more boys to work, more men to cut wood, and the chalceus to see that the smelting goes as it should. By spring there will be a load of tin that will be so heavy we will have to throw all of the ballast out of the ship. We will return to Mycenae, the Argolid will be united again, Atlas will be driven into the sea and sent to its bottom this time.'

The men of Mycenae complained mightily of the bitter cold, yet they worked. Ason put aside his axe for the first time and directed the building of new huts, while the chalceus shook their heads over his smelting techniques and set about their own operations. The days were bright but the sun had little warmth. Inteb and Ason grew closer once again, talking of the return voyage, but Naikeri withdrew inside herself and would speak to no one. Only Inteb seemed aware of this and he smiled at her back. Things were going very well.

On the eighth day after the arrival of the Mycenaean ship there was an alarm from the men on guard at the mouth of the valley. Ason, in good armour now that shone brighter than the weak winter sun, went out with his new and sharper sword to find out what the trouble could be. From the top of the embankment he could see three Yerni warriors standing hesitantly at the edge of the forest, peering up at the armed men above them. They must have recognized Ason because they came forward slowly when he appeared. When they were closer Ason saw that it was Ar Apa and two of the warriors from his teuta.

'Ason abu,' Ar Apa called out, raising his axe but looking uncertainly at the armed and armoured Mycenaeans at the same time.

'My friends are here,' Ason shouted back. 'There is nothing to fear.'

With this reassurance the three men came on and entered the guarded area of the mine. They squatted before the fire in the house and were given food, and Ar Apa produced only a token amount of bragging about their journey before speaking his mind about his true reasons for coming.

'It has been a bad winter. There have been many cattle raids and many warriors are dead. First by men from Dun Moweg to the north of our lands, and then from Dun Finmog far north of them. They do not raid each other, or Dun Uala which is in between, but pass instead through the grazing lands of the other teutas to steal our cows and kill our warriors.'

Ar Apa beat on the packed earth floor with his axe-handle as he said this, almost shouting the last word, and the men with him stamped their feet as well and groaned aloud. The Yerni believed in expressing their emotions at all times and Ason, who had seen this sort of performance often before, waited patiently for it to end. Relieved of some of his feelings, Ar Apa brushed at his stiffened moustache and finally continued.

'Now I know why this was done. Now I know who arranged all this and who sits in Dun Uala and gives gifts to people when they do what he wants them to. Now I know.' He looked up quickly at Ason, then away.

'The Dark Man,' Ason said, speaking aloud the name that Ar Apa still found so hard to say. 'He is causing trouble again? How do you know this?'

Ar Apa looked up at the ceiling, examining with great interest the hole where the smoke escaped. Then he brushed at his shield, scraping away a hardened bit of mud. Inteb came in and listened silently in the background.

'Someone came to me,' Ar Apa finally, reluctantly, said. 'Uala himself came with some warriors and did not want to fight, wanted to talk instead. The druid made the henges that are made when bull-chiefs meet and we hung them with our treasure and we talked. He showed me gifts he had from . . .

130

the one whose name you said. We talked ...'

Ar Apa's mouth stayed open and he had run out of words. There was a beading of sweat on his forehead, perhaps from the fire. But Ason now knew the path of the other's thoughts and spoke the words Ar Apa was unable to say.

'They are trying to make another raid on the mine, like the last one with many teutas together. That's what it is, isn't it?' Ar Apa nodded and looked away. 'You were right to tell me and not join them. Where is the Dark Man?'

'At Dun Uala.'

It was so simple and so right. The chalceus were here now to tend to the mine, freeing a warrior for a warrior's work. This Dark Man, this trouble-maker, man or spirit, must be stopped or there would be no end to the trouble of the mine. Ason knew how to stop him.

'I have armed men to follow me,' Ason said. 'Armoured and unbeatable. I am leading them against Dun Uala to kill the Dark Man. Will you bring the warriors of your teuta and fight beside us?'

'The Dark Man ...' Ar Apa was so troubled by the thought that he spoke the name aloud.

'Uala and his men cannot stand before us. We will kill them. There will be cattle, revenge, gold and treasure.'

'We will join you,' Ar Apa said in sudden decision, thinking now only of the treasure of Dun Uala, largest, richest, strongest of all the duns of the Yerni. Saliva filled his mouth at the thought of all it contained and he spat into the fire and laughed aloud.

17

It was imbolc, the happy time, the first sign that the grip of long winter had lessened even the smallest amount. Inside the duns, in their pens underneath the women's apartments, the cattle and sheep were finishing the last of the green boughs and brush cut for them in the autumn. The first grass was beginning to appear. Lambs and calves were born. Life was starting anew and that was something to celebrate. There was fresh milk to be fermented and that was something to celebrate with. The ale made from the grain of the previous year was long since finished, and drunkenness was only a dim and happy memory. Drunk again, the warriors could lie in the sun and watch the women carry out the sheep and cattle, weak and unable to walk after a winter of short rations and immobility, to restore their strength on the bright green grass.

Dun Moweg was like all the other duns of the Yerni, with the warriors' apartments on the outside overlooking the ditch. The embankment outside their doors was a fine place to find the sun on the good days, and this was a good day with plenty of freshly fermented milk. The warriors lay there and the bull-chief Moweg himself was sprawled in their midst bragging of past exploits, raids and slaughters, when the armoured men arrived. They came quietly for all the weight of metal they carried, and behind them were the white-haired, boar-toothed figures of the warriors of Dun Ar Apa. It was not a nice thing to see or to have happen and was very shocking. Imbolc is not a time for cattle raids or warfare and everyone knew that.

'You are Moweg,' Ason said, looking coldly from beneath the lip of his helmet at the open-mouthed man on the dirt outside his doorway.

'He is,' Ar Apa said coming up to join him, and could not resist a fast kick in Moweg's ribs that brought him to his feet bellowing in pain. The bowl he was drinking from spilled. Brewed from milk from stolen cattle. Ason pushed Ar Apa away before battle was joined.

Moweg needed very little convincing to change sides. He really had loyalty only to himself and had received fine gifts from the Dark Man for the raids he had carried out. That was in the past. The future looked even brighter with a victorious assault on Dun Uala, the fat and the rich, the largest dun and the most powerful. How would that power stand against the might of all the warriors of two teutas—led by these frightening men in their hard armour? He remembered, and it was not a good memory, how much killing just three armoured men had done when they had been attacked at the mine. And now there were one, two, three—more armoured men, more than on two hands, to fight with them this time.

They all stayed that night at the dun and drank every drop of the newly fermented milk. Aias, who had little work to do now at the mine with the chalceus in charge, had come with the war party and had promised to use his sword instead of his fists. Inteb was no fighter, though he did look impressive in his borrowed armour. And he would even fight if he had to to be here, with Ason, away from Naikeri's influence. They sat together by the fire drinking in moderation, while the others tasted all the pleasures of imbolc.

'There is no doubt that we will win,' Inteb said.

'We must do more than win. The Dark Man must be taken and killed. If he escapes again there are other teutas of the Yerni far to the north, and he will go there. With his treasure he will cause us trouble as long as he is alive. After this battle I want him dead.'

'What do you plan?'

Ason sketched a circle in the dust with his forefinger.

'They say that Dun Uala is like the others, only larger. There will be one or two entrances and the warriors' rooms with all their doors. We must take them by surprise, from all sides at once, and stop every one of those rat holes.'

'How will you do that? Come up by night and attack at dawn?'

'No. That would be impossible with this great number of men. We would be seen or heard and the warning would go out. What we must do is move fast. They say it is an easy day's march to this dun. If we leave at dawn and go quickly we will arrive ahead of any warning.'

Inteb looked around at the drinking men. 'They won't like that.'

'That is of no concern. Fighting the battle and taking the dun is only half of what must be done. I must have the Dark Man.'

The sky was still black when the men were roused up. There were groans and more than one thud as the drunkest were kicked to life. Ason permitted them to eat and drink quickly, and they were straggling away from the dun at first light. The Yerni complained bitterly about the sad state of their moustaches and hair, and Ason promised that they would have time to make repairs before the battle. Then he set the pace, first trotting smoothly, then walking, never stopping. There was some rain in the morning that added to their discomfort, but it stopped by noon when they crossed the river that was the boundary between the land of the two teutas. The hills rose up to a high down, flat and stretching to the horizon on all sides with few trees to stop the eye. They reached the home of one of the retired warriors of the teuta, and he tried to run away towards the dun but was caught and cut down. Here they made a brief stop and ate what food there was in the house, then hurried on. Distantly across the plain could be seen the circular wall of the dun with the smoke fires rising up from it. There was another halt, much to Ason's annoyance, while the Yerni chalked their hair and moustaches before the battle. Then they went on.

The warriors of Dun Uala were on top of the embankment and waiting for them; they had received the alarm. The attacking Yerni stopped to shout insults at the men above them but Ason was too angry to wait for this ritual. He spread his Mycenaeans out in a line so no one could interfere with another's sword-arm and led them in the attack. They went down into the ditch and up the embankment, shields raised when the warriors above threw a sudden barrage of the rocks that each had in a socket in the back of his shield. These bounced without effect from armour and shields, and then the Mycenaeans were among them.

Those who tried to stand were cut down. With steady butchery the swords swung back and forth and men died. Even Inteb, paces behind the others, managed to reach past Ason with his sword and push the point of it into a Yerni stomach. It went in easily and the man dropped his axe and groaned in a terrible manner and fell to the ground, holding his middle with both hands that quickly dripped with blood. Inteb felt a little sick at this and stayed behind the others, and was almost knocked down in the rush of their Yerni allies who now felt inspired to deeds of violence when they saw the enemy being killed so efficiently.

The battle spread into knots of fighting men who shouted and screamed at one another, who were wounded and died. The warriors of Dun Uala were numerous, more than the other teutas put together, and they were fighting for their lives. They could easily have won if the armoured Mycenaeans had not done their butchery so well. They fought bravely but were killed, and very quickly the survivors broke and fled for their lives. Some of them ran through their rooms into the women's apartments inside the dun, and the howling victors rushed after them. Ason stabbed at a man, but only punctured his back slightly which made him run the faster. They stumbled through the sleeping quarters and out on to the balcony beyond, with shrieking women running on all sides. The wounded Yerni vaulted to the ground below but Ason, in his heavy armour, followed slowly by climbing down the notched log to the ground. Once on the ground he pursued the man who was cowering behind a tall, bluish stone that rose like a pillar from the ground. Wounded and in pain the warrior hurled his axe away and fell to the ground and begged to be spared. Ason turned and saw that other warriors were doing the same and the fighting was almost over. Individual battles did continue, in and around the double crescent of great stones that stood inside the dun, but when the other Dun Uala warriors saw what was happening they threw their axes aside as well and the fighting was finished.

'Take me to the Dark Man,' Ason said to the warrior on the ground before him and pressed the edge of his bloody sword against the man's skin. The warrior, his eyes as round and as white as his chalked hair, scrambled to his feet and hurried out of the entrance of the dun with Ason just behind him. They pushed through the victorious Yerni who shouted with joy as they used their daggers to saw off the heads of the defeated, while the women of the dun wailed with anguish on all sides. One warrior, unlucky enough not to have killed any of the enemy, was exacting some small victory by mounting one of the women on the ground among the slain and wounded; a circle of children stood close by, chewing on their fingers and watching.

There was the same dark doorway Ason had seen once before, and the same smell of some alien scent. And the same absence of any occupant.

'He must be here!' Ason shouted, hurling the warrior to the ground and striking him in the face with the edge of his shield. The man howled and tried to roll away, babbling in answer.

'He was here, I know he was. But someone came, they saw you coming, told us, so we took up our axes. Maybe then he ran away—don't hit me—I don't know.'

As some of the anger ebbed away, Ason began to think

again. The Dark Man could not be far away, there could not have been that much warning, he could be followed. Where could he go? To the next dun to the north, Dun Finmog; there was no other place he could find safety. He could be overtaken. Ason kicked the man to his feet.

'Take me on the trail to Dun Finmog. The shortest way.'

There was no place to hide on the open plain. Ason ran, ignoring the weight of his armour, and the point of his sword kept the wounded Yerni running before him. They came over a small rise; far ahead three dark figures could be seen moving away from them, and Ason shouted a victorious cry. He burst forward, knocking the Yerni aside, running as he had never run before, forgetting his fatigue and his heavy armour, spurred on by the sight of the fleeing people. One of them must be the Dark Man.

As he came closer Ason could see that two of them were women, their skirts flapping about their calves as they ran clumsily beneath the burdens on their backs. One of them looked back and squawked and the two of them stopped and screamed, dropping their bundles to the ground and running off in different directions. The man ran after one, hesitated, ran back to the fallen bundles—then stopped. He bowed over, bent almost double as Ason jogged up breathing heavily. When he straightened up he touched his hands together before his chest and spoke in a high lisping voice.

'I greet you here, oh noble Ason son of Perimedes, some day King of Mycenae. All hail Ason.'

He was old and fat, his skin dark olive, his black beard shot through with grey and curled and oiled, as was his long hair, cut off straight above his shoulders. He wore a colourful and richly embroidered cap on his head, brimless and tight-fitting, and his ankle-length gown of dark blue was also embroidered in black. There were dark tassels on its bottom and tassels as well on the length of cloth worn like a cape across his shoulders. A richly decorated sword, with jewels set into the pommel, swung from his waist—and Ason lifted his own sword when the man reached for it. But he only pulled it free and threw it from him.

137

'Who are you? How do you know me?' Ason asked.

'All men know of Ason of the great deeds. I am Sethsus, he who would help you.'

'You are the Dark Man who has been raising the Yerni against me and it is your time to die.' Ason swung the sword high and stepped forward. Sethsus fell back, his eyes wide with fear now, his skin ashen and drained of colour.

'No, Ason, champion of the Argolid, you must listen. I have many things to tell you and I can help you. There is gold and rich treasure you can have.' He fell to his knees by the nearest bundle and tore it open with trembling fingers, pulling out a handful of golden jewellery that he held out to Ason. 'This can be yours, I can aid you.'

'Where do you come from—and why are you here with your gold?'

Sethsus was calmer now, with death withheld for the moment, and he stood with the golden axes and discs still in his hand.

'I am a simple trader, a man who buys and sells and thereby makes a small profit to live by. My city is Troy, so distant it pains me to think upon it, but I am no longer welcome there. There are such things that you, a mighty warrior, should not bother your head with; politics is one, and the struggle for power, a curse. Others rule there now; Sethsus is not welcome and must travel the ends of the world to stay alive. I voyaged and traded with many along the rivers and in the camps and cities. I came here to this land, to Dun Uala, where the trade-routes from the east and south, with its amber and bronze and fine things, cross the path from the north that brings the Albi with their red gold from the green island. Here I stayed, using what little skill I have in trading to stay alive.'

'You lie to me, great ball of grease from the rotting walls of Troy. I know the people of your city, and their tongues are as twisted as a snake's spine, until the truth is harder to speak than the lies that fall from your painted lips as rain falls from the clouds. Look at this—do you think me a fool.' He

138

reached out and tore the little golden axe from the Trojan's hand. 'The double-headed axe of Atlantis. You are here on their bidding.'

'That I trade with Atlantis is true, one does business where one can ...'

'More lies. You came here for gold, you just said that. Do you *bring* gold with you for that purpose?' Sethsus was wordless for the moment and Ason smiled without humour, knowing he was coming near the truth. 'You were in Dun Der Dak until I came, and not for trade but to watch the mine. Of what importance the tin? What use the tin?' Anger welled up with the memory of the raid, and he pushed out the sword until it dug into the Trojan's cheek and a thin trickle of blood started forth.

'You had the mine watched, and when I left you told the Geramani, who then came and took the tin. Truth?' He pushed the sword hard until it penetrated Sethsus' cheek and grated against his teeth.

'Yes! Great Baal save me, I speak the truth, only the truth! That I am wicked I know—do not kill me merciful Ason. I sold information to the Geramani so they could take the tin, which they value, knowing how to work it. Yes, I took presents from Atlantis, a poor man must take what he will. They do not like the tin-mine here being worked for the good of Mycenae. You cannot blame them, can you? It is a matter of policy. I was wrong to aid them, I see that now. But I can change, a wiser man crawls before you, mighty Ason. I can aid you, be of much aid, there are things I know ...'

'No.'

Ason said the word coldly and swung his sword high.

'Have you forgotten my dead kinsmen so quickly? The Yerni did that because of you. Die, Trojan.'

Sethsus screamed as shrilly as a woman and fell away, raising his hand to protect himself. The sword slashed, catching him in the wrist, almost severing it so that his hand—still clutching the gold—hung dangling and spouting blood.

He looked at it, dumbfounded, screaming all the louder, and stopped only when the sword swung again and severed his neck.

18

It was dark by the time Sethsus was brought back to the dun. Leather ropes had been tied about his ankles so he could be dragged, but even in death the Dark Man still exacted a sense of fear from the Yerni who pulled the ropes, so they had run faster and faster, hauling him over the hard chalk of the plain. His corpse was stretched out near the council fire and no one sat near it.

The looting was in progress. Never had so much treasure been gathered in one place before, and the victorious warriors began to squabble among themselves for the gold. Some slipped away into the night with their wealth. Ason put a stop to this, and his armoured Mycenaeans drove everyone, victor and vanquished alike, into the circle of the dun where amid pained cries he ordered the dumping of the loot. The invading warriors kept the heads they had severed and personal jewellery removed from men they fought; everything else was gathered in one place before Ason. He sat cross-legged before the fire on a great black bearskin, drinking ale and chewing on cold greasy mutton. Inteb sat beside him, exhausted by the day's events, looking on unbelievingly as the amber discs and drinking-cups, gold collars, armlets, pins, coiled wire, plaques and lock-rings, copper daggers, pieces of bronze armour, beads and figurines, mounted before them.

'They work the gold and copper here,' he told Ason. 'I was in that round building, over there against the far wall.' He pointed out through the broken circle of high blue stones.

'There is a forge, tools, a workshop such as we have in Egypt, though not as grand or well supplied of course. They work stone too; look there, one of those large stones is still being dressed. I wonder what they are here for?'

Ason shrugged and chewed on the meat. It had been a good day. The Dark Man dead, a host of the enemy dead, even Uala killed, slain in single battle with Ar Apa, who was swaggering around with the head bragging to everyone he came across. Uala was old; it had been no great deed. So there was no bull-chief for the dun and the warriors and members of Uala's family were already squabbling about the succession. It did not matter. Right now he, Ason, was leader of all the Yerni, chief of all the Yerni. They followed him—or they fought against him and died. He was at peace.

Inteb went over to the nearest stone, clear in the firelight, and ran his hand over the surface. It had been worked and smoothed, a fair job on a stone this big, reaching high above his head. Sat square in the ground too—he closed one eye and looked along it—or at least squarely enough. The upper, rounded end had been painted bright red, but the thick pigment had chipped and washed off in places during the winter rains. Two rows of the stones were arranged in the shape of a double circle that was not completed. Years of labour here. Even the stone wasn't local. With a builder's eye he had noticed that the only stone they had seen on their way here were the great slabs that lay about on the plain. Greyish white, a different kind of stone altogether. Inteb walked around the upright column and almost stumbled over the man who sat slumped against it on the far side.

'What are you doing here?' Inteb asked, sharply.

'My stone, mine,' the man muttered.

'Come out where I can see you.'

The man crawled around the stone, dragging one leg and fell once more against it. He was a Yerni warrior, one of Uala's defeated men with broken moustaches and drawn face. A club had shattered or bruised his leg and it was black with clotted blood. Inteb was curious.

'What do you mean, *your* stone?'

142

'Mine!' the man answered, some of his spirit returning as he felt the strength of his claims. 'I am Fan Falna, the one who kills but cannot be killed, who has eaten the bear, the deer, the wild boar, the horse, killed them all. My stone. A warrior's stone. When I took my first head it became my stone, and I put the head on it, hung my jewellery from it, painted it myself. The women cringe before it and are afraid to look because it is as big and red and hard as I am.' He clutched at his groin when he said this, then sighed wearily and slumped back again. 'I am Fan Falna,' he mumbled, all spirit gone with the memory of defeat.

'Do all the warriors have a stone like this?'

He didn't answer until Inteb took him by the stiffened hair and banged his head against the stone.

'Only the best, the finest,' he sighed again. 'Uala my kinsman, I saw him killed. There will be a burial but his head will look down forever from some different dun.'

Inteb went back and sat beside Ason who was staring into the fire, his eyes growing red from the fermented milk.

'We shall stay here until spring, until the ship is ready to return with the tin,' Ason said. Inteb lifted his eyebrows but said nothing.

'The chalceus work the mine, I am not needed there.'

'You are certainly needed here,' Inteb said, putting his hand on Ason's thigh, on the firm warm flesh. Naikeri was far away and would stay far away. 'You are a man of war and wage it as it has never been seen on this island. You have captured a royal treasure here, and now three teutas follow you. You can do what you want with the Yerni and they cannot stop you—in fact they cheer you. Stay here, you are right, keep them from more mischief. The Dark Man is dead but they are great ugly children and capable of anything. Stay here. There is more food and drink than at the mine— there were tears in my eyes when the last amphora of wine was emptied.'

There was a wailing and shouting from the darkness where a smaller fire had been lit; dim figures could be seen silhouetted against it.

'What is that?' Ason asked.

'The druid, Nemed, is calling to the Earth Mother,' Ar Apa said. 'He is calling to her to take the dead which are hers now. The dead go to her and She of the Mounds guides them to Moi Mell.'

'Bring the druid here,' Ason ordered.

The Yerni warriors drew away and turned their faces to the darkness and made as if they didn't hear him. The Mycenaeans laughed at this and two of them went to drag the old man to the fire. Nemed came willingly enough, he had no choice, but there was hatred in his eyes when he looked at their hands upon him. He was grey-haired and had a good-sized belly that bulged through his white robe. A heavy gold lock-ring held back his hair, better than the leather bindings the other druids wore, and no one had dared or even thought to take it from him. He stood before Ason and looked over his head into the night.

'I know of you,' he said suddenly and everyone close fell silent. 'Man from across the waters with the long bronze knife. You have killed the Dark Man and that is a good thing to do. Because of that I do not curse you for what you have done here ...'

'You do not curse me ever,' Ason said in a low voice, leaning forward with his hand on his sword. 'You obey me because I am not one of your boar-toothed warriors but a man who will let your guts out in a moment if you cause me any trouble.'

The druid did not answer but was silent, which was answer enough.

'Your bull-chief is dead. This place is no longer Dun Uala, but Dun Dead-man.' The listening circle roared with laughter at the rude joke but the druid did not change expression and continued to stare into space.

'There will be a new bull-chief,' Nemed said. 'He will be from Uala's family and that is how he will be chosen, that is the way we do it here.'

'That is the way you used to do it here, old man. You will not do it that way anymore. Perhaps I, Ason of Mycenae, will

144

appoint the new bull-chief. I may do that. Now go back to your wailing.'

The druid was angry. He drew himself up and stood on one foot.

'One foot!' he called out, and silence fell through the dun. A prediction, a prophecy, a curse, this was the way it was done.

'One hand,' he pointed.

'One eye ...'

'And next you speak—but I speak first!' Ason shouted, jumping to his feet and drawing his sword at the same moment. It stretched out straight to the bulge of the druid's belly and stopped not the thickness of a leaf away.

'Speak, but think carefully what you say. I will not be cursed. This sword has eaten men today and it will happily consume more. Your power is no power against its bite, druid. Remember that, then speak.'

There was a long silence while the druid stood, still poised immobile on one foot. Then he spoke.

'There has been an ending in this teuta. Now there will be a beginning. This beginning will have an ending too.'

Ason smiled and lowered the sword.

'Well spoken, grey one. Just enough—but not too much. All things end and that is right. Now go.'

There was very little sleep that night while the warriors, filled with the enthusiasm of victory, drank and ate and bragged about their exploits. The beaten Yerni were defeated in spirit as well as flesh, and vanished one by one into their apartments, the wounded being nursed by their mothers and sisters. Ason sat with the bull-chiefs of the two teutas he had led to the victory, but they would only drink and brag and talk of nothing else until things were done in the proper manner. The hurried attack on Dun Uala had been one thing, taken on in a moment of enthusiasm and greed, a war-party, a raid. Now more portentous matters would be discussed and there was a correct manner for this as for everything. When the sky began to lighten the chief druid, Nemed, was sent for and he in turn ordered out the wrights who worked in wood. They cleared the rubble from the post-holes where the bull-chief's henge was placed, and when night had ended they put the uprights into position. The bull-chief sat in this place of honour, the first one to be touched by the warm sun of a new day, his back to the setting sun so that the others would have to squint and shield their eyes when they talked to him. Because the bull-chiefs of two other teutas were here they would have their own henges, smaller ones of course, on each side, with the more favoured bull-chief to the right. Holes were dug for these, and logs with their bark removed were dragged from their place of storage under the second-storey dwellings. They were thickly stained with animal droppings, but the white painting would cover that.

Inteb had slept during the night, while the others drank, and now sat awake with the two bleary-eyed Mycenaeans who had been assigned the morning's guard duty. He watched the construction of the henges with great interest. Up until now all the buildings he had seen on the island of the Yerni had been of the crudest, fit only for the construction of Egyptian chicken-coops. The duns themselves were simple structures. Their wooden frames were supported by the main circle of heavy logs set upright in the ground. These logs gained support from the circular bank against which they rested and were spaced at one apartment's width. This none too secure structure was held together by the wooden flooring of the second-storey apartments. The walls between the uprights were made of wattle, plaited withes, which filled the space but added nothing to the supporting strength of the structure. Dun Uala was built in the same manner, though it was much larger. As in all the duns, the bull-chief's residence was located in the large second-storey apartment that spanned the broad entrance. An overhanging roof gave some protection from the weather and kept most of the rain out of the building. In addition to the main construction of the dun, two circular buildings stood inside the outer walls, both workshops inhabited by the numerous cordwainers, goldsmiths and wrights.

146

These people worked in stone, too, unlike most of the other teutas. The work was of the simplest, of course, smoothly dressed stones set into holes in the hard chalk, but even that was something. And they worked well in wood. Inteb looked on with interest while they shaped the lengths of timber that would form the henges.

Using their stone hammers and wedges, they split away one surface of each log until it was flat, dressing it even smoother with copper adzes. While they did this, other wrights were busy shaping the ends of the uprights—one in particular, an old man with swollen knobby joints, who did the most skilled work. With quick, precise strokes of a short-handled axe he worked around the end of the log until a knob the size of a man's fist was left. When this was done he had the log that would form the horizontal lintel of the henge rolled over to him. After careful measurement he used a hammer and a sharp fragment of a broken bronze dagger for a chisel to dig out a matching hole into which the knob of wood fitted as well as a man's finger into his ear.

Under the watchful eye of the druid, Nemed, the posts were raised for the first henge with much shouting and cursing, being secured with lumps of chalk that were hammered into the hole around them to hold them into place. The lintel crossbars on the top required more labour, and a log platform had to be put together to enable the men to raise the lintel of the largest henge. The prepared log was rolled on to this platform and the wrights climbed up beside it. Nemed shouted the signals that directed them to pick it up, to raise it above their heads, to lift one end after another that extra amount which enabled the projections of the tenons to fit into the hollows of the mortars. There were shouts of victory when this was done, and the builders strutted and felt very proud of themselves.

While the construction had been taking place the Yerni warriors had begun to watch the ceremony. When the wooden troughs of chalk and water appeared they shouldered aside the builders and grabbed up the tied bundles of grass themselves. Nemed pointed out which were the henges of

147

each teuta and the warriors from each one began industriously to wash the structures with white, shouting for possession of the grass bundles and dipping out handfuls of the white mixture to daub their own hair and moustaches.

When the assembly began, early in the afternoon, Ason made it very clear who had won the battle. With a show of ceremony he led Ar Apa to the right-hand henge and with his own hands slung Ar Apa's shield from the crosspiece. Moweg was conducted to his station on the left in the same manner, and all were watching the largest henge, the empty arch of the dead Uala. Ason walked towards it in a growing silence, drawing his sword as he came close. He turned once in a full circle to look at the Yerni warriors, his own Mycenaeans, the druids and craftsmen of the dun. Only then, with a sudden and powerful overhand swing, he drove his sword against an upright of the henge. It bit deep into the wood and hung quivering when he released it.

'Mine,' he said, and sat down before the archway.

No one spoke up or made any move to challenge his right to sit there and speak for the warriors of the dun. He had defeated them and until a new bull-chief was appointed his word would rule.

There were shouts of appreciation now from the warriors as the bull-chiefs put their spoils on display. The recently severed heads of the defeated were placed on the crossbar of the henge, jewellery hung from the posts in rich profusion. Before sitting, each bull-chief slung his axe from the henge by his hair-belt; the axes were sharp, the daggers shining, the jewellery rich. And Ason's was the richest of all. His bronze armour hung from the henge, his shield glittered from it, his sword impaled it. A flood of gold ran down the whitened wood to the ground. And on top where all could see it, though they only looked with quick glances then turned away, was the round and greyish head of the Dark Man, black hair now unkempt and blowing.

No one was even certain of how many nights and days had passed when there came the unwelcome interruption. It was the women and children working near the gate who started it first, squealing and running. Their noise disturbed the warriors in the outer circles, who turned and strained their necks to see what was happening, shouting inquiries. This uproar penetrated to the centre of the ceremonial ring, where Ar Apa was holding forth on the necessity of returning with a number of cows that had been stolen from his dun. He grated his teeth and stamped with anger at the interruption. The crowd of people moved towards the council and was stopped by the warriors on the outside, who slowly moved apart to make a pathway for the two people who came haltingly forward.

Naikeri was first, her clothing dirty and scratched where she had pushed her way through the forest. She had a thong in her hand, the other end of which was held by the man who stumbled after her. He had but the single hand that clutched the thong; the other, his right hand, had been amputated, and recently because the arm was still dark with blood which also coated the cords that bound the stump tightly at the wrist. He had been blinded as well; the blisters on his cheeks and forehead showed that his eyes had been burned out with hot pokers. His feet were bare, his limbs scratched and he had only a few rags for clothing. Therefore it took Ason a few moments to recognize him, and, when he did, he sprang to his feet and shouted the man's name:

'Atroclus!'

The Mycenaean stopped at the shout and turned empty eye-sockets in his direction.

'The Atlanteans have come,' he said, swaying as though he would fall.

19

The blinded Mycenaean noble was taken to Ason's rooms, the large apartment over the entrance to the dun that had belonged to the bull-chief Uala. Ason would not permit another word to be said until they were behind the closed door and his own men stood outside it, occupying the connecting apartment of Uala's relatives as well. Atroclus lay unmoving, his skin pale, his chest heaving as though each breath would be his last. Naikeri had tried to talk but Ason had silenced her with his raised hand. Now he knelt by Atroclus and raised him in his arms and put a cup to his lips and urged him quietly to drink. He did, thirstily, and Ason lowered him gently back to the soft furs on the bed.

'I am going to die, my kinsman,' Atroclus said in a calm voice.

'So shall we all, but tell me first the name of the one who did this.'

'That is why I am here. There is no place in this world for a warrior of Mycenae whose sword-hand is gone and whose eyes are gone as well. When I have told you what I know, you will put your sword into me.' It was not said as a question, and Ason responded in the same calm voice.

'That will be done as you ask. What of our kinsmen at the mine?'

'Dead or enslaved. Though it was a good battle. Some days after you left, we had the warning from the Albi who live in the forest that two ships of armoured men had landed and were on the way to the mine. A man was sent to warn you of what had happened but I saw him killed. We stood to arms and formed a line. The enemy marched up to the distance of a spear-cast and we saw that indeed there were enough to fill two ships and they were three, four to our one. I called to the men to die bravely and to take with them as many as they could of the Atlanteans, and they shouted that they would and struck their swords against their shields and stood ready. They fought well, even the chalceus, but all were killed except two chalceus kept to work the mine. This was done on orders, for they were so many they could pick and choose whom they would kill or would save. They had many spears which they threw in volleys heavy as rain. In the end we made a circle and stood together behind our shields and many of them died before we did. They would not let me die but pushed me with their shields and prodded me with spears, until I went down and was captured. I did not wish it that way. Then a spear was thrust between my elbows behind my back and my arms bound to it, and I was taken to the one who had sat at a distance bearing weapons but did not fight. His name is Themis.'

'Themis the Atlantean, son of Atlas, is dead,' Ason said, looking at his palms. 'I killed him with these hands.'

'No. He lives. He spoke your name and said that you had struck him down once with a coward's blow, and when he said this his face became red and he babbled and there was froth on his lips. He took off his helm and pointed to his head which now has no hair, it all having been removed, and to a gold plate that was held in place by linen wrappings. There was much he said that I could not understand, but he lives, that I can assure you.'

'Was the wound here,' Ason asked, touching his fingers lightly to Atroclus' head.

'That is the place.'

'Then Themis lives. The blow should have killed him.'

'He shouted much about that, about the pain and how he now cannot box or battle and drags his leg when he walks and has been made an old and near-dead man by you. There was much about surgeons of Atlantis and how they drilled away the broken bone and removed it, but I could not understand all that he said.'

'I should have struck harder. That blow would have killed any ordinary man.'

'Would you had. But we topple like an ash, felled by bronze on a mountain-top, bringing our young leaves to the ground, and, once fallen, the tree cannot be raised again. What was done cannot be undone. I do not think that Themis cares for the tin he captured or the tin he is mining, that is merely something to do while they are there. It is you he wants ...'

'I want him,' Ason said softly and took Atroclus' hand.

'... and all else is nothing to him. As the son of King Atlas, he commands ships and brought them here through the spring storms to find you. He tied me and tortured me, did the things you see here to make me speak. Though I am of as noble a line as he and told him only the truth. He would not believe me and threatened to cut off my sword-hand if I did not tell the truth about you. I spoke the same words again and one of his men with a great axe did this, then tied cords about my wrist so I would not bleed and die at once. Still he said that I lied, and I would no longer talk to him. When he came close I bit my tongue and gathered blood and spittle in my mouth and spat it full into his face. That was my last word to him and I would say no more. Then he did to me what you see, and told the girl to lead me to you, to carry the message that he was here to find and kill you, though it is my hope that you will be the finder and the killer.'

'It will be!' Ason swore and bent to kiss the burnt, blistered cheek of his kinsman.

'Then what has needed to be said has been said.' Atroclus swung his feet to the ground and struggled to stand erect. 'Your sword now, kind Ason. You will tell them in Mycenae that I died well?'

'None has ever died better.'

Ason drew his sword from the slings and held it before

152

him, guiding Atroclus' fingers to the point so he would know where it was. The blinded man raised his head, his lips drawn back from his teeth and shouted 'Mycenae' loudly before he hurled himself forward on to the blade and was dead before Ason could lower him to the floor.

When Ason came out of the door he ordered the two Mycenaeans there to remove Atroclus' body and to ready it for burial. Then he stood on the high mound looking across the plain at the blood-red disc of the afternoon sun behind the gathering banks of clouds. Two black ravens flew by, cawing loudly to each other, and settled in the ditch to pick at some refuse. There was an omen here but he did not know how to read it. When he turned away he saw that Naikeri was sitting against the wall, waiting for him. She stood and with both hands pressed down her clothing so the round fullness of her stomach could be seen.

'The Atlanteans fought only against your warriors. They have need of slaves, they said, so did not kill us. If they had known I was carrying your child they would have killed me.'

Ason started away and did not stop when she screeched after him. Finally she ran and held him by the arm.

'I am sure this child matters little to you but it is of some importance to me, do you hear?' He raised his free hand to strike her but stopped when she released him.

'Listen,' she said. 'Hear what I have to say. I am a woman, which is nothing in your eyes, and also not a Mycenaean which makes me even less. But I can help you and will bear you a son who will be a warrior like you. There are things about these Atlanteans that Atroclus does not know, that he could not tell you.'

'He is dead.'

'Alive he could not tell you. There was one man who came with the Atlanteans whom I have seen before. He led them on the path from the beach and stood behind with Themis during the fighting. Once before he came that way with others of his kind, no Atlantean but a trader, a Geramani, He was with the men who took the tin.'

153

Ason swung about and clutched her by the jaw, pulling her to him.

'Do you know what you are saying?' he shouted. She smiled, her smile a grimace as her face was twisted by his fingers, and would not talk again until he released her.

'Of course I know. We all heard that Themis was there to kill you, had come across the world to do so. He shouted it often enough. He was guided here by the Geramani who had means of knowing where you were, just as they knew where the tin was.'

'The Dark Man, Sethsus, I killed him too quickly. There are much slower ways of dying. Even dead he attacks me. It was more than the tin he took, but the lives of all those who came after it. The tin went to Atlantis as did word that I was here.'

'I am with you still,' Naikeri said, putting her arms about him. 'You are still my king.'

'Themis must die. We must retake the mine.' He was unaware of her presence.

'I can help. The Albi can watch them, tell you when they leave or are weak.'

'I have Mycenaeans. I have the men of three teutas to fight with me.'

'You have me.'

'We must attack. Now.'

'I will be with you always.'

He pushed her aside, unaware, and hurried away. She fell back against the wattled wall of the dun and watched him go. Was there no end to this killing? Would it stop only when every man in the land was dead?

The ravens rose up, calling loudly, and she shielded her eyes from the sight of them.

20

The summer sun was hot, the wind that blew across the plain as searing as the molten breath from the tin smelter. At night it was cooler, but only slightly, and there was just a brief while before dawn when a breeze came up that could be called comfortable. Then the light would wash the east again, the stars fade, and the great hot trembling sun would lurch over the horizon for another day. There had been no rain for thirty days; the grass was burnt yellow and the streams were only a trickle. The cattle went twice a day to the narrow stream of the Avon nearby and broke down its banks and trampled in the mud until it was only a bog with a slow-moving, mud-laden surface in the centre. The women, when they went to get water for the dun, had to walk upstream a long way before it ran clear and they returned, sweating under the weight of the jars on their heads, complaining in high voices that reached Inteb where he lay in the shade on the bank above. For the most part there was silence inside the dun. The animals lay quietly chewing their cud, and even the children were still. The copper workers could not fire their forges for the heat and also lay in the shadows chewing on straws and talking to each other in low voices. One of the masons had rigged some hides on a frame to give him shade, and sat beneath them smoothing the surface of a bluestone column. He would raise the round stone-maul over his head and bring it down to bruise away some fragments of the column. Then he would wait before doing it again. This slow thud, then a space, then another sharp thud, was the only sound other than the constant high whine of the flies. Inteb yawned and waved the insects away from his face.

Suddenly bright sunlight shone from bronze armour and he saw the men in the distance. He felt a great thudding in his chest—they might be Atlanteans. Had Ason been defeated? Were they all dead? And the Atlanteans now come to kill the remaining few of the enemy? The heat of the day drove these fantasies into his head and made the air shimmer so the approaching men were unclear. Only when Inteb was sure they were Mycenaeans did he quickly strip off his heavy armour and go out to meet them.

They were alone—and fewer returned than had left. Their faces were drawn with exhaustion, and most of them walked with their heavy helmets slung with their shields because of the heat. Ason came first and the others followed, with Aias bringing up the rear and half-supporting one of the wounded.

'Are the Yerni warriors here?' was all that Ason said when Inteb came up to them.

'You are the first.'

Ason nodded and would say no more but walked on stolidly and entered his own quarters. Naikeri opened the door for him. Inteb felt a sharp stab of hatred for the woman, then turned to Aias.

'The others can help their comrade. Come with me and I'll give you some freshly fermented milk.'

'By the great horned bull those are the finest words I have ever heard,' the boxer said in a cracked voice. His face was covered with dust that was traced through with wet rivulets of sweat. He tore off his armour in Inteb's doorway and dumped an entire jug of water over his head. The first bowl of fermented milk was drained without stopping for breath, and he dropped, gasping, on a couch against the wall and sipped at the next. Inteb sat beside him.

'A lot of fighting, Egyptian,' Aias said. 'All for not much good. Two evenly matched boxers, that's what it was like. Swing a lot, do damage, no one wins. If we had had twice as many men we could have done it. But every morning there

156

were less Yerni than the night before. They had heads to bring back to their duns, treasure too. They had been fighting a long time. And were in no hurry to impale themselves on the Atlantean swords. There were only a handful from each teuta when we did attack. They ran at the first sight of bronze. We couldn't break their line. Then we stayed in the woods and when they came out we attacked. Drove them back. Nobody wins, nobody loses. In the end Ason saw that and we force-marched here before the warriors came back alone.'

Aias lowered his head after that and slept, not waking even when the bowl slipped from his fingers and spilled the sticky dregs across his legs. Inteb sat, staring across the plain and lost in thought, and was still there at sunset when Ason emerged.

'Aias told me,' Inteb said, standing and stretching his cramped limbs.

'There are too many Atlanteans and the Yerni run. They know there is little they value at the mine and have no desire for swords in their guts. It was no victory.'

'It was no defeat either,' Inteb said, trying to find a brighter side to look on because Ason was in the darkest of humours. Even as he said it he realized that he was speaking only the truth—and the truth was larger than either of them realized. As they walked to the council circle inside the double ring of bluestones he was silent, lost in thought. Only the smallest fire had been lighted because of the heat and they sat well away from it, Ason at the base of his henge in his proper place.

'We have been thinking too much of the mine and only the mine,' Inteb said. 'It hangs before our eyes like a fog, blotting out everything else.'

'There is nothing else. Mycenae needs the tin and the tin is at the mine.'

'Your father's words—and not wrong words. But there is more that can be said. Mycenae will not fall for want of this bit of tin, not at once. You will get it, but only by admitting that you have done something else, are something else.'

'You are talking in riddles tonight, Egyptian, and my head is still thick from the heat of the day.'

'Then think of this and you will find your pulse faster. Here is the Island of the Yerni, a rich land with cattle and sheep, many people, grain for ale and honey for mead, sweet milk and good cheese, great centres for trade, where many men gather from far away. Of all the tribes and people in this land the Yerni are the most warlike and rule where they will —but one teuta is stronger than all the others. And the dun of this same teuta is the richest and the largest where the traders cross paths and meet. And you, Ason, are king in this land.'

'Say more, Egyptian,' Ason called out when Inteb stopped, and there was sharp interest in his voice.

'There is much more to say. You could be bull-chief in this dun and none would oppose you. Once you were bull-chief here you could do what your father is doing with the cities of the Argolid.'

'Make all the teutas of the Yerni one?'

'It could be done. You could do it. No longer bull-chief but king of this land. The king could take the mine away from the Atlanteans. The king could rule a rich country and, as king, you could bring the entire land to the aid of Perimedes. Give him an ally as well as a mine.'

'Of what use, the distance ...'

'The distance did not stop Sethsus from doing Mycenae harm and in the same manner you could do her good. The Geramani are friends neither of Atlantis nor of Mycenae but, like all men, befriend only themselves. Perhaps they can get tin to Mycenae. Perhaps they can guide you to the Atlantean tin-mines. Perhaps many things—all possible to a king. All yours for the taking.'

'I'll take them!' Ason shouted and laughed aloud. The Mycenaeans across the fire smiled that their leader could be in such spirits, and the first of the Yerni warriors, coming in from the darkness, wondered at the sound.

'You must unite the tribes,' Inteb said in a rush of words, carried away as well by his vision. 'Make them all one tribe,

158

one teuta, give them a nation, give them a city to hew to as the Mycenaeans hew to the great walls of rock-girt Mycenae.'

Ason smiled at the thought.

'We are both far from home, Inteb, and there are no Mycenaes or Theras or Thebes in this land. A city of wooden huts is all we have.'

'Tear it down—they work stone here.'

'Enough? You tell me, if we used every stone in these two circles, could we lay the foundation or build a single wall of a city?'

'No, you are right.' Inteb laughed. 'I saw Mycenae on this plain. But if not Mycenae, a greater circle then. Every bull-chief has his stone; we could make a greater circle of pillar stones, circle within circle perhaps like the canals of Thera, so every great warrior here could have his stone. And the bull-chiefs' stones would be here and they would have to assemble here, all the bull-chiefs together, and you king over them all.'

'I'll need my pillar stone.'

'And so shall have it, mighty king. The grandest, largest, most glorious stone these people have ever seen. They will come from everywhere to gape at it. I'll shape it as only Egyptians know how to shape stone, and will rise it behind you here at the council fire for them to stare at, right behind you.'

Inteb swung about in his excitement and pointed to the bare ground behind Ason, pointing between the uprights of the henge. And stopped, frozen, his jaw open. A dawning expression of delight swept over his features and he clapped his hands together before him at the strength of it, bending to seize Ason by the shoulders and pull at him and beg him to turn about.

'Look,' he shouted. 'This silly little arch of wood these people think so precious, white-painted and adorned, the henge of a little cow-chief. It is nothing. But look at it grow, watch it with your eyes as it swells up higher and higher, wider and stronger, reaching for the sky. As high as one man, two, three—four even. Too wide to span, too high to reach,

159

too solid to move, a henge that will drop their jaws to their chests and start the eyes from their heads.'

His hands traced the unborn shape in the sky and Ason could almost see it there.

'And not wood either,' Inteb said. 'Stone, good solid stone, a henge of stone mightier than any. It will be your kingdom and your city, Ason, right here ... *I will build it for you!*'

Part Four

21

Unable to contain his excitement, Inteb woke Ason at dawn, shaking at him until he crawled up from the depths of sleep. Naikeri looked on accusingly from the bed beside him but said nothing when they left. The air was still cool and the morning star bright in the east when they walked out across the plain. Inteb led the way to the area nearby where the great blocks of stones lay about in the greatest profusion. He hurried to the nearest and peered at it from all sides, even dug like a hound to examine its underside at one spot. Ason smiled and sat down on the stone, yawning broadly.

'What do you see?' Inteb asked.

'Stone.'

'Nothing more, and that is right because you are a warrior. But as you see skill with a sword in a man, or strength, endurance, other warlike qualities, so can I look beneath the surface of a stone. You know the walls of Mycenae and the lion gate there, you have not forgotten?'

'Never. And I know who built them.'

'I am the man who did that, so when I speak now you will know I speak the truth. Notice the way these great slabs of stone are thrown about on the ground as though left there for our purpose.'

'A great mystery.'

'Not at all, we have the same in Egypt. Hard stone concealed beneath the earth that is disclosed when the dirt is cleared away. Here the rain and wind have done that, exposing this stone for us to work with. Now notice the shape and the straight edges and these little lines here.'

'They mean nothing.'

'They do to me. This rock is grained like wood and when worked in the proper manner will split just as wood does. We shall take the two largest columns and shape them and bring them to the dun and seat them in holes in the ground behind the speaking-stone. Then we will work and raise up a third stone and place it across their tops high in the air and everyone will marvel and will wonder how it was placed there.'

'How will you place it there?' Ason asked, looking doubtfully at the immense size of the stone, aware of its incredible weight.

'With skill Ason, the same skill that raised and fitted the walls of Mycenae. We will begin today.'

Ason lay back on the rock, still cool from the night, and dozed as Inteb scouted among the great white slab of stones, nosing in and out like a questing hound. He finally raised Ason with a shout and led him through the stones to a long slab that rose chest-high.

'This is it,' he said, slapping it with the flat of his hand. Ason looked on doubtfully.

'You are a master builder, Inteb, that cannot be denied—but what can you possibly do with this giant of a stone that bulks as big as a ship, bigger than the largest stone in the walls of Mycenae?'

Inteb smiled at the question and they climbed up on to the slab. It stretched away from them not only as big as a good-sized galley but shaped very much like one, bulging out towards the centre and narrowing at the far end. Inteb paced it out and it was four paces wide at the widest and over ten paces long.

'As high as five men, perhaps higher,' Inteb said proudly. 'This top side you will notice is flat and will need little dressing, and we must hope the bottom will be the same. The two outer sides must be straightened and that great bulge knocked away.'

'Do we have the lifetime for that?' Ason asked unbeliev-

164

ingly. 'Do you propose that all that stone be removed here, without the tools and instruments and devices I saw you employ in Mycenae? Can it be done?'

'I will do it, Ason, and if you wish I will do it *today*.'

They returned to the dun and ate and drank and made their plans. Naikeri served them on the mound outside the door and listened but said nothing, not understanding what was being planned. When they were finished Ason put on his newly polished armour and went to get his men. Inteb scratched diagrams in the dirt with a stick, then searched out the stonecutter.

'Your name?' he said. The old man glanced over his shoulder and to both sides to be sure he was being addressed then looked at the ground. Inteb spoke more sharply a second time and the man squeezed his swollen knuckles and reluctantly said, 'Dursan.'

'Are there any in the dun other than yourself who can work stone?'

Dursan looked around for some release from this dark stranger who spoke with such a thick accent that many of his words could not be understood. But there was no escape. He pressed his hands together and mumbled answers and finally and reluctantly admitted that there were two others who aided him in his work. Inteb sent for them and while he was waiting ran his hands over the bluestone that Dursan had been working.

'Where does this stone come from?' he asked. 'I've seen none like it on the down.'

'Far away.'

'I'm sure of that or I wouldn't have asked. Can you try to give me a little more detail than that?'

Under verbal prodding Dursan told him how the bluestones were brought from a distant mountain where they waited to be seized by any warrior strong enough to do that. The story seemed true enough; the man did not have enough intelligence to concoct such a complicated lie. A warrior would take men with him and pull the stone down to the shore and

165

then on to a raft of logs. It took a long time to paddle this out of the harbour and along the coast because the ocean was wild there many times of the year. The sea voyage was ended when they reached the mouth of a river. Apparently the stone was brought up the river, across country for a bit and down another river that became the Avon and passed by near the dun. All in all a great labour, and Inteb marvelled at the things men do to assure their own importance.

'But why this particular mountain?' Inteb asked. 'There must be good stone a lot nearer than that.'

'It has always been done that way. They did it like that before we drove them out—in my father's time it was.'

'They?'

'The Donbaksho. They used to keep cattle here, but they don't know how to fight. Now *we* have the cattle and they give us the grain we ask for. They used to trade here; now we trade here. They used to have someone always on the mountain where the stones come from, watching for the Albi when they came from Domnann—you can see all the way across the channel from the top there. Now the Albi come here with their bronze and gold to trade with us and we don't even need a watch on the mountain.' Dursan snorted with pleasure over the superior fighting ability of the Yerni and pointed to the large stone almost completely buried in the ground.

'See that? Our speaking-stone. Do you know how it got there? My father did that. It was the biggest stone the Donbaksho had, the chief's stone, and they all wanted to come and touch it. My father had the pit dug, pushed it over, buried it. Now we stand on it, stand on the Donbaksho.'

Then Dursan's two assistants arrived and the first of the Yerni warriors were already beginning to climb down the ladders and notched poles from the balconies above.

Very soon it was like a disturbed ants' nest, with the warriors milling about and calling to each other, cradling their battle-axes and smoothing their moustaches. The women followed behind, keeping their distance, yet curious, too, as to the reason for this activity in the heat of the day.

166

All they knew was that the Mycenaeans were going about the outer bank and hammering on all the doors with their swords and calling the warriors to the council fire. They came and settled, those who had pillar-stones of their own leaning against them or sitting in their shadows. Then Ason appeared, marching at the head of his Mycenaeans and, as always, the Yerni stared in admiration at this incredible sight. Men in bronze from head to foot, eye-hurting shining bronze, bronze swords in hand and brazen shields on their arms. Ason led them to the speaking-stone set into the ground within the ring of bluestones; they stood behind it and he upon it. When he raised his sword the noise died away enough so that his voice could be heard.

'I am standing on the speaking-stone and I am telling you something. Today you will see a thing that you have never seen before. Today you will see something that you will tell your children about and they will tell your children's children and there will be no end to the telling. Today you will see something done that you know cannot be done. And after it is done I will tell you something that you never thought you would hear.'

The rising hum of voices drowned Ason's voice and the crowd stirred with excitement. No one knew what the words meant but everyone knew that something incredible was going to happen. What Ason said he would do he did—they had learned that much about the man at least. He called out again and they grew silent.

'Follow me,' he called out and went out through the entrance of the dun, with his Mycenaeans behind him. The Yerni warriors came next, pushing and jostling and shouting at each other angrily in order to stay close, while the rest of the inhabitants of the dun, women and children, metal- and wood-workers, even the druids, followed after. Ason led them the short distance to the field of jumbled rock and climbed upon the great stone that Inteb had selected. The Egyptian clambered up beside him and reached down to take a heavy rock that Dursan lifted up to him. A hush fell as Ason spoke.

167

'Now listen to Inteb who will do the promised thing for me.'

Inteb rolled the round, greenish rock with his foot and pointed to it. The warriors strained to see.

'This is a maul,' he called out, and they pushed and craned their necks as though they had not seen these stones in the dun every day of their lives. 'It is a hard stone, harder than any other, and Dursan and his helpers use stones like these to dress the stones of the warriors. They do it like this.'

He bent and strained to lift the rock—it was a third of his weight—and struggled it as high as his waist before he dropped it. It smashed into the surface of the white stone with the familiar dull thud. Inteb rolled it aside and scraped up a little rock dust with his finger.

'This is what the maul does. Every time it strikes the larger stone it breaks off a few grains. After many blows a stone can be smoothed or grooved, or even hollowed away. It takes day after day to smooth even the smallest stone and that is all that can be done. But not any more. Today we are going to do something new.'

He slowly paced the entire length of the immense slab and back, and every eye was upon him as he did this. He pointed down at the immense bulk and they listened with unbelief.

'Today we are going to break this stone in half, the warriors and I, and it will become Ason's stone when we bring it to the dun. We will shape it and move it and raise it and it will be the mightiest warrior's-stone ever raised. There will be more after that but I tell you only of this stone now ...'

Someone laughed and Ason leapt forward, pushing Inteb aside and stabbing his sword at the crowd so that the nearest drew back in fear.

'Inteb speaks for me,' he called out with a deadly anger in his voice. 'His words are my words. If you laugh at him you laugh at me. I will have the head of anyone who even smiles in my direction. Have you heard me?'

They had, well enough. The women covered their faces

and many of the children ran away. The warriors stayed, they were warriors, but their faces were as expressionless as the stone before them.

'I will need only the strongest warriors to help me cut Ason's stone,' Inteb said in the silence. 'Each warrior will need a maul, and the heavier it is and the stronger he is, the more honour will be his. There are some mauls here and Dursan is looking for others.'

Now it was a matter of pride and strength and the warriors put their axes in their hair belts and went, shouting and pushing, to find the biggest mauls they could lift. Most of the stones they found were the wrong kind, only the hard green stone could be used, and they cursed and dropped the stones when they were told this and went to find others. One by one, sweating and grumbling in the heat, they came back with the mauls until there were more than twenty warriors who had them and Inteb called a halt.

'There is room for no more. The honour is for these warriors who will do what no one has ever done before.'

They swaggered when he had them climb on to the great slab with him, calling out boasts to the scowling warriors left behind. They brought the mauls with them and, with the aid of the Mycenaeans, Inteb pushed the Yerni back in a line against the far edge of the stone. Shoulder to shoulder they stretched the length of the slab, listening with pained attention as Inteb explained what they had to do. It was not complex, but they were not used to working together and had never done anything in unison before in their lives. It was a concept they found difficult to understand and he made them repeat the motions over and over many times before they got it right. Small stones, no bigger than a man's fist, were passed up and they used these as they practised. Inteb had drawn two lines with charcoal the length of the slab, a pace apart, and he kept redrawing the lines as their shuffling feet obliterated them. There were mutterings of complaint over the stupid hot thing they were doing—but no one smiled. Inteb repeated the instructions with a voice rapidly growing hoarse.

'That's it, all in a line, your feet on that marked line. Not standing in front of it or behind it but *on* it. Good. Raise your mauls, as high as your head, hold them there ... *hold* them until I give the word and all together, just for once, *drop them!*'

The small rocks clattered down, most of them on the marked line in an irregular fall, rolling about and some dropping over the edge to the ground. The watching crowd had been cleared back by the Mycenaeans but small boys ran forward to retrieve the fallen stones and pass them back up. They were enjoying themselves if no one else was.

'No, leave them there,' Inteb ordered. 'And throw the rest of the stones away. We'll do it now with the mauls.'

There were excited shouts at this announcement and the warriors called to one another as they kicked the small stones away and bent behind them to pick up the waiting mauls. It was an impressive sight, the tall, sweat-drenched warriors, shoulder to shoulder the length of the great slab, with Inteb standing behind them. The crowd was silent.

'Lift!' Inteb called out, and they bent, and a ripple moved down the line as they straightened and the green mauls rose in the air.

'Hold, hold!' he shouted, since some of the warriors were slower than the others and one, cursing, dropped the stone on his foot. Then they were all up, high, higher ...

'*Drop them!*'

The great weight of hard stone fell with a rolling thunder and the warriors jumped back.

Nothing happened. Inteb shouted hoarse orders above the growing murmur from the crowd.

'Not good enough, not at the same time, not on the line. Do it right or it can't be done at all, you great hulking dim-brained animals. Lift together, hold together, drop together ... *drop!*'

Again, nothing—but a rising growl of anger from the warriors as well as the crowd. The Mycenaeans raised their weapons and shields and Ason jumped up next to Inteb and paced behind the warriors' backs.

'Killers of dogs!' he shouted. 'This is harder than killing. This is something you must do right or I will slay you all. This you will do.'

By force of will he kept them there, now shouting aloud in protest, and they raised and dropped the mauls again with no result. With the flat of his sword Ason drove back the men who tried to turn away and cursed them in three tongues so that they once again grabbed up the mauls.

'Over your heads, you eaters of turds!' he called out. 'High, higher, hold them there, all of you, do what I tell you, do it right, because this time they fall together and they fall on the line the correct way, bring them down ... *now!*'

Shouting angrily the Yerni warriors hurled the stones down with a crashing roar and the solid rock beneath their feet shivered.

With a growing, crackling, rushing roar it sheared in half, fell away, a great broken slab that dropped and cracked and sprayed fragments out at the screaming running crowd.

Dumbfounded, the warriors looked down at what they had done.

The immense slab of stone had broken along its entire length, along the line Inteb had drawn upon its surface.

22

There are some things that are unbelievable. Even when they are seen to happen they cannot be accepted. The warriors who had done this thing could not credit their labour with the mauls as having had any connection with the splitting of the great stone. It would have been easier to believe that lightning had struck down from the sky and done this thing; they had seen the carcases of animals and riven trees that lightning had struck, so knew its strength. Just as they knew their own, and knowing this could not believe what they had done. They jumped down and pushed the crowd aside and stared with open mouths at the fresh white surface of the sundered rock, bent to pick up fragments of it from the ground. These they turned over and over and examined, tapping them, even touching them to their mouths as though taste might reveal something the eye could not see. But they were rock, good solid rock, and could not be broken again. Some tried with the mauls with no success other than a few bruised fingers and crushed toes. The stone which had given way and fallen apart before them was still stone; hard, intractable, unworkable.

'Listen to me,' Ason called out, standing alone on the rock above them. 'This is a day that must be remembered and what was done here today must be remembered. Ason's great stone was cut this day. The council fire will be built high, and sheep and cows will be roasted and ale will be drunk and all the warriors shall sit by me.'

This was greeted with roars of approval, and when they had died away Ason said, 'And tonight, before these warriors, I shall be named the new bull-chief of this dun which will be Dun Ason now.'

There were more shouts at this, and dark looks only from the family of the dead Uala from whose ranks the new bull-chief should have been selected. They dared say nothing aloud because the other warriors saw only honour and victories for the teuta led by a man like Ason. He was the strongest among them, the deadliest warrior, and now commanded great stones to be cleaved at his word. He would be a bull-chief they could follow.

'We could cut the other face now,' Inteb said, the niceties of politics forgotten in the pleasure of once more working with stone.

'I think not,' Ason told him. 'There is enough wonder here for one day. The women must prepare for the feast, the druids have their work as well. Tomorrow will be a day for labours.'

While the warriors had been away the Donbaksho had continued to bring their tithe of grain to the dun and the women had prepared it in the squat, wide-bottomed pots. Because of the heat it had brewed and matured with bubbling efficiency and now great quantities of ale were cooling in shaded corners. A fat-flanked cow was dragged to the killing area, bellowing at the smell of blood, its eyes rolling in agony. The first butcher, an ugly bondman with a fearful squint and great-muscled arms, swaggered over in his blood-drenched leather apron with his heavy stone hammer over his shoulder. While two men hung from the cow's horns he waited, then swung the hammer with practised skill against the flat of the beast's head just in front of its horns. It collapsed to the ground, dead instantly, where the old women severed its throat with sharp flint knives and caught the spurting blood in pottery bowls. Other beasts were dragged up and the preparations for the feast got under way. Well before dark the first warriors were in their positions and the drinking had begun.

It was the druid, Nemed, who conducted the bull-chief rites and if he still bore any ill will towards Ason he was silent about it. Now he was wearing his finest robes and a tall, cylindrical head-dress that grew narrower towards the top, a wonder as long as a man's arm and made of beaten gold into which designs of lines and circles had been worked. He stood between Ason and the fire, arms folded and waiting as the crowd grew quiet. When they were silent he began his chant in a high toneless voice that gradually deepened as he warmed to the subject. Much of the material was familiar, old lines repeated and used in different ways, but this increased the warriors' appreciation rather than lessening it and they nodded at the parts they knew well.

Sound of thunder and rushing wind,
A crashing, a breaking,
Rock tearing, ground ripping,
Such sounds to deafen the ears.

The sounds that I heard were men at war,
Shield shock of shield against shield.
Axes striking and breaking,
Skulls crushed.

What fighting was done then,
Deep voices of heroes,
And battling warriors, raging with anger,
Grim wild men, great bull-chiefs.

There was Ason,
In the midst was Ason, quick eagle,
Striking hound of gore, seeking blood,
Man of the long knife, bellowing bull.

Then they met,
Then Ason struck.
Cleft Uala's head,
Drove the blow to his navel—

Then a second cross-wise stroke
Brought him down in three pieces.

Nemed drew a deep wavering breath, loud in the silence,
and shouted the remainder without stopping or even pausing.

Drenched with blood and grey with brains,
He cut away
jaw from head,
head from trunk,
arms from trunk,
bend from arms,
wrists from bend,
fists from wrists,
thumbs from fists,
nails from thumbs,
legs from trunk,
knees from legs,
calves from knees,
feet from calves,
toes from feet,
nails from toes,
And he sent these limbs and parts
Flying front and back like bees
Buzzing about in the sunlight.

Loud shouts of appreciation followed this and buzzing
sounds that would not stop until Nemed had regained his
breath and repeated the part about the bees again. There was
more like this, often repeated, far more interesting to the
Yerni warriors than to Ason, who could see no interest in
the lying and the bragging that they all knew could not be
true. It went on a long time and Nemed built the tension carefully until the moment when he spun about and pointed at
Ason.

'You have a question?' Nemed shouted.

'I have a question,' Ason answered as he rose and stood
before his henge. 'Is there a different purpose for this day?

How can this day be different from all the others?'

As he said this, two of the other druids dragged up a man who struggled weakly in their grip. A captive, imprisoned for what reason? Ason neither knew nor cared. The man was held with his back to Nemed who was handed a sharp bronze dagger. He nodded once and the prisoner was released, the druids stepping back. Before the man could take a step, Nemed plunged the dagger into his back with a hard upward thrust beneath the ribs that penetrated his heart. The captive shuddered all over and fell, writhing for a moment on the ground as he tried to reach back for the dagger still in his body. Then he convulsed again and died.

Nemed stood over him, his face set and flintlike, reading omens from his thrashing then and the positions of his limbs after he was dead. The movements of a man already part way through the gate of death are far better augury than clouds or the flight of birds. What he saw there must have satisfied him, because he straightened up and pointed carefully at Ason and began the ritual questions that would make Ason bull-chief.

The thing was done.

'You rise with the first light, Egyptian,' Aias said from his perch on the ramp above as Inteb hurried by. Mist still hung over the plain and the birds were waking and calling.

'The first light of dawn can show things in a stone that are not normally seen.'

'I know. It is the shadows.'

Inteb halted and looked up quizzically.

'For a boxer you seem to know a good deal about stone-working.'

'As a slave I learned a lot about a number of things that require a strong back and little thought. Boxing took me from that. I have been in the galleys and in the stone-quarry at Karatepe.'

'Kizzuwatna sandstone,' Inteb snorted. 'You can chew it with your teeth. Come along and I'll show you what real stone is.'

176

As the dawn sun burned away the mist and shone across the stone, Inteb hurried from one end to the other, mumbling to himself and marking quick strokes with his piece of charcoal. Aias watched, scratching and belching sleepily; he had not slept that night.

'This side should be even easier,' Inteb said. 'The stone is thinner for one thing and it will break cleanly away. And the Yerni now know that it can be done so it might be possible to get them to work together.'

'A touch of the whip made from the skin of the water-horse helps with that.'

'Only with slaves and peasants, Aias, and I wish I had a few here. An axe in the head is what I would get if I tried it with these Yerni. When the time comes for the final shaping I will have to find bondsmen, or perhaps the Donbaksho from the farms, for that work. It is simple enough and requires only strong arms and the repeating of the same process from sunrise to sunset.'

When the boys drove the cattle out to pasture for the day they saw Inteb at the stone and word was quickly passed. All the warriors who were sober enough to walk hurried out, led by the ones who had not had a chance to work a maul the day before. Laughing aloud, they climbed on to the slab, smiling at Inteb when he cursed them for obliterating his marks, fingering the stone-mauls and comparing their fine points like experienced masons. There was a warrior for every maul. Soon the crowd was pushing close, and Aias went to bring Ason for the spectacular moment.

'One cut for each side,' Inteb told him when he appeared. 'That is economical of labour and time but is also a mark of skill that few possess.' There was no conscious boasting in this, but only truth, and Ason nodded agreement. 'The stone shall be wide at the base and will taper on each side as it rises, much like the temple of Ni-weser-re next to the Nile, or the pillars in the courtyard of Sahu-re. This is a much admired line and one I much prefer to the straight angularity of the walls and columns executed for King Khephren in his temple. That is not for you—even if I had the means here

177

to work stone to that degree. Yours will be a living and warm stone that takes its unpolished form very much from the earth from which it springs. Now we begin.'

This time the warriors listened intently, straining to hear and understand, remembering that it could be done. The crowd of watchers moved far back and climbed on other rocks for a better view. Aias helped Inteb to place the men correctly and to order their movements. The practice with the pebbles did not take as long as the first time, and one of the warriors shouted 'Ason abu!' when they were told to pick up the mauls, all the others joining in the war-cry.

High they held them, tensely waiting the word, and hurled them down at the given moment.

With a sharp crack the stone split and the great jagged piece fell away.

The watchers were struck dumb for a moment, remembering the frenzied labours of the day before and not expecting anything yet. Then they burst into shouts and ran forward, pushing and milling about to examine this new wonder. In the middle of the broken stone, fallen away slabs and forgotten mauls, Ason's column lay neatly shaped and ready.

'Now to move it,' Inteb said. 'No excuses today about banquets, this work must be accomplished.'

'Everything shall be as you say,' Ason agreed. 'Though how you intend to move this mountain is beyond me.'

'But not beyond me, which is why I serve you. In Egypt stone-working is older than the memory of man or his writings. The art we practise is known to no others and I am skilled in that art. But I need the proper materials and labour.'

'Labour there is enough. The warriors themselves fight for positions to help. They will tire of this, I am sure, but there will be others to replace them, you have my word on that. What materials do you need?'

'Something unknown on this treeless plain. Strong wooden beams as thick as your leg or thicker. Lengths of logs, many of them, and rope, more rope than I have seen anywhere on this island.'

178

'The wood is easy enough. The dun is made of wood and you will have every splinter of it if you need it.'

'Not all, not quite yet—'

'Then take my apartment. There are lengths of log bridging the entrance that should suit you, and the walls and floors. Do you wish it now?'

'As soon as it can be obtained.'

The new orders were received with joy by everyone but the woodworkers and Naikeri, who cursed and threw things at the people who came and began to tear at her walls, stopping only while Ason himself came to drive her out with their personal belongings. The woodworkers, many of whom had helped to build the dun with great labour and time, thought even less of tearing down their handwork. But it was coming down, whatever they felt, so eventually they moved in and supervised the destruction.

Inteb stayed at the site and directed the digging out of cavities under the stone. Here, as everywhere else on the plain, the hard chalk lay just under the surface soil and could not easily be dug or shovelled away. Sharp-pointed deerantlers were driven into it with rocks, then levered sideways to crack out a piece of chalk, this process repeated as long as was needed. When the first beams and logs arrived the pits were ready and heavy stones had been pushed into positions before them.

'This beam is used as a lever,' Inteb called out. 'You do not have to know why, but a lever increases the strength of men and enables them to do things thought impossible. We will now use the levers to lift this stone. This will be done a little at a time, and each time the stone is lifted these logs will be pushed under to prevent it from falling back down. When it is tilted enough these other logs will be pushed all the way under it and that will be the first step. We will do that now.'

Once more aided by Aias, Inteb instructed the men on the great levers, putting their hands in the proper place and explaining over and over what they were to do. Aias and two Mycenaeans manned the chocks that had to be pushed under when the stone was lifted since this required instant decision and action of a nature too technical for the Yerni.

There were twelve men on the three longest poles, eight men on the four shorter ones. They clutched the wood and waited anxiously while Inteb surveyed the arrangements and then, at his ordered command, threw their weight on to the levers. They did it unevenly, of course, some hanging from the beams, others pushing in the wrong direction. One of the poles was rotten and cracked, dropping a half-dozen men into the dust where they were laughed at for their pains. Another pole was fitted, more explanations given, even a demonstration by six Mycenaeans as to how a pole should be pulled on. The Yerni spat on their palms and went back to their labours.

This time there were excited screams as the great slab trembled and tilted ever so slightly. The chocks were quickly thrust home and all work stopped again as everyone went to look at the black opening, laughing and grabbing up the beetles and disturbed insects that emerged. Inteb waited until they had all seen enough, then ordered them back to work. The rock fulcrums were moved closer and changed for higher ones and, ever so slowly, the immense slab of stone tilted into the air.

'Enough,' Inteb called out. 'Bring the logs.'

The Yerni were hesitant about coming too close to the stone, sure that it would fall back to the earth or perhaps roll over and crush them at any moment. It was Aias and the Mycenaeans who placed the logs as Inteb directed, until they filled the space under the stone completely, their round ends projecting along the side in an unbroken row of circles. The sun was low and evening approaching before Inteb approved of the arrangements and prepared to lower the stone on to the rollers.

'Slowly,' he called out, 'a step at a time, the reverse of lifting it. If it breaks loose it will turn those logs to splinters when it falls and we will have to start all over again.'

The creaking poles levered up the unimaginable mass and, one by one, the supporting chocks were removed. When the last one was taken away all the weight came on the platform of loose logs, which groaned with the weight. Some of the logs, over irregularities in the ground, were crushed with loud snapping sounds—but the others held.

Inteb would not permit the excited Yerni to take more time to run around the stone and admire it, but they did anyway, kneeling down and looking beneath it at the light on the far side. Under his direction more logs were placed on the ground before the small end of the stone to form a solid mass of rollers. Inteb climbed up on the slab to direct the next step and Ason came to join him.

'We will move the stone,' Inteb said. 'Just a few paces today to see that it can be done, so that in the morning we can begin its path to the dun. Poles over here.'

The great beams were once more angled under the slab, but this time at the large end and not the sides. On the given signal the men on the poles heaved and the great stone shivered.

'Again—harder!'

They pulled with all their strength and the stone slab moved forwards over the first log and then the second. The position of the levers was moved forward, and the men heaved again. Slowly, the last log emerged from the rear of the stone. The stone had moved forward twice the span of a man's hands.

'The beginning of the journey,' Inteb said proudly.

23

News of what was happening at Dun Ason spread quickly
to the other teutas and by word of mouth to the Donbaksho
farmers in the forest and to the isolated Albi settlements. It
was the dry part of the year; the crops had been harvested
and the animals were well fed. There was time to see this new
wonder in the world, and many came to do just that. Each
day when the work began there was no shortage of observers
and volunteers if they were needed. And they were. Bringing
Ason's stone to its resting-place was a great labour.

A track had to be smoothed across the open down to the
gateway of the dun. More of the walls were sacrificed to
obtain logs to be placed side by side to fill in the swampy
spots and to level the ground. A smooth roadway now
stretched from the field of broken stones the short distance
to the dun—and along it the ponderous stone made its
voyage.

Everything was organized now. Every bit of leather available had been gathered and braided into ropes to tie about
the stone. These were the anchor lines for two long, thick
leather cables that stretched out ahead, well rubbed with
fat to keep them soft and supple. Other leather ropes were
attached to the stone near the front so more men could haul
at the same time. The mass of the stone was so great that
if any progress were to be made, other than a simple crawl
by using the levers in the rear, a great number of men would
be needed. When they finally assembled to begin the move,

182

their numbers were too large for the Yerni to count.

'My counting does not go that high either,' Ason admitted. 'Is all this needed?'

'It is,' Inteb said with a calmness he did not feel. Would it really be enough? His calculations were accurate and he had gone over them many times. 'To move the stone easily and keep it moving even up the small grades here we will need at least five hundred men on the ropes.'

'A number beyond imagining,' Ason admitted.

'It can be imagined. All the fingers and toes on a man number twenty and the count of five men is one hundred. We need the count of twenty-five men.'

'It is still a very large number.'

'It will be larger still. To keep the stone moving steadily we must have log men, two to each log since they weigh as much as two men for the most part, and the count here will be two hundred. They must seize the logs as they emerge behind the stone and move quickly ahead to lay them down ahead of the other logs to act again as rollers when their turn comes. All of this must be organized to a very high degree. I will supervise the hauling-team, Aias will make sure the logs are taken forward properly, and someone must ride the stone and supervise and order everything.'

'That is my position.'

'The highest, Ason; none other dare fill it. Shall we begin?'

Although they had started at dawn the sun was nearing the zenith by the time the order to move was finally given. The ropes were laid out along the ground by Inteb himself so the pull would come in the proper direction. The rollers stretched ahead of the stone and men stood ready in the rear to seize them as they emerged. Inteb raised his hand and Ason called out loudly:

'We will begin.'

The men bent to seize their ropes and lifted them to their shoulders and stood there, waiting Inteb's orders as they had been directed. Inteb stood on a rock to one side to see that they were all in the correct position, then spoke the commands.

'Hold the ropes firmly. Lean forward. Do not pull yet but lean forward so your weight is on the ropes. Feel that weight. Do not pull with your arms, your arms and hands are just for holding the rope—it is your legs that will do all the work. Now, crouch forward, bend your knees beneath you so that you are ready to push. Be ready now ... ready ... slowly as you can straighten your legs, push—PUSH!'

They did. The ropes stretched and grew taut and the logs beneath the massive stone creaked.

And then it shuddered and moved forward.

As soon as it did some people fell, others turned to look— while the rest kept pulling with no effect, the veins standing out in their foreheads. Ason called out for them to halt and they did. The routine was repeated.

After many false starts the necessary coordination was achieved and the stone moved forward with deliberate and steady motion. One log after another emerged from the rear to be grabbed by eager hands, lifted, and carried ahead to await the arrival of the stone again. The men hauling on the ropes sweated and strained; Inteb kept them moving, a slow step at a time—and Ason rode his strange stone ship through the entrance of the great dun and across its spacious interior to the prepared pit next to the council fire. When the signal to halt was given some of the men dropped to the ground on the spot, while others called out for ale to slake their thirst.

Ason rested too, sitting in the shadow of the great stone, feeling it against his back, a part of him, eating the food that Naikeri brought to him. She wanted to talk about their new rooms but he waved her away. The stone filled his thoughts.

'Do we go on?' he asked the sweating Inteb, who crawled up out of the pit and dropped to the ground next to him.

'At once, while everyone is willing. I was making a final check of the dimensions and all is as it should be, the stone will fit. You will notice that Dursan and his assistants have pounded the base, rounding it slightly. This will enable us to position the stone exactly after it is in the pit, rock it back and forth, and even turn it if we must.'

'By what magic will the stone enter the pit at your bidding?'

'No magic. Art. You will see that this side of the pit is cut in a sloping ramp. The far side is straight up and down and those large stakes have been put in position against it so that when the stone slides home it will not bring down the chalk on the other side and destroy all our labours. What we will do now is draw the stone forward very gently so the base projects over the side of the hole and the ramp. When more weight is over the hole than is on the rollers the end will swing down and the stone will slide in and seat itself.'

'Leaving this great handsome thing standing at an angle half in and half out.'

'You can see in your mind like an artist, Ason. You are correct. When it is down I will then bring it to an upright position against the far wall, and we will hold it there while chalk and rubble is quickly shovelled into the hole to fill it and secure the column. Your first stone will be in place. The first upright of the henge that the druids call Mother Earth, the first planted.'

Inteb had prepared the stone for its descent into the pit in other ways. As it had been brought closer and closer to its resting-place, he had arranged that larger logs be used as rollers so that the stone would be as far above the surface of the ground as possible. This was vital as Inteb knew from experience, and he made many measurements and calculations before he would allow the stone to proceed, surveying it from all sides and squinting along it. He would not permit the operation to go on until the angle of approach had been moved slightly to one side. This proved to be harder than rolling had been, and there was much straining and cursing at the levering beams before Inteb was satisfied. Only then were the ropes picked up once more and the signal given to take up the strain as slowly as possible. The stone moved forward.

Moving alongside it, Inteb kept one hand on the stone and watched its progress carefully. The end was over the pit when he stopped the hauling and brought up two heavy wooden stakes. These were driven into the ground at the very edge of the pit, after the last log had passed that point and had been pulled quickly aside before it fell into the opening. The forward movement was started again, and the pivot log was drawn across the ground to the stakes where it stopped. But the stone kept moving, scraping across it, and the crowd murmured and pressed back as the massive end of the column moved out into the air, overhanging and shadowing the pit below. Farther and farther it went, until the men on the ropes felt a shiver along them and dropped the ropes and scrambled away. The stone hung there, its immense weight pulling it down, the chalk on the lip of the cutting crumbling and falling away, more and more, the pivot log next to it splitting and cracking as it was crushed.

With a sudden swooping rush the great length of stone hurled itself into the air, blotting out the sky, sliding down with a crashing roar to seat itself in the waiting socket.

The ground shook beneath their feet and a great cloud of dust rose up.

Tilted at an angle, like a giant's finger pointing at the sky, the stone was seated in its opening in the ground.

While the others celebrated and danced around it Inteb went back to work, pulling out his helpers from the mob and pushing them to their positions, with Aias at his side when a little violent persuasion was needed. Shear-legs had been prepared days earlier, and these were carried over and laid on the ground next to the straight side of the pit opposite the angled stone. They were simply made, of four lengths of wood, but most cunningly designed. The shear-legs themselves were two tall tree-trunks that were wide apart on the ground but angled towards one another as they rose so that they crossed at the very top, and were tightly bound together there. An arm's length below this crossing, a short crossbar had been lashed into place between the two legs and another, longer one, connected them at ground level. The exact placement of these crossbars was essential to its operation. Before
186

the wooden framework was raised, two pits were dug into the chalk for the bottoms of the legs so they would not be able to move about once seated there.

Again Inteb did what no other could do, laying out the ropes in the proper manner. A heavy log was lashed to the back of the angled stone just below the top. Ropes ran from the small crossbar near the top of the shear-legs and over this log to the ground. These ropes would first be used to lift the shear-legs into position. But before this was done the hauling-lines that would lift the stone were tied securely about the shear-legs where they crossed at the top.

Lifting the great wooden form from the ground was a labour in itself. Two teams of men pulled on the ropes that ran over the log at the top of the stone, while others raised the top of the frame, pushing with poles when it lifted above their reach. Slowly the shear-legs rose until they were standing vertical next to the pit. The ropes that had been used to lift the legs were now lashed securely to the log behind the stone, and the lifting was ready to begin.

One hundred and fifty men picked up each line. They would pull the top of the shear-legs away from the stone, and the lines tied to the short crossbar would pull the stone to a vertical position. If everything went correctly Inteb ordered the slack be taken up on the lines, then walked about examining every detail before turning to Ason.

'We are ready,' he said.

'Begin.'

There was a great creaking from the wooden frame when the pressure came on it as the men hauled with practised strength. The great stone stirred from its resting-point— then slowly heaved free of the supporting ramp and rose to the vertical.

'Stop!' Inteb shouted when the stone pressed against the flat wall of the pit. 'Hold there, keep holding!'

They held, sweating and straining, as Inteb walked up to the stone and pressed a strange instrument to its surface. He had supervised its construction when the wrights had made it, and none other than he knew its function. A half-section

187

of a small log had been hollowed out to make a trough, almost a duplicate of the large chalk troughs, and this was secured to a vertical length of wood. There was water in the trough, and when Inteb pressed the trough and wood to the stone he divined some mysterious knowledge from this water, perhaps as the druids read signs from the tortured positions of stabbed prisoners. Everyone marvelled at this, even the gasping, straining men holding the stone in position.

Inteb was aware of the tension and knew there was a limit to the length of time they could hold the strain, but the column had to be vertical before it was secured in position. The water level told him all he needed to know. He had scratched a deep groove into the wood and when the water level was at this mark the surface against which it was resting was vertical. With careful patience he made his measurements and ordered the men on the poles to push at the top of the stone, so it rocked on its base, to align it vertically. They pushed from one side, then from the other, then back to the first again. He shouted instructions at them, which Aias passed on with curses, and the weakest men had fallen from the ropes to be replaced by others before he was satisfied.

'Now,' Inteb called out. 'Fill in the hole!'

Shouting with excitement, the workers shovelled the dirt and lumps of chalk back into the hole, mixed with rocks and broken mauls, anything that would fill the space. It rose quickly to the ground level, was tamped down with heavy logs and filled some more. When this had been done the second time the order was finally given and the exhausted men let go of the ropes.

The column stood by itself, reaching up into the air, casting a great pointing finger of a shadow across the dun, a shadow that had never existed before.

24

Soon after dark the moon rose and shone on the banquet that was already well under way. This was a signal for more admiring of Ason's stone—it had never been seen by moonlight before—and a pacing out of the immense shadow that the moonlight threw. The most venturesome warriors came close to the rock and some even touched it; Ason stood with his back against it and feared nothing. Ale was brought to him there and he drank. There were no women at the banquet, of course, other than those who served the drink, nor was their presence permitted at so important a function. Ason ignored the woman's voice calling to him, but he could ignore it no longer when Naikeri appeared, still speaking his name.

'Away,' he called out, raising his hand to strike her if she came any closer.

'There is something you must know, something important.'

'Another time.'

'It is important now. Shall I come to you—or would you have me wait away from the council ring.'

Ason jumped forward to seize her but she escaped him. Angrily he followed her from the fire, until they were well away from the circles of men when she turned to face him. Her belly was large, pushing its mound up through her clothing, and when he saw this he lost some of his anger thinking about his son to be.

'I have word about the Atlanteans,' Naikeri said, 'though perhaps they are no longer as important to you as your stone.'

189

He turned to admire the column from this new angle, ignoring her waspish tones; women were often like that. 'What have you heard of the Atlanteans?'

'They will march out of the valley of the mine to attack you here, and a kinsman of mine is leading them.'

For the first time in many days the stone was forgotten and Ason turned all his attention to her. With the excitement of the stone-raising the Atlanteans had been out of his thoughts of late.

'Tell me all you know,' he said.

'So now you have attention for me? Only when you need me do you even speak to me. At all other times you treat me as though I were as dumb as that stone you have there.'

'Speak about the Atlanteans, woman,' Ason said between his teeth. 'You can flay me with your sharp tongue some other time. What has happened?'

In a sudden change of mood she went to him, her arms about his back and her face against his. 'I wish only to help,' she said. 'What I do I do for you, my king. There was no one before you and there will be none other than you for me, this I promise. I carry your son and this is what I want.'

Not untouched, Ason put his hand to her hair and felt its softness against his ribbed callouses. Standing close like this she told him in a whisper everything she knew, everything she had done.

'The men of Atlantis are stupid and think only of slaves. Most of the Donbaksho from nearby are gone, and now when they capture any they put collars on them and lock them up so they cannot run away. But they know the Albi as traders who can help them, and supply information as well as food and other things they need, so do not enslave my people. Not yet. It is the cousin of my father Ler, a man named Turi—you saw him once in my father's house—who has been helping them. But he reports everything that he does and I learn about it. The man Themis has been asking him to guide a force of men against you, but Turi has been afraid of being killed. But they have given him many gifts

190

and he has agreed. He will bring them out—but his family will go north as soon as they leave, and other Albi as well, because he will take them through the forest to a spot where you and your men will be in hiding. He will be going ahead of the others and you must let him escape. Then everyone else can be killed.'

'When will this be?' Ason asked, speaking quietly despite the excitement he suddenly felt.

'In three days' time, in the valley you know, before the hills, beyond the meadows of Dun Ar Apa where we rested once. A kinsman of mine will meet you there and show you the path that the others will take, and will point out the cousin of my father so he will not be harmed.'

'No harm shall come to him—but I will not say the same for the Atlanteans. If we can surprise them we can take them one by one and wipe them out. We must leave tonight if we are to reach the spot in time.'

Ason returned to the banquet place and stood once more with his back against his stone, his mind working steadily as he thought about what must be done. The men of his own teuta were here, but there were many other Yerni as well. Maklorbi himself, thick-armed and gnarled, had come down from the north with eleven of his warriors and all had helped in the labour of the stone. There were warriors from Dun Finmog and Ar Apa was here with many of his men. If all these warriors would fight together it would be the largest striking-force he had ever had. They would accompany him, he was sure of that. He would give the bull-chiefs rich presents now and they would want to come. He would tell them all about the long column of soldiers going through the forest and how they could be attacked and killed, how their bronze armour and bronze weapons would be shared out afterwards. Not one warrior in ten now owned a bronze dagger for the taking of heads—how they would value a sword! He knew that this could be done and he would tell them how they would fight and win and they would follow him.

'Listen to me,' Ason called out, stepping forward. 'Listen

to what I have to say.' He waited until they were quieter then told them what could be done.

They reached Dun Moweg just after dawn and here they drank and rested. When Moweg saw all the men and heard what was planned he put on his axe and hair-belt and took up his shield, and all of his warriors there did the same. They were hunters, and could appreciate the difference between attacking a heavily armed enemy on his own ground or surprising a column of men strung out through heavy forest. When the attacking force marched out of the dun soon afterwards they were much larger. They straggled out across the plain, the armoured Mycenaeans first and the men of Dun Ason just behind them. All the others marched as they wished, singly or in groups, some taking parallel tracks while others lagged behind, then ran to catch up. A great sprawling, disorganized mob of men, joined together only by greed and a pleasure in battle and killing.

They came to the edge of the open down the following day and there, at the forest's edge, a small dark man was waiting for them. He came forward reluctantly to meet Ason, tremblingly aware of all the axes and swords.

'I am Gwyn, son of the aunt of Naikeri,' he said quickly. 'I am the one who waits for you.'

'There is nothing to be afraid of—it is the Atlanteans who should be fearful. Are they on the march?'

'A day behind me, they do not move fast in the forest, along this same path. Turi leads them and he goes in fear that he will be killed.'

'His life is in my hands and I will hold it safe.'

As his disorganized army straggled up, Ason climbed to the top of a large boulder and they gathered around it, Aias and the Mycenaeans closest with the bull-chiefs, while the warriors pressed in on all sides.

'This is the way the Atlanteans will come,' Ason said, and the men stirred and craned their necks to look at the opening in the forest wall. 'The trees are thick here and there is a hill as well which is difficult to climb, with a stream and a

192

swampy area below. When they arrive the Atlanteans will be strung out along the trail and we will be in the forest on each side. They will march by us and will not see us. You can do that because you are hunters and invisible if you wish to be. You will lie there and will not attack until the signal is given, not because I will kill any man who is greedy and attacks too early—though I will—but because it is the best way to surprise the Atlanteans and to destroy them all. They will pass between us, and when the leaders reach this spot I will give my war-cry and we will attack, and every man hearing the cry will shout it himself and attack as well.'

There were cries of agreement and axes were waved in the air. Ason led the way into the forest, posting the men himself as he went along. The Yerni warriors moved carefully off the path through the dry crackling leaves and called enthusiastically to each other. Down the hillside Ason went, with the men vanishing into the shade of the great trees behind him, to the swamp at the bottom. There was even more cover here among the reeds, and the warriors bent them carefully aside instead of breaking them and moved off into the muddy water. Ason watched while the last of them vanished from sight, then started back up the trail to the far end. His Mycenaeans were in the forest too, spaced out one by one where they could do the most good by attacking the Atlanteans singly, drawing their attention so that the unarmoured Yerni could cut them down.

In the forest there was only silence. The wind moved the branches in the treetops high above, but nothing else stirred. An army was hidden close by, yet there was no sign of it at all. The Yerni lay silent as the trees themselves. Aias and Gwyn, waiting for Ason where the trail reached the open down, were the only ones to be seen. They moved off between the trees and settled down on the cool moss behind the trunk of a giant oak. Gwyn crouched down and Aias dozed, muttering in his sleep, then jerking awake to look around, while Ason sat with his sword in his hands and listened to the small sounds of the forest. The day slowly passed.

A distant shout.

Ason sat up silently, cocking his head to listen better, wondered if he had heard it. But the others were awake as well, listening just as intently. Then it came again, a man calling out something and someone else answering, far back down the trail.

'They are coming,' Aias whispered, fingering his stone-headed sledge. He had seen the cattle butcher using it and had admired it, a short-handled heavy hammer of death, and had given a good copper pin for it. It was better than a sword, more like a fist, and more to his liking.

They silently moved closer to the trail and slid behind a thick tangle of hawthorn, looking out through the heavy branches close to the ground. Another voice could be heard, and a moment later the shuffle of feet. There was the first flicker of motion down the trail. An armoured Atlantean came into view, walking just behind the brown-clad form of an Albi.

'The first one is Turi,' Gwyn whispered.

They were here—and unalarmed. Which meant that the entire Atlantean column was strung out through the forest in the midst of the hidden warriors. The trap was ready to be sprung. As the first Atlantean passed, Ason rose and stepped from behind the bush, then ran forward.

He was halfway to the trail, with Aias right behind him, before one of the Atlanteans saw him and called a loud warning—drawing his sword from its slings as he did. As soon as he spoke, so did Ason:

'Run, you fool, run!'

The Albi ran even before the words were out of Ason's mouth; he had been expecting the ambush. The Atlantean who was guarding him was an instant slower and his sword cut only air. He started to chase the guide, then realized that Ason was almost upon him and turned to defend himself. Ason swung his sword down and shouted as loudly as he could:

'Ason abu!'

Then his sword struck the Atlantean's shield, and he pushed the other's sword aside with his own shield and twisted his sword up into a belly jab, hearing the echo of his words that sounded down through the forest. *Ason abu*. As the words started from one man's mouth another picked it up, and another, from both sides of the trail, and the attack was launched.

'Ason is here!' the Atlantean shouted, and choked as the sword caught him in the stomach, up, under his breastplate, and tore out his life.

Screams and the crash of metal sounded from the forest. Ason withdrew his sword and turned about to fight for his life. All the nearest Atlanteans were ignoring the Yerni rushing towards them from the forest and were attacking him. Five, six of them at once. Swords and spears and a barrier of shields. He drew away, slashing at them, until his back was against a tree.

'To me, to me!' he shouted and his call was answered. Aias was there, his great hammer swinging, and the warriors of Dun Ason behind him. All Ason had to do was to hold.

He was the man the Atlanteans wanted, the man Themis hated, the one they had come so far to find. They attacked him in overwhelming force, battering at him. One went down, then two, they were being attacked from behind, they could not hold out. A few instants more.

A few instants too many. A sword crashed against Ason's sword with all the weight of the man's body behind it, pressing him. Ason's shield was up to block another sword.

The spear thrust in over the shoulders of the nearest man, jabbing like a deadly fang.

Ason pulled his head aside, but not fast enough.

The bronze speartip, honed and sharp, caught him full in the throat and pressed home, through his neck, pinning him to the tree.

Blood filled his throat, he could not shout.

Everything ended.

25

Against the white-banked clouds in the pale sky the pair of hawks moved, soaring in lazy circles, each separate, yet each always close to the other. The male saw a movement in the grass below and halted in mid-air, hanging stationary under rapid-beating wings while he turned his head from side to side until he saw the motion again. There was something there and he closed his wings and fell downward like a stone, spreading his wings wide only at the last moment, with his great clawed toes out before him. Never touching the ground, he beat his wings and was up with something wriggling in his talons, his mate soaring close to see the captive mouse. They swirled away into the distance over the grey down like leaves before the wind.

There were leaves as well, turned red and yellowed-brown, pulled from the branches by the cooler winds of autumn. They banked in the hollows, and some even blew far out across the plain to fall among the cattle cropping the sere remains of the summer's grass, to blow on again until they lodged against the woven lattice wall of the dun that rose solitary from the plain. The wind was not cold, not yet, but there was a crispness and a bite to it that presaged the winter soon to come.

Even the light touch of that moving air and the pale brightness of the sky made Ason's red-rimmed eyes water and he blinked away the obscuring tears. The furs on the low couch on which he lay were soft and warm; softer furs lay across him. Memories of days and nights and unending pain came to him and he remembered waking like this and sleeping again even before he knew he was awake. It had been a long illness. There was a low crooning and he turned his head with caution to look at Naikeri who sat, cross-legged, nearby. She had the front of her garments undone and with her hand guided the fullness of her breast to the baby's mouth. It smacked its mouth industriously and made little kneading motions with its tiny hands. She rocked slowly back and forth while it fed, humming the wordless song. There was a sudden shadow in the doorway and Inteb bent to enter.

'Awake, Ason?' he said, seeing that the other man's eyes were open. Ason nodded—he talked as little as possible—and pointed to the cup of mead nearby on a wooden chest. Inteb handed it to him and he sat up on his elbows to drink it.

'You progressed as far as the door yesterday,' Inteb said, taking back the drained cup. 'Shall it be outside on the balcony today?'

'He should not move yet,' Naikeri said, shaking her shoulders angrily at the thought. Her breast fell from the baby's mouth and he gurgled and sucked air, then began to howl with hungry anger.

'He has the voice of a lion,' Inteb said. The wailing cut off sharply as the baby began to feed again.

With Inteb's arm about him, Ason managed to climb to his feet. Everything swam in circles when he did this and he had to stand, leaning on the Egyptian's shoulder, until the motion stopped. Only then did he take a first shuffling footstep, then another. His legs felt strange under him, and he knew that the flesh had fallen away from his body. It would be rebuilt; it must begin now. Sweat broke from his skin with the effort but he kept going, one sliding step after another, through the connecting apartment to the inner door. Inteb kicked this open and they went out into the clear air, looking down at the centre of the dun, at the hubbub of daily activity. There were the animals and the playing children, the craftsmen labouring outside the door of their workshop to catch the light, the hundred and one activities that were the life of the dun.

And something else, something new that Ason had heard about but had not seen until this moment. His fingers dug into Inteb's flesh and he pulled himself up straight, smiling with pleasure at the incredible sight.

Where one great stone had risen from the ground the past summer, there now stood two. Matched and beautiful they rose, white and glistening. Two immense columns planted in the earth and stretching up towards the sky. At their bases they were close together, almost touching, but their sides were angled so they grew narrower towards the top and the space was larger there. They were solid, strong, powerful; their presence spoke this message with firm majesty.

'Yes—' Ason said in a rough hoarse voice, his fingers going up to his throat at the same time, touching the edges of the great red puckered scar.

There was more he wanted to say, much more, but the pain was still in his throat when he talked, only a tiny memory of the immense pain that had bathed him for so long, but it was still there. And he was tired. Inteb helped him as he slid down slowly on to a wooden chest and sat with his back to the wall, taking pleasure in the light warm touch of the sunlight.

'There is more done than you realize,' Inteb said, pointing to the summits of the stones. 'If you look at the tops of the columns you will see that they have been worked. I had old Dursan up there on a scaffolding for so long that he said he felt like a bird in a tree. But he is the only one who can do the fine finishing work. He took down the tops of both stones so that a raised tenon remains on each. This will be built just like the wood henges; they would do it no other way.'

Ason blinked in the strong light and looked again. Yes, there on the top, in the middle of each upright, was the solid projecting bulge of the tenons, carved from the stone just as they were carved from wood.

198

'The lintel is almost ready to be raised, you can see them working on it over there by the wall. It was squared before we brought it in and now they are hollowing out the sockets for the tenons. I had a wicker form made—you should have heard the women scream when we made them climb the scaffolding to the top—an exact duplicate of the tenons on top and the distance between them. Dursan's men are using the mauls to hollow out the sockets so that the form fits into them. This is almost done.'

'And by what magic ... will you raise that great stone into the air?'

'An important question.' Inteb paced the length of the balcony and back, his fingertips together before him. 'In Egypt there would be no problem. One thing my dear country has more than enough of is sand. This can be shovelled, carried, heaped into a mound, made into a ramp or a road-way up which the stone can be dragged. That is not possible here. This white chalk is almost as hard as rock to break and we would labour for a year getting enough for a ramp. There is another way but it would require wood, immense amounts of wood, almost a forest.'

'Or a dun?'

Inteb turned slowly, squinting in thought, to survey the apartments and walls of the dun. 'Yes, the wood is here. But I might need all of it. And your people live here—what about them?'

'They can build houses nearby, just as the retired warriors do when they marry. There will be no hardship. But before you tear down my dun, tell me what is the need?'

'It is a technique we call raising. It is used inside tombs and buildings to lift large stones or statues into place. I will raise the stone with levers, just as we do when we lift a stone to put rollers beneath it. But instead of rollers we put a solid platform of logs under it—like this.' He held his hand out, flat, before him. 'Now the stone rests on the platform and it is levered up again. When this is done a second log platform is placed across the first, going crossways—like this.' He put his other hand flat on the first, fingers going at right angles. This makes a sturdy support to work on, and the levering-up continues, with more and more platforms being built beneath the stone until it has reached the top of the columns. It is then pushed over and dropped into place. But, as you see, a great amount of wood is needed.'

'You shall have it. My entire dun if needs be. Then I will have my stone-henge and I will call a meeting of the five teutas here. I will have my strength back, enough to talk to them about what will be done, and behind me will be the strength of the stone. That will speak louder than I can.' His face set suddenly into harder lines. 'What about the Atlanteans? Any reports?'

'From the Albi, nothing. They stay away from them since the murders of many of them. Some even blame you.'

'Naikeri told me this. She also said that it is not important.'

'Probably so, but it does shut off that source of information. But the warriors who go to the mine to throw stones at them and shout insults report that the outer wall is even higher and that a wooden palisade is being built across it.'

'Defence works. They know Yerni can't get past something like that.' He hit his fist against the wall in sudden anger. 'This wound—if I had not fallen we would have gone on and surprised them at the mine, finished them all at once.'

'None would march without your leadership. But the Atlanteans we trapped were killed to the last man, chased through the woods and pulled down like stags. There were heads for every warrior, armour and swords. It was your victory, Ason, and they know it. They will follow wherever you lead now.'

'I will lead them. This quaking body will be strong again, and when I am strong there will be one people here and they will be stronger. Will this henge of stone and wonder be finished by samain, when the cattle are brought in and the traders arrive?'

'It will be, even if we have to work as I have done before, in shifts. By moonlight, someone always working. It will be done.'

'Then the word will go out now. The assembly of all the

teutas of the Yerni will be held here. Here before the stones. It will be the beginning. Will they come?'

'They await only your word.'

'Then give it to them.'

26

There was a loud chuffing in the undergrowth and the sharp snap of twigs. The circle of men crouched low, spears pointed and waiting, muscles taut and ready to jump instantly. When the boar came out it could emerge in any direction, fast, low and dark. And deadly. Its white tusks could rip a man open with a twist of the massive head, disembowel him or strip the flesh from his legs. This was the deadliest creature in the forest. And now they had driven it from its forest refuge into the open down, to temporary safety in the large clump of bushes.

'He's wounded,' Aias said, crouching and alert like the others, but carrying his hammer instead of a spear.

'A scratch,' Ason said, panting heavily. The hunt had been a brief one but his first since he was wounded, and he was barely able to keep up with the others. His throat hurt as he gasped the air into his chest but he ignored it. He was getting stronger, that was the only thing that counted.

'Boar, boar!' someone shouted from the far side of the bushes and there were excited cries and an angry squealing. More crackling in the brush and then, like a dark thunderbolt, the boar hurtled from under the bushes at the waiting men, twisting and dodging towards the spears, its hooves throwing up clods of dirt as it spun. With an angry squeal it twisted about and raced towards Ason, hooking its tusks at his legs.

There was not time to spear it, just to leap aside. Ason did this, felt the rough hairy flank brush against him and heard the sharp cry from Aias who leapt to meet the beast.

Fast as the boar was, the boxer was faster. The hammer chopped in a short arc and caught the beast in its shoulder with a loud crack, bowling it over. For one instant it was on its back, black hooves waving, and Ason lunged. As it rolled back the spear point caught it in the side and plunged deep, almost pinning it to the ground.

It screamed in agony and fear, writhing and trying to snap at the spear, its red angry eye glaring at Ason. Then another spear plunged home and another and it kicked spasmodically and died.

'Your tusks,' Aias said, as Ason dropped to the ground next to the beast, breathing as loudly as it had done.

'The first blow ... was yours,' he said between gasps.

'The kill was yours, oh king. What does a slave need with tusks? I'll have the tail, a more fitting part.'

Aias took his dagger and sawed the twisted length of tail off at the root; then he brushed smooth the tuft of hairs on the end. He stuck it in the back of his belt so it hung down behind. 'Now I'll be safe in the forest,' he said. 'They'll take me for one of them.'

The Yerni howled with laughter and slapped their legs and hit one another on the back. Even Ason smiled slightly, breathing slower at last. There was the sharp crack of stone on wood as one of the men chopped a sapling from a nearby grove. Another was lashing the dead beast's feet together with strips of leather. Aias prodded the boar's flank with a thick knobbed finger.

'Filled with acorns and rich with white fat. I can taste it already. Mead, ale, boar-meat. This is a good land you rule, great Ason.'

Leaning on his spear-butt, Ason climbed to his feet and they started back to the dun. The others slung the boar from the pole and followed behind, laughing and bragging to each other, comparing the fine white curve of their moustaches to the sharp thrusts of the dead beast's tusks. And as they always did now when they came in sight of the dun, they marvelled aloud at the changes. Any physical change was so rare in their lives that something as major as this had to be talked about over and over to fix it into reality.

It was a change. The palisade of tall logs had been taken down completely as well as the rooms and apartments that were fixed to it. Now the dun was just a circular bank, cut by the entrance and the building of the workshop which had not been touched. All about the embankment now, some pushed up against it, stood the buildings and shelters where the warriors and their families and the many workers stayed. There was some crowding, and occasional fights, but no real complaints from the Yerni warriors about this. A new dun would be built, Ason promised that, and they were comfortable enough. And none of this really counted. What was important, the thing that made Ason different from any other bull-chief and made them better than any other teuta, was the great structure in the centre of the dun. The two stones that reached the sky and the third smaller stone now rising into the air, lifted by the Egyptian's magic. Once again there were shouts of amazement when they saw the great creation, even though the rising balks of wood all but hid it from sight.

Inteb was waiting at the foot of the great timber construction when Ason came up.

'We are ready,' Inteb said.

Ason led the way up the tall ladder to the top, past layer after layer of logs notched and fitted together into an immovable whole. On the platform that formed the top section lay the great stone lintel, and next to it, and sitting on it, were the workers who had raised it this far. Cut into the bottom of the stone, not visible now, were the two sockets that would fit over the upright tenons that rose from the top of the two columns. Ason admired these constructions, running his hand over the smooth bulge of their surfaces, realizing how much stone had had to be pounded away to leave them here.

'Notice the tops of the columns,' Inteb said, coming up behind Ason. 'Notice how they are hollowed so the lintel stone

204

will settle firmly into place and will not be able to rock or shift in position.'

'A great work,' Ason said with conviction.

Not too much of the top of the great stone could be seen. The logs that made up the upper three layers of the platform had been extended out to rest on the tops of the columns, as well as being held up by the platforms beneath them. Using the stones as supports, the platform was now much bigger and extended out over the stones.

'We will move the lintel now,' Inteb said, and ordered up the leathern buckets of grease. Animal fat had been rendered until it was thick as mud; Inteb himself threw down the first handfuls.

'I want it here, all the way across the platform and on these logs. Not close to the edge or you fools will be sliding in it and falling off. It is for the stone, not for you.' He handed over the bucket and supervised the application.

When an even layer of grease had been applied, Ason and Inteb stood to one side while the workers grabbed up the long levers. Holes had been chopped in the top layers of logs so heavy stakes could be driven into them. A thick log was placed against the stakes, running behind the back of the stone and leaving just enough room for the levers to be inserted. They pressed against this log and levered against the stone. When they were all in place Inteb shouted the beginning of the chant that kept them working in unison.

'Seat the lever, seat it deep.'

'*Bu!*' the workers shouted in answer.

'Weight on the wood and ready to pull.'

'*Bu.*'

'Pull now, pull, pull!'

'*Bu.*'

Chanting together, they applied their strength and the wood creaked beneath them. The stone slid forward a small amount. The chant went on until they had moved it far enough to get a smoothed section of wood in between their levers and the back supporting log. As the stone moved, more and more of the greased area came under it and the going was easier. There was grease about the platform now, and Inteb halted the operation while he sent down for buckets of sand to throw on it. The men needed a firm footing—a fall from this height would surely be fatal. Then the work went on. Slower and slower as the lintel approached the correct position over the supporting columns, and Inteb ran back and forth peering under the stone and calling out instructions. It was levered from one side, and then from the end, while Inteb crawled about it and hung over empty space to check the alignment. He was finally satisfied and ordered a halt.

'One last step,' he told Ason, wiping the sweat from his forehead with his arm, his hands black with grease and bark. 'A supporting timber is removed from under each end of the stone, and in their place a stack of these flat boards, adzed down out of split logs, is substituted. When the stone is resting on the stacked boards we lower it just as we raised it to this height—only in reverse. One end is raised, a board is removed, it is lowered on to the remainder. Then the same process is repeated at the other end. Light as a thistle, the great stone will sink to its resting-place.' He muttered a prayer to some animal-headed Egyptian deity as he turned to direct the final stage. It was the most delicate of all.

Once the weight was on the stacked boards the supporting logs were slid out from under it and dropped to the ground. Then, with careful efforts, the stone was levered up again just enough to pull out a board before being dropped back on to their support.

Whatever went wrong happened very quickly. The lintel had been lowered so that the tips of the tenons were just entering the sockets in the stone. Ten men hung from the lever that held the stone while two others steadied the planks and a third man withdrew the top plank.

There was the sudden crack of breaking wood and someone screamed.

The men on the lever fell in a tangle, the length of wood no longer supporting the stone. It dropped on to the pile of boards, and the one board half removed, and shuddered there

206

for an interminable instant on the uneven support.

Splintering and crashing, the supporting pile bent and broke, and the massive weight of the stone dropped, angled down, fell heavily on one end, on to the supporting column.

When it struck, the crushing impact was felt and heard; bits of stone flew. The supporting bulk of timber swayed and a shudder went through the stone upright, Ason's stone, the first stone.

Everything moved, lurched sickeningly like the solid ground during an earthquake. Men shrieked and dropped, one falling from the timbers, sure that everything was collapsing, crashing down to destruction.

Time flowed steadily where it had rushed a moment earlier, instants passing with the slow precision of drops of water falling from melting ice. The world trembled and moved.

Then everything was still. The horrified men stared into each other's faces, seeing their own terror mirrored there. But the movement stopped and they looked around them, numbed.

The boards at one end were gone. The lintel angled down from the precarious balance of the boards at the other end to the solid stone of the column on which it rested. The tenon was out of sight and fitted neatly into its socket. The stones still stood.

Screaming, pained screaming, drew them back and Inteb jumped forward.

'Supports!' he shouted. 'Get them under here. Now. Before this other end goes. Jump, jump!'

The screaming went on and Ason saw that one of the workers had been under the stone when it dropped, his body and head smashed between the stone and the wood. He was silent. Forever.

But another man was still alive, shrieking in agony, over and over again as fast as he could fill his lungs. He had been pushing the board out of the way and his arm had been under the stone when it dropped. It was still there, crushed, flattened, and trapped.

After the accident the men were unnerved enough; the screaming did not help them to do the precise work needed if a greater tragedy were to be averted. Ason understood this as he stepped forward and drew his sword from the slings. He reversed it and struck the man in the temple with the solid pommel.

It was a flybite, perhaps unfelt in the greater agony, but the man did recoil and try to pull away, still screaming. Ason was not as gentle the second time and the bronze knob struck with a heavy thud and the man was instantly still.

A little blood dribbled over the lip of the stone, but very little, so tightly sealed was the arm between the column and lintel. Most of the man's lower arm was trapped and crushed there, to within a handspan of the elbow. Ason tore one of the leather slings from his back and wrapped it tightly around the arm just above the elbow.

'Hold his body so he doesn't fall,' he ordered the nearest man. He tested his footing, making sure there was no grease on the platform, and raised his sword above his head.

With a long downward chop, hitting true in the joint of the elbow, he severed the trapped arm from the body. Unconscious as he was, the man's body contracted when the sword struck.

'Pull him away and lower him to the ground,' Ason ordered.

'Secure now, I think,' Inteb said, trembling, his face pale. Ason put his arm about Inteb's shoulders.

'There are always losses, they should not bother you.'

'For an instant there I thought—the entire thing ...'

'But it didn't. You build well, Inteb. The stone-henge is almost finished.'

'Blood. That arm, it will be in there forever, the bones.'

'There is nothing wrong with blood to set the stones in place. There is a slave under each of the column of the gates of Mycenae, put there when they were built to hold the stones firm. This should not bother you. Will the work go on now?'

Inteb pulled away, clutching his shaking hands together.

'Yes, of course. It must be done. Now, at this time. There is very little left.'

Some of the men were reluctant to resume the work but Ason showed them his bloody sword in silence and it spoke louder than words. Carefully, slowly, stopping and starting again many times, the boards were slipped from the other end and the stone levered lower until the last was removed and stone grated on stone. Inteb rested his hand upon it.

'Here is your henge of stone, Ason, ready for samain. Something that has never been seen before. You will be king, Ason.'

The men did not understand the meaning of all of this, but they understood what they had done and they shouted and called out their cries until they were hoarse and everyone on the ground below did the same, except the man who had fallen from the top and lay crumpled and dead against the base.

27

Coming across the plain from any direction the great dark form was clearly visible against the sky, rising above the circular mound and the buildings outside that only served to contrast its looming size. The warriors from the other teutas saw it and shouted in amazement to one another while their bull-chiefs fingered their moustaches and chewed at their tips. This was a henge. Albi with packs on their backs admired it; they knew the handling of stone from their great tombs, so appreciated it all the more. Donbaksho trudged many days, with trade goods or without, just to look upon it, and even wary Hunters wriggled across the down in the dark to seek a hiding-place where they could watch it for all of a day before returning to their swamps and forests.

In single file, the women as tall as the men and carrying packs as large or larger, the Geramani came west for their landing-places on the coast and knew that there was something new in the land.

Samain. With the year drawing to a close and winter on the way the teutas gathered. This was a time for cattle slaughter and feasting, trade and drink, time for the making of bull-chiefs and the burning of captives in the best manner. Time for everything.

Time for an assembly of all the teutas of the Yerni of the high downs. This had never been done before and it had been thought about over and over. But the bull-chiefs had warm gold and soft amber discs to wear to show that Ason wanted them, and each had been told that all of the others had agreed to come. This was a political suggestion of Inteb's, who had much experience in this sort of thing, and decided any of the bull-chiefs who might have been wavering. How could one stand against the united power of all the others? They polished their ornaments and their bronze and they came. They brought with them all that they had to trade, and others, who would have traded at different duns, now came to Dun Ason. They came and they kept coming and never in the memory of living man had there ever been a samain like this.

Four henges had been built for the bull-chiefs of the four visiting teutas. Two on one side and two on the other, facing across the fire, with Ason's henge at the head between them. Ason had been generous and had taken eight of the largest logs that had formed the circle of logs supporting the dun. These had been planed and painted and sunk deep into the ground with four large crossbars above, so that each bull-chief could now sit before a truly majestic henge of his own, a henge twice as big as any he had ever had before.

While above them loomed that which was of white stone like a new mountain, white-daubed with chalk and red-painted with designs, hung with gold and weapons and heads. Stone, not wood. Stone, hard as any axe-head. Stone. The bull-chiefs drank in silence for the most part and wherever they looked, sooner or later their eyes would return to those massive stones and gaze up, up at them.

In the round wicker-work building just outside the embankment, Ason was putting on his armour, newly polished and gleaming. As he tied the leather thongs, the baby, lying on furs on the floor, caught sight of the shining shield and crowed with excitement. Ason pushed it over with his foot so the tiny hands could touch the gleaming bosses.

'The bull-chief Maklorbi has been talking to the druid Nemed,' Naikeri said. 'I have not seen it but some of the women told me.'

'I have no care for women's talk.'

'You should care, because Nemed still talks to people in

211

Uala's family and reads signs for them.'

'The bull-chief is dead and can no longer hurt me.'

'The living can when they consult with the dead.'

'I do not fear the living or the dead, bull-chiefs or druids. I have a tooth that bites them all equally deep.' He slapped the sharp blade of his sword as he said this, then slipped it into the slings.

'It does not hurt to notice these things. You have become bull-chief here instead of someone from Uala's family. They don't forget this, that they were once the highest and now they are nothing.'

Ason settled his helmet on his head and did not bother to answer as he left. The baby began to cry when the bright shield was taken away and Naikeri snatched him up and held him to her.

The other bull-chiefs were there before their henges and the meat was brought from the cooking-fire when Ason appeared. He would make the first cut and take the hero's portion and the feasting would begin. An appetizing smell of crackling flesh greeted him, as the immense sow, smoking and rich with fat, was placed on the hurdles. She had been captured that summer and penned and fed heavily until she was round as a tree-trunk. Her litter had long since been eaten, and now it was their dam's turn. Ason drew his dagger and tested the edge with his thumb.

'I am Maklorbi,' the bull-chief from the northern teuta said, climbing to his feet. 'I have marched a hundred and a hundred miles to be here for this banquet and have brought a hundred men. I have more heads over my door than a hundred men can count. I have killed a hundred warriors in battle. I will make the first cut of the meat.'

There was sudden silence after he spoke. He brushed at his moustache and slapped his chest, a short but solid man, with muscles that stood out gnarled as weathered bark. His arms were as thick as most men's legs and he was known as a formidable warrior in battle. He was challenging Ason at his own fire. Naikeri had been right; here was trouble. Ason looked around at the silent faces and staring eyes and knew that he could not refuse the challenge. He did not want bloodshed but it could not be avoided. Maklorbi would have to die.

'I cut the meat,' Ason said, holding up the dagger. Maklorbi swung about to look at him directly for the first time.

'I am Maklorbi and men fear my name. I sleep at night with the head of a bull-chief beneath my knee. I will cut the meat and I will sleep tonight with the head of Ason beneath my knee.'

The challenge was there. Ason put away the dagger and slowly drew his sword from the slings. Maklorbi, still looking at Ason, pointed back over his own shoulder at the henge behind him.

'I have my gold and it is here on my henge for everyone to see. I have captured armour and helmets in battle and they are here for everyone to see. I fought the men from the sea and captured these things. I fought as a Yerni fights with my kirtle around my waist, my hair-rope and my dagger, my axe in my hand and my shield on my arm, my arms bare, my chest bare, my legs bare, my hair and my moustache white as a Yerni warrior. That is the way we fight. That is the way a bull-chief of the Yerni fights. We are Yerni.'

There were shouts of agreement from the warriors of Maklorbi's teuta who slapped their hands against their legs with approval. Some of the other warriors in the circle did the same but others murmured and looked about.

Ason stood silent as a sudden chill touched his skin. Now that it was too late to do anything about it he knew what had happened. He had enemies and they had planned well. He still did not have his full strength after his sickness and Maklorbi was the strongest of all the Yerni. In armour, with his sword, Ason could defeat any man. But now he had defeated himself. He had become a bull-chief of the Yerni and if challenged to battle he must fight as a Yerni; there was no other way. All these thoughts went quickly through his head and he knew what had to be done. There could be no excuses that he was weak; a bull-chief could never be weak. There were neither excuses nor a way out.

'Maklorbi comes to my fire with a mouth that gapes open like that of a dog in heat,' Ason said. 'Maklorbi wants to sit at my fire and cut my meat first and eat the hero's portion. I will tell you what Maklorbi will get. He will not eat, ever again, he will not drink, ever again, for I will kill him and with my knife take his head and tonight his head will be beneath my knee.'

As he said this Ason dropped his sword and his shield to the ground and tore the laces from his armour and his greaves. He threw these aside, and his helmet as well, and stood unarmed except for the dagger on the cord about his neck. Then he picked up the shield and slipped his hand through the loops on its back.

'I am Ason of Mycenae,' he called out. 'I am Ason of the Yerni of Dun Ason and this is my henge. I am a killer of men. I will kill Maklorbi with an axe. I call to my friend Ar Apa of Dun Ar Apa and tell him I will do honour to his axe and will battle Maklorbi with it.'

Ar Apa jumped to his feet and swung his arm in a slow circle so his axe flew across the fire and Ason grabbed it from the air.

'Maklorbi abu!' Maklorbi shouted, clashing his axe against his shield and running forward.

'Ason abu!' Ason called out and stepped forward to meet him.

Axe struck shield and the battle began.

After the first blows it was clear who would win. Maklorbi was the stronger, and with axe against axe little else counts. The stone head of his axe thudded against Ason's raised shield and Ason felt the shock of it in his arm. His own blow was caught and brushed aside, and even while his shield-arm was aching from the first blow a second and a third rained down. Ason backed away and, relentless as death, Maklorbi followed him, his axe-blows as continual and strong as though he were chopping down a tree. He was chopping down a man and with each blow Ason felt the strength going from him; he panted with the effort to stay alive. His reactions were slowed and his shield tilted so that with the next blow the axe glanced off it and cut into his shoulder drawing first blood.

At the sight of this all the watchers roared aloud and Maklorbi stopped and stepped back, shaking his axe and shield over his head and shouting his war-cry.

Ason felt the wound. It was not deep but it bled and more of his failing strength seeped away with every drop. He would die—and he did not want to. Maklorbi spun about to shout his war-cry again and, as he did so, Ason slipped his arm from the loops inside the shield and grasped it instead with his hand.

'Ason abu!' he shouted in his hoarse voice and leaped to attack.

Maklorbi braced his legs and stood waiting, smiling broadly so his yellow teeth could be seen. Ason swung a wide, full-armed blow that whistled about in a great wide arc aimed at Maklorbi's side. The bull-chief moved his shield out to catch it and at that moment Ason threw his own shield full into the man's face.

The edge of the shield caught Maklorbi square in the mouth and he fell back bellowing in pain. Ason's axe bounced from the other's shield and he swung it over in a quick blow that struck Maklorbi's right arm. But the edge of the axe did not strike, though the weight of the stone was enough to jar the axe from Maklorbi's fingers.

Before Ason could recover and strike again, Maklorbi had hurled his own shield aside and dived forward, his fingers locking into Ason's throat.

The pain was overwhelming and almost drove awareness from Ason's brain. Through a haze he saw Maklorbi's face, mouth gaping, spitting blood and teeth. A roaring was in Ason's head and he tried to swing the axe, but the other was too close for him to do anything. He let the axe drop and struck with his fists but it did little good. He was aware of shouts and loud voices and one familiar voice shouting louder than all the others, Aias bellowing something, something about fighting, something he could barely understand. Then the meaning of the words penetrated the sickness and pain

215

and Ason reached out his hands in obedience. Not to Maklorbi's throat, because in an even contest of strength Ason would die, but to his head, to his face, his fingers crawling up to seize the sides of his skull. His thumbs to dig into Maklorbi's eyes.

Something that slaves did when they fought without weapons, something a warrior would never think of. Thumbs digging deep into eye sockets, gouging, blinding.

Maklorbi's battle cry turned into a cry of wavering pain, and his hands dropped from Ason's throat as he clutched his ruined eyes.

Ason drew his dagger and in the same motion plunged it up under the other man's ribs and into his heart.

Gasping for breath, his head swimming with pain so great that his vision was fogged and he had to blink to clear his eyes, Ason bent over the corpse and, while all the watchers shouted *Ason abu* over and over, he sawed through the neck until the head was separated from the body. He was red to his elbows with gore before he was finished and the dagger slipped from his fingers. Seizing the decapitated head by one long moustache, he straightened up and walked, step by slow step, to the great stone henge. He reached up and wedged the head between the uprights where they narrowed so it stared sightlessly out at the council fire.

'I am Ason, bull-chief of the Yerni,' he said hoarsely, leaning back against the cool stone so that he would not fall.

28

Ason drank thirstily of the ale, then of mead rich with honey that brought some relief to his throat. Little by little the pain ebbed away, and he saw the three remaining bull-chiefs drinking in silence while the great roast-pig cooled on the hurdles. When warriors of Maklorbi's teuta came to take the body, he stopped them and ordered them back to their places. Then Ason rose and went to cut the first portion of the meat, and the headless corpse remained there for the rest of the banquet as a silent reminder.

Despite the presence of the body, humour improved under the onslaught of food and drink and in a little while there was much shouting and bragging across the fire. When it grew dark this fire was fuelled with pine-logs dripping resin, until it sparked and crackled and flames rose high into the air. By their light the stone henge loomed even larger and more impressive, and when the bull-chiefs and the warriors walked close to it none could resist the impulse to reach out and feel its grainy-smooth surface. Ason was not unaware of this and when the proper time came he stood and touched the henge himself and everyone was silent.

'I am Ason. I have killed a hundred times a hundred men. I have killed bull-chiefs. I have killed Atlanteans. I have killed every animal that roves the land and caught every fish that leaps in the sea. I am bull-chief of this dun. I have built this henge.'

The truth had more effect than any number of boasting

217

lies. He had done these things. The great stones were here to prove it. Not a voice was raised in dissent.

'Today the five teutas of the Yerni meet together for the first time at samain. You are all here because you are bull-chiefs in your own duns and that is the way it will always be. But we are something more. We are the Yerni and together there are none who dare stand against us. I ask you to join me here in a union of the five teutas. I ask you to do this here in a dun of all the Yerni, a dun of a kind never seen before. Made of stone. If you join me here your wooden henges will be taken down and in their place you will erect a stone henge just as I have done. This will be done.'

They looked, all of them, at the wooden henges and at Ason's of stone, and in their minds they could see great stones rising in their places. This was something! Seated before his henge, Ar Apa saw the stones and shouted with happiness at the thought.

'Ar Apa abu! Ason abu!'

'Ason abu.' More than one voice shouted it, and, when they quieted, Ar Apa called out again:

'Ason—will you be bull-chief of all the Yerni?'

Ason put his hands flat against the stone and said, 'I will.'

There were more loud cries at this and all of them seemed in favour of the plan. The bull-chiefs and their teutas would lose nothing by it—and would gain a lot. There were other tribes to the far north, beyond the forests, who raided for cattle here in the south. Now they could be attacked in force; there would be rich booty. And the henge, there would always be that. When they were most enthusiastic Ason called for quiet again and pointed to Inteb.

'This is Inteb the Egyptian, the builder. It was he who shaped and lifted these stones for me. He will tell you of something else that will be done here.'

Ason had been doubtful of Inteb's plan at first, but the more he thought about it the more appealing it became. He needed more than just the bull-chiefs' allegiance; he must have the warriors' as well. Inteb knew how to accomplish this.

218

'The five henges for the five bull-chiefs will be here.' Inteb pointed and their eyes followed his hand. 'Around them shall be a stone dun for the warriors. A ring of stones joined together at the top by other stones, with doors for the warriors to enter.'

There were gasps, then cries of approval for this, and Inteb waited until they had quieted. 'As the warriors of Dun Ason each now has his stone, so shall the most valiant warriors of all the duns have doorways in this stone dun. They will put the heads they have taken on the lintel above, and during feasts will hang it with their prizes and arms. This will be the dun of all the Yerni. In stone.'

After this no one held back. There was shouting, war-cries; axes were brandished and boasts drowned out boasts. In the excitement and noise Ar Apa came over and sat by Ason and they drank together. Ason returned the stone axe.

'You were there when I needed you,' Ason said.

'You did good service with this axe and it will be remembered. But there is something I must ask you. Your Egyptian did not say how many doors there would be in the stone dun.'

'No one asked him.'

'That is true. But I have been thinking of my dun and the doors for the warriors and thinking of all the warriors here. This stone ring will be a very large one?'

'It will be, though not that big. The bluestones will be moved back and the ring will be built here. There will be thirty doors in it, or so Inteb says. It will be a great labour.'

'Is thirty a big number?'

Ason held up the fingers of his right hand. 'This is the number five. There are five teutas.' He added the thumb of his left hand to the others. 'This is six. There will be six doorways for each teuta and six doorways five times is the number thirty.'

Ar Apa frowned and scratched at the dirt with his finger. 'There are more than six warriors in my teuta.'

'There are. But only six will be honoured. They will be from among your kinsmen, they will be the strongest warriors. To have a doorway will be a very good thing and warriors will work very hard to be one of those six. They will work hard to help you and you will always know you can count upon their aid.'

Thinking about this, Ar Apa nodded and almost smiled. It is sometimes harder to remain a bull-chief than it is to become one. There were rivalries and feuds within the teuta that never stopped. The six stone doors would help, they would help him very much. He went back before his henge and drank some more, glad he had come, thinking that a teuta for all the Yerni was a very good thing.

Ason was happy to lean against his stones and drink quietly. He was tired and his throat still ached. Yet Inteb had been right. They were all with him. The henges would be built.

The warriors grew very drunk as the night wore on and Ason almost wished he could lie down and sleep, but he could not leave while the others were still here. Much later Inteb came and sat beside him and had some ale from his cup.

'There has been an accident,' Inteb said. 'The druid Nemed is dead.'

'That is pleasant news.' Ason touched his throat. 'How did he die?'

'He was found on the ground with his head on a rock. He must have fallen and struck his head on the rock and died.'

'What a thin skull the man had. I wonder if he could have had any help in embarking on this voyage?'

'Such things are always possible, I suppose. But no one will speak the thought aloud. He and Maklorbi plotted your death, and both of them are dead instead on the same night. I think the plotting will stop for a while.'

'I think so too. The druid must have a very large funeral with many funeral games.'

Ason looked across the fire to the place where Aias sat. Had he been there the entire evening? He could not remember. The boxer was drinking from a cup that looked small in that great fist. A fist that could break a jaw and kill. Or a head? Perhaps it would be better not to know. The druid would no longer plot against him and that was all that really mattered.

'I have amber from the north here, great Ason. Brought by trails through the dark forest and down the river Rhine and across the sea to you.'

Ason looked up to see that one of the Geramani was bending over before him and opening a roll of leather on the ground. He sat on his heels behind it and arranged the display of lumps and plates of amber of all shades. 'I am Gestum and I lead my clan.'

Ason picked over the pieces, holding up the finest ones and looking through them at the fire.

'They are good. My workmen must see them.'

'I know that. I only show them to you so that we can talk. There are many eyes on us. Do not reach for your red-stained dagger to have it drink at my heart when I tell you I have dealt with the Atlanteans.'

Ason held up a piece of amber but looked beyond it at the other man for the first time. He was tall, well dressed in a long cloak sealed by a curving gold bar, rich and heavy, that held it away from his body, the bell-shaped ends of the bar peering brightly through the fabric. There were gold bracelets on his arms and gold as well on the bronze of his wide-horned helm. A short sword of bronze was in his belt and a bronze-headed axe was beside him on the ground. His cold blue eyes stared into Ason's and he was not afraid.

'You know I war with the Atlanteans?'

'That is why I am here, though others do not like it. I have said my people deal with the Atlanteans and that is because we must. They have camps and mines for tin on the lands in our valleys. They are too strong to fight and by working with them we gain many things. We work our own bronze now and our traders go along the rivers both east and west. We know of the war between Atlantis and Mycenae and that is a good thing. We know that you are a Mycenaean and have now united the tribes of the Yerni.'

'You know a good deal,' Ason said with no warmth at all

221

in his voice. 'Perhaps you learned a lot from the Trojan Sethsus and even helped him?'

'We did.'

Gestum rose when Ason did and they stood there face to face.

'I will not lie to you,' Gestum said. 'I work only for the Geramani. We sold information and did work for the Trojan and were repaid and received tin. Now he is dead. You are the power in this island now and we will work with you. We can help each other.'

At times there was little pleasure in being a king. Knowing what Gestum had done, Ason, the warrior, would have happily plunged his sword into the man's middle. Ason the ruler could not. Everything the man said was true. They could help one another and each would profit. Perhaps a way could even be arranged to get tin to Mycenae down the Danube. The gold of Dun Ason would pay for it.

'Sit and drink with me,' Ason said. 'I admire your amber.'

'I will drink. I admire your decision.'

29

It was a winter long remembered, a winter well enjoyed. The labour on the stones was interrupted only by raids on the Atlanteans and both were most satisfying. Until the Atlanteans grew wary, their hunting-parties were easier to ambush and trap than the game itself, and produced the double benefit of meat and heads. It was a fine winter. When spring and the warmer weather returned the warriors were loath to return to their own duns and their duties and stayed among the great stones as long as they could.

The construction went ahead rapidly. Once the five henges were constructed the men turned with equal enthusiasm to the erection of the outer stones, the doorways of the warriors. These doorways would eventually make a complete ring of stones, though they little resembled that now. Since each warrior chose his own place to enter and to face in some favoured direction, the twenty-four completed upright stones formed a very ragged circle. Three together, three isolated, solitary stones, and then a cluster of eighteen. Only six of the lintels that connected the upright stones above had been completed. These were harder to shape and fit—and to raise—and only five were in position, while a sixth rested on a rising mound of logs. The work progressed.

On a morning, very much like many other mornings, the work was going ahead steadily just as it had since the first stone had been raised. It was then that Ason heard the shouts in the distance, as though someone were calling his name. But the shouts were lost in the voices closer by on the top of the timber construction, as the careful operation of lowering one of the lintel stones of the circle of doors got under way. These stones had been shaped with great skill, not only hollowed underneath at each end to fit on the tenon of the upright, but a projection had been left at the end of each lintel that would fit into an opening in the next. Settling these stones into place was an exacting operation. The shouts came again and this time Ason heard his name clearly. He turned, wiping the sweat from his eyes so he could see, and looked across the plain.

Three men were running through the entrance in the embankment. Two of them were warriors of his own teuta, and they half-carried between them the brown-clad form of an Albi. They had their hands under his arms or he would have fallen; his head bobbed about and he seemed to be in the last stages of exhaustion. It was Turi, Naikeri's cousin. One of the warriors saw Ason on the timbers, cupped his hand to his mouth, and called out loudly :

'Atlanteans!'

Ason sprang to the ladder and slid down it, two rungs at a time, turning to face them. They had been running hard in the heat and were all gasping for breath; the Albi had fallen to the ground as soon as they stopped.

'We found him this morning,' the warrior said. 'Out on the plain. Stumbling along, coming this way. All he would say is your name and told us that the Atlanteans were on the way.'

'I wish they would,' Ason said. 'We have lost enough good men trying to get over their wall. Bring that water over and we will find out what is happening.' The Atlanteans could not threaten him, Ason knew that, yet he still had a hard knot of worry in his middle. Something must have happened to send Turi running all this way.

The exhausted Albi gulped at the water, drinking half, then raised the bowl with shaking fingers and poured the rest of it over his head.

'The Atlanteans march in this ... direction,' he finally gasped out. 'Coming over the wolds, being led.'

'We will welcome them,' Ason said.

'No ... more ... more landed. They marched at once.'

The hard knot was now a weight of stone. Ason shook the man so hard his head bobbed back and forth.

'More of them—how many more? Do you mean more ships? How many ships?'

'This many,' Turi said, holding up the fingers of one hand and two fingers of the other.

Seven ships. Ason released him and he sank back to the ground. Seven ships. How many men in each? All of them armed, armoured, fighting-men of the sea king. Themis had commanded. That is why he had sent away the captured Mycenaean ship with such a small crew. That had been reported to him: he had paid no attention. To send back the tin, yes, but even more important to send for men. Ason was suddenly aware of his silence and that the warriors were watching him.

'You,' he commanded the nearest, 'go to the place where we get the stones and tell the bull-chief Ar Apa and the bull-chief Moweg that I wish to see them at once.'

The man left at once, passing the bondsmen and warriors who were hurrying up, aware that something was happening. Ason looked at them all and came to a quick decision. He called two of the warriors to him.

'Comn, you are a tracker of game and of men. Korm, I have heard that you could run a deer into the ground if you wished.' He raised his hand to silence the instant boasts that sprang to their lips.

'Here is what you must do. I have been told that the Atlanteans are on the way here, more Atlanteans than you have ever seen before. They seek to attack us by surprise but that is a game that two can play at. It is said that they come from the mine over the wolds. Do you know that track?'

Both men did and he questioned them about it until he knew what sort of a track it was.

'They cannot march too fast, not with that many men or

225

through that kind of country. So here is what you two must do. You must take a skin of water and some meat and leave and go down the track as silent as a hunting fox. You must not be seen. You must find the Atlanteans and stay with them until they make camp for the night. When they do this Comn must stay and watch them and Korm must return here to tell us where they are. We will march against them. Do you understand?'

When they had each repeated the instructions he dismissed them and they left at a run. Ar Apa and Moweg appeared, pushing through the excited crowd. Inteb had finished with the stone and had descended from the wood and was as curious as everyone else. There were no secrets here; all actions of the teuta and the warriors were decided in public.

'What of the Atlanteans?' Ar Apa called out.

'They come in force,' Ason answered. 'Ships have brought more men and they are on their way to attack us here, in our dun.'

There were cries of outrage at this and bloodthirsty boasts of what would happen to those who dared such a thing. Ason let them speak their wrath before he called for attention again.

'They have come a long way to die,' he said and there were shouts of agreement which faded quickly so they could listen as the bull-chiefs talked. 'They come through the wold and the going will be heavy. There is very little chance that they will be here before dark, so they will have to stop somewhere for the night. I have sent men to find the place where they stop. We must send for all the warriors to follow us and we must march at once with the warriors who are here. We will find the place where they are camped and like the wolves we will attack by night. We are hunters of the forest, we are hunters of men, we are killers of men ...'

His words were drowned out by excited war-cries and the thud of axes against shields. The Yerni did not usually fight during the night, but they welcomed a battle at any time and shouted their enthusiasm.

The messengers were sent. Ason called to the bull-chiefs

226

and they went with him to his house and Inteb followed after, the only one who showed concern for the future. Naikeri was waiting for them and Ason ordered her to bring fresh ale, and meat and salt. They sat and Naikeri brought the trays with short legs to set before them so they dipped the meat into the salt and ate and passed the cup around and drank. Here, away from the crowd, Inteb was aware that Ason was as concerned about the future as he was.

'I am the one the Atlantean Themis wishes to kill,' Ason said. They nodded their heads in agreement; the battle and the escape and the ships made a good story that improved in the telling. They had heard it many times, never often enough. 'I will call him out and do battle with him before the warriors.'

'No,' Ar Apa said. 'He is now drag-leg the cripple and no longer a man. He will not fight. We must fight them all.'

'It is my battle.'

'It is our battle,' Moweg shouted angrily. 'They come to our lands, they attack our duns, they seek the death of a bull-chief. Our battle.' He bit savagely on the meat, his teeth crunching through the gristle. Ar Apa nodded agreement. So it was done.

'How many ships?' Inteb asked.

'Turi said there were seven.'

'That is very bad.'

'That is the way it is.'

'Must you fight them now?' Inteb said.

Ason was surprised. 'Of course. What else is there to do?'

'Many things,' Naikeri cried and stepped back when Ason waved her to silence with a chop of his hand. 'They cannot find you on this island if you do not wish to be found. What madness is it to go to them and seek death—'

'Be quiet, woman.'

'—because death is all you will find. Other things are possible.'

'This is the way it will be done.'

The Yerni bull-chiefs chewed their meat and looked out of

227

the doorway; women are not permitted to talk at such times. Naikeri called out to Inteb.

'Help me, Egyptian. No, do not help me, you will do nothing for that reason. But help Ason. You know nothing but twisted secret ways. Find another way to fight the Atlanteans. You can.'

Inteb nodded reluctantly and turned to Ason.

'I know that women are of little importance to the Yerni, or to the men of the Argolid for that matter. But in Egypt we are aware that through women different voices talk, and we listen. A way can be found to fight the Atlanteans other than by headlong combat.'

'We surprise them at night and kill them,' Ar Apa said.

'If that could happen we could hope for no better result. But can you be sure? If all are not killed and they are as strong and as numerous as we think, they will still come on in the morning ...'

'This time I cannot use your counsel,' Ason said. 'This is a time for battle.' The bull-chiefs nodded their heads in solemn agreement.

'Kill!' Naikeri screeched, and hurled the pouring vessel to the floor where it broke and splattered ale in all directions. In the other room the baby complained lustily and began to cry. 'Kill. Do you know anything but killing? Is that all you can do? We of the Albi live without your wars and killing, and find that life can hold other things. Swords, axes, killing—is that all the world contains?'

Ason was insulted by her words and actions, and turned his back; the bull-chiefs all found the open door worth examining. Inteb spoke for them, angry himself now.

'It contains more—but if that were all it contained it would be enough. Mankind has a nobility that the lowest animals can never obtain, and in the life of the warrior and in battle it reaches its highest point. That is something that you, a *woman*—' he spoke the word like a curse— 'will never understand.'

'There is nothing to understand. It is a madness like the stags in the spring who fight and lock their horns and die

228

fighting. Lock your horns and die—I don't want to understand. Die—'

Ason sprang to his feet and seized her and dragged her from the room and pushed her through the door and sealed it shut behind her. Her words were like a curse, and there was a bleakness now that pressed against him.

'You are a warrior, Ason,' Inteb said quietly. 'The man of battles stands highest in the ranks of man, and you stand highest of them all. Hundreds come running to follow where you lead. Where will that be?'

Ason touched his hand to the pommel of his sword.

'To battle of course. If we must die we will die as heroes and men.'

30

From the top of the embankment around the dun the figures could be seen coming across the plain while they were still far away, dark blurs on the horizon. The sky was low and solid with clouds, and from time to time lightning would flicker, followed by the deep rumble of distant thunder. Rain would be a relief—it was so hot and close—but it did not come.

As they came nearer, the dark shapes separated into groups of men making their way towards the dun. Warriors, all of them. Some with trophies, some with wounds, all of them tired. The first of them dropped into the shade of the buildings outside the embankment and called loudly for ale.

'What a battle,' one of them found the energy to shout.

'Killed a hundred, took a hundred heads,' another said, although his only prize seemed to be a bloodstained dagger shoved into his hair-belt.

There was much boasting and swaggering, for that is the Yerni way, and Inteb ignored it all until Ason and the other bull-chiefs finally appeared, coming in with the last of the men. They went to the centre of the ring of stone to the great stone henges, and each sat before his own, gaining strength from it.

'Neither a victory nor a defeat,' Ason said, licking the golden drops of ale from his lips.

'A victory,' Ar Apa insisted. Inteb sat next to Ason and passed him the ale beaker.

Ason shook his head. 'A victory is when the enemy dies or flees the field. We killed many—but even more still live and will follow us.'

'If we had had more men,' Finmog said darkly. Ason agreed.

'If all the warriors had been there the outcome might have been different. But many have not arrived yet. We attacked at night and we surprised the Atlanteans, that much we can agree on. But the attack was confused in the darkness and they soon fought back well. Our warriors lost their way in the dark, or stopped for loot or heads, so the attack lost its momentum. We withdrew. The enemy still comes on. We must not deny these facts.'

'It was a good battle, hundreds died,' Ar Apa grumbled and the others nodded.

'The next battle is the one that will be the important one,' Ason said, and they had to agree although they did not like to do so. 'It will be fought here, in this great dun of the Yerni, and many will die.'

'More warriors are on the way from our duns,' Ar Apa said. 'They will be angry that they missed last night's battle and will fight all the harder. We will all fight the harder for the great dun of the Yerni.'

They were in complete agreement about that, and it seemed to settle any differences of opinion. Most of them were asleep within a few minutes, as were the other warriors who had fought the previous night, and Ason's head was nodding too. Inteb put his arm about Ason's grimy shoulders and smelt the acrid sweat and fatigue.

'Will we win?' he asked.

Ason looked about at the four bull-chiefs and lowered his voice.

'There can be no thought of winning. We must kill as many as we can to avenge the slaughter. And to help Mycenae. You must leave now, my Egyptian. Turi will take you to the Albi and you will be safe.'

'Will you come with me?'

'I cannot.'

231

'Then neither can I,' Inteb said and held his hands tightly to his knees so that their shaking could not be seen. 'We have come this far together and I cannot leave you now. I can use a sword.'

'Not very well.'

'You speak the truth, Ason—even when it is hurtful. Not very well, but it will still be a sword. And I will be fighting beside you. We have journeyed a long way to reach this place and I do not wish to leave it without you.'

'Nor I without you, Egyptian,' he said, and embraced him and lay back to sleep. Inteb left to get his armour and weapons, and met Aias at his door.

'I see you have armed yourself for battle, slave. Shouldn't you be fleeing?'

'I'll flee as far as you do—what is that sword doing in your hand?'

Inteb looked at it ruefully and shook it so it shimmered even in the dim light. 'I wish I knew. My work should be for my Pharaoh, erecting great temples to his glory. So what am I doing here putting on armour to battle in this far-away place?'

'You follow a man, Inteb, the same one I do. Perhaps you have paid a higher price. Mine was no price at all. I was a slave. Now I am a free man with honour. I can even talk to Egyptian nobles.'

'Killing you will soon end that. You are a strange slave, Aias, with hard death in your fists. I reluctantly admit— though I will deny it if anyone asks—that it has been good to know you too.'

After this there was very little to say, so they went to stand on the embankment and watched the warriors coming across the plain, fewer and fewer now as the last stragglers and the men from the distant duns arrived. The afternoon was well advanced and the thunder still growled on the horizon when the solid mass of the attackers appeared. Their warhorns could be heard, distant and small but soon to grow louder; Inteb and Aias went down to the stone henges where the warriors grouped around the bull-chiefs.

232

Ason stood before his henge and a silence fell.

'They are coming. We will stop them here. There are no city walls to fight behind but there is the embankment of the dun. We will be on the top of the embankment and they must come up to us and our axes will be ready. Ar Apa, take the men of your teuta and seize all the logs and pile them into the embankment entrances so it will not be easy to enter that way. The rest of you—come with me.'

Ason shouted the last words and the warriors echoed his cry.

'*Ason abu—abu!*'

They streamed to the embankment, to the top, and looked out at the marching ranks of the men of Atlantis. They came on in three columns, and the greatest warriors were at the head of the columns. Gold and precious gems decorated the bright sheen of their armour, and the Yerni pointed to this and swore oaths that they would be wearing all of it before nightfall.

Thunder still rumbled, closer now, and a thin rain began to fall. The Yerni welcomed this, turning their faces up to let it run into their mouths. Now the chalk of the embankment would be slippery and that much harder to climb. The Atlanteans came on, straight for the dun, calling out to one another and pointing to the waiting men and the great stones rising up behind them. They were almost to the embankment, dark, hard men in solid bronze with swords in their hands, when it happened.

Light burst and blinded them, and an instant later the roar of noise beat at their ears.

Men cried aloud and looked, their eyes still burning with the tracery of lightning that had seared down from the sky to lick at Ason's henge. It had struck full upon it—but had not harmed that solid stone. Steam rose where rain had been before, and a cow which had been close to it lay gutted and dead at its base.

'An omen,' Ason shouted above the roar of the rain. 'An omen! Lightning itself cannot harm the henge of the Yerni.'

The warriors stirred themselves now and beat their axes

against their shields. It was a good omen; nothing could harm them. They shouted and threatened, and when the Atlanteans reached the foot of the embankment they took the throwing-stones from their places in the back of their shields and hurled them down upon the attackers. Men fell in the deep ditch, bringing others down who tripped over them, and then—shouting war-cries and with the horns bellowing behind them—the Atlanteans charged to the attack up the high bank.

On the top of the embankment the solid ranks of Yerni stood as a barricade against the advance of the bronze-armoured warriors. There was a sound almost as loud as the thunder when the two hosts met and weapons crashed on shields. And so the slaughter began.

In the rain, slipping and falling in the white chalk mud, the desperate engagement went on. For a short while the embankment was held, not so much by force of arms but because the Atlanteans could not both climb and fight at the same time. But the uneven ranks of the defenders were soon breached and once this had happened the armoured horde poured over this barrier and into the dun. The fighting broke into individual engagements, while in the centre the bulk of fighting warriors retreated step by step through the rings of stones, fighting all the way, dying as they retreated, back to the great stone arches of the henges where the final desperate battle was fought.

Inteb was there, not through any strength of arm but because of the lack of it. He stayed near Ason and there were always others, stronger, who pushed past him to do battle. In this milling, screaming, dying mob he was perhaps the only observer.

He saw the litter being brought up, surrounded by rows of guards, and guessed that this must be Themis, crippled and carried to battle. Aias must have seen it too and recognized his one-time master and boxing student. Swinging his great hammer, he ploughed through the ranks of the Atlanteans, not trying to kill them but only to drive them aside,

234

until he reached within a few paces of the chair, shouting above the clatter of arms.

'Come out, Themis, you cowardly boxer. I could beat you any time I wanted to though I never let you know. Come out so I can do it now!'

Themis simply made a chopping motion with his hand; a slave is a slave. The Atlanteans closed in and, although some fell, at least one with a skull broken by a fist, they did their work quickly and efficiently. Aias went down as their swords plunged home, one fist rising up for an instant as they went about their butcher's work, then this dropped as well.

There were few defenders left among the stones, and Inteb now had his chance to fight. He stabbed through at the attacking men and felt his sword sink home more than once. Then the circle of Yerni warriors was broken and Inteb stood alone. His first sword stroke was easily parried by a massive Atlantean with black beard and blood-soaked armour, who struck out in return, driving the sword from Inteb's arm and cutting into his flesh at the same time. He pushed Inteb down with his shield, chopped at his body and legs as he fell, then trampled over him as he rushed towards Ason.

Ason. The Atlanteans pushed and almost fought one another to get at him. Inteb tasted salt blood in his mouth, clutched at the other gaping red mouth of the wound in his leg, and looked up through the falling rain at the men at bay.

His back to the stone, Ason hacked at them, his sword never stopping, slashing across an arm, darting under a shield to find flesh. Fighting, fighting. And losing against their numbers.

Their swords went up and came down and he vanished from sight beneath them.

Envoi

The small, dark-skinned man came first, the brown of his clothing the same brown as the tree-trunks of the forest they had just passed through. A bronze-armoured warrior walked at his side, a man no longer young but still upright, and bearing easily the weight of his horse-tail plumed helm, the richly decorated breastplate and greaves, the long sword in his hand. Behind them more and more armoured warriors emerged from the forest in loose formation, coming on steadily despite the burden of their armour and packs, calling out to one another and singing songs. The column emerged like a writhing golden snake and wound across the plain, more than a hundred men.

When the sun was at its highest they stopped to eat and drink, then moved on again after only the shortest rest. By mid-afternoon the brown man who was guiding them pointed to a mound on the plain ahead. There was the smoke of cooking-fires rising from it and the grey forms of immense stones at the centre. The march continued, with the men shouting to one another about the strange sight in this empty plain, until the mound was seen to be a ring-shaped embankment and they went towards the opening that had been cut through it, crowding through this entrance.

Rough huts and small wooden buildings had been built against the inner wall of the embankment and people were in the doorways, looking out with frightened eyes. Some men appeared with stone axes but drew back farther and farther as more armoured warriors appeared. Their leader ordered them to halt and went on alone to the ring of capped stones, with the even greater stone archways in the centre. There were five of these, massive and brooding, and he felt dwarfed when he stood before them, looking up at their height.

'You will see nothing like them in the rest of the world,' a voice said and he turned quickly, his sword ready.

A raggedly dressed man, as small and dark as his guide, hobbled towards him and he let his sword fall. There was an old scar on the man's face that pulled at his cheek and an even deeper one on his leg that forced him to walk painfully.

'You are not of Atlantis,' the man said, his clear voice and good diction out of place in his tattered form. 'Tell me who you are and why you come here, if you please.'

'I am Phoros of Mycenae. These men are Mycenaeans for the most part, though some are from Asine and Tiryns and other cities of the Argolid.'

'Then I bid you welcome, warm welcome. I thought your face familiar. We met once. I am Inteb the Egyptian.'

'The builder?' Phoros looked closely and shook his head. 'You resemble him in some ways. Yet, still ...'

'Still many years have passed and many strange events have overtaken me. Shall we sit? My leg is not good for much. Over here, on that long stone in the ground. It was called the speaking-stone once and we can speak there. Speak, yes, we shall.'

Phoros shook his head again as he followed Inteb's limping progress. The way the Egyptian talked his senses seemed as scarred as his body. They sat and looked up at the stones that rose above them.

'I did this,' Inteb said, and there was more strength in his voice when he did. 'I raised these stones for Ason. This place is Dun Ason of the Yerni.'

'Where is Ason? We come seeking him. There was trade with a tribe to the north of the Argolid, the Geramani, who carried messages from him to King Perimedes.'

'You are too late.'

'There have been wars, travel is not easy.'

240

'There are always wars, it is what men seem to do best. There was a war here, with the Atlanteans. I fought in it; these are noble wounds you see here. It was a great battle even though we lost.'

'Ason was killed?'

'No, captured, though he killed many before they took him. I saw him carried away, wounded and unconscious. I heard later that he was still alive when the Atlanteans left and he was taken in their ship. He is surely dead by now.'

'When did this happen?' Phoros asked, speaking softly so that his excitement would not be seen.

'When? I have lost track of the months.' He looked around him. 'This must be the dry month of Payni, by Egyptian reckoning. It would then be thirteen months, perhaps, since it happened, in the month of Epiphi.'

Phoros rose to his feet and paced back and forth excitedly.

'We hoped to find him alive, but I think that even Perimedes understood he must be dead. We knew the Atlanteans had come here in force, that is why I came with seven ships. But they are gone now; just a few left at the mine, now dead. And Ason went back with the others, to Atlantis.'

'Where else would Atlantean ships go?' Inteb said testily, rubbing at his leg.

'Where indeed. And with good sailing they could have reached Atlantis in time. My cousin Ason is dead, but he died nobly. He died knowing that Atlantis would die as well.'

'You are talking in riddles and I am very tired.'

'Then listen, Egyptian. You knew him—'

'I loved him.'

'Then know how he died. The world has changed. There was a day of fire and the sun turned red and black and the earth shook and in Mycenae ashes fell from the sky. Here is what we discovered when we went down to the ocean. The water rose up and washed into the sea all those cities on the shore, waves such as no man had seen before, destroying cities as far away as Troy. Every ship at sea sunk, every coast ravaged. We built new ships and armed them and sailed to Crete. Thera, their holy home is no more. Their coast

241

is wiped out and their ships sunk. Mycenae now rules in Atlantis and in the Argolid, mighty Mycenae on her rock far from the sea has descended and now rules them all.'

'I do not see.'

'Don't you? Don't you see Ason taken to Atlantis and dying there with all of his enemies and knowing that their death would mean life for Mycenae? He would know victory.'

'He is dead. It matters not how he died. He left this, these henges of stone, and they will live after him and be his memory. Men will see them and know that something great happened here. You will return to Mycenae?'

'Yes, soon. Perimedes must be told.'

'Will you take me? I think I have served Mycenae well. And I wish to see green Egypt again. I will pay for my passage with something worth more than treasure to Perimedes. His grandson.'

'Is this true? Ason married?'

Inteb grinned crookedly. 'Married by local custom, to a princess of her people. She and I both loved Ason, and in the end learned not to hate one another. She kept me alive. Ason's seed already lived in her but I could not return the life she gave to me. She is dead along with the daughter who would also have been Ason's. But his son lives. There, behind the stone and watching us, bolder than the Yerni children.' He raised his voice and called out.

'Atreus. Come meet your kinsman.'

The boy came forward slowly; if he was afraid he did not show it. Already wide-shouldered and strong like his father, with his same steady gaze.

'I have taught him the Mycenaean tongue,' Inteb said. 'In case this day should ever come.'

His thoughts wandered then, and so did his attention. He would be leaving here soon and although Egypt pulled him with golden memories he knew that part of himself would always remain in this place. These great stones were Ason's and if any part of Ason lived on it was here. He limped slowly among them, touching their cool surfaces with his fingertips, hearing dimly the war-cries of the Yerni warriors, the crash of weapons on shields.

It was all over. He must leave. His dragging footsteps brought him to the single stone where he had laboured so long. What magnificent hard stone this was—his hand went out to the face of the column. With his own hands he had done this. With stone mauls, swung until his fingers bled, and with a broken bronze sword for a chisel, and sand, hammered until the metal was worn away. But the harder the stone the longer the inscription would remain.

'Ason,' Inteb said. This was the stone before which he had fallen.

He moved his fingers to trace the dagger he had so painfully incised and abraded in the stone. The square hilted, diamond-bladed dagger of Mycenae. The royal dagger that was Ason's due.

The royal dagger of Mycenae.

Filled then with fatigue Inteb turned and limped away, a small figure among the great ones of the stones. Turned his back and walked away from them a final time. Left them behind, and Dun Ason, and the Island of the Yerni. Left behind the Yerni, dispersed and slaughtered, their power broken. Darkness fell then, and lasted a long, long time.

AFTERWORD

The first great political and military event to colour Western history is the Fall of Troy, a not very important event.

Far more important is the fall of Atlantis, which heralded the breakthrough of the Mycenaeans into the eastern Mediterranean. Troy, the end of the story, is remembered in Homer, but the poets who sang of its beginnings are not.

Thus has the irony of time raised Troy into brightness and kept Atlantis in the dark, to be dimly remembered through Plato and only recently verified by archaeology.

Plato describes Atlantis as a kingdom of two islands. One. round, has circular harbours at the centre which are reached by a canal across its radius. The description fits the remains of Thera, an exploded volcanic island seventy-five miles north of Crete, the other island.

Plato got his story from Solon who in turn got it from Egyptian priests. The priests said that Atlantis was destroyed 9,000 years previously, at some time near the end of the Ice Age, when man everywhere was a hunter and a gatherer of wild food. No civilization existed then, no Egypt and no priests. Atlantis is a Bronze Age civilization, with sailing ships and commerce, metallurgy and court artisans, stately palace buildings and great temples. Solon must have transcribed thousands for hundreds, an easy mistake in reading Egyptian numerals. The priests meant 900 years before Solon's time. This is more like it, and would place the event near 1470 B.C., the estimated year of Thera's eruption.

Our novel begins three years before.

The Egyptians had good reason to record the destruction of Atlantis; apparently they were shaken by it. For the Mycenaeans, it meant the opportunity to occupy and rebuild Knossos in an eastward thrust that eventually carried them all the way to Troy.

The Mycenaean-Atlantean civilization is a variant of the same Bronze Age order derived from its original in Mesopotamia and Egypt.

The wheel and the sail, writing and smelting, were inventions which made for a more complex reorganization of the preceding Neolithic way of life. The Neolithic order, in turn, was founded on plant and animal domestication, permanently settled village life, and the basic crafts of carpentry, ceramics, and weaving.

The Bronze Age introduced a new community type, the city, that lived off the produce of the surrounding Neolithic villagers and housed the quarters of royalty and its attached craftsmen. Kingly establishments work as centres that take in all valuable commodities and then redistribute them, after keeping a share, to important people by way of winning them as clients. In the original centres of civilization the intake came from peaceful trade and commerce; in the derivative areas, by war and piracy.

The areas covered by the original Bronze Age civilizations were small—a narrow strip along the Nile and another along the Tigris-Euphrates. But the search for copper and tin, both necessary for bronze-making, carried traders, prospectors and adventurers far from home to acquire metal for carpenters, sculptors, jewellers and soldiers. This quest brought news of power and wealth to the surrounding Neolithic world.

Among the first Neolithic peoples to be impacted were those of the Mycenaean-Atlantean area. The effect here was to create a barbaric version of civilization, an imitation based on piracy and city-sacking. Indeed, Mycenaeans were rather more barbaric in this respect than their Atlantean neighbours, who had the advantage of an island retreat in which to cultivate refinements.

Least refined of all the Europeans were those located north of the Alps. The distant influence of civilization so militarized these barbarians that Julius Caesar in his time described them as 'madly fond of war, high spirited and quick to battle'. These were the Celts of Gaul, essentially the same barbarians of Celtic Britain who built Stonehenge.

Stonehenge was built in 1470 B.C., by our reckoning. It was built by the same kind of Celtic war-lovers described by Caesar about 1,400 years later, some fifty years before Christ. In prehistoric times, things changed slowly on the non-literate fringes of civilization.

During the mid-third millennium B.C., a copper-working population crept up the Atlantic coast of Europe to the British Isles, as colonists and prospectors traded metal back to their homeland somewhere in the Mycenaean area. Their tombs, huge upended boulders capped with massive slabs of undressed stone, are the only mark of their passing.

The island on which Ason is wrecked is covered with such tombs. Known as the Scilly Islands, it is today not one island but several, now that the sea level is higher. The tomb-builders are the Albi of our novel, who lived in what is now Cornwall and Devon. The copper lodes of south-west Britain often occur in tin-streams, so that Uncle Lycos, in search of tin for Mycenae, had only to look for operating copper mines among the Albi.

The tomb-builders, the immediate heirs of Mediterranean civilization, made their *own* impact on the Neolithic peoples of Europe. Within the Iberian peninsula the result was the emergence of barbarians known as the Bell Beaker folk, who, as warriors, lashed back and destroyed the fortified towns that had called them into being. The Beaker folk were archers and degenerate metallurgists who quickly spread throughout northern and eastern Europe, seeking domination over the Neolithic peasantries as a kind of primitive warrior aristocracy. They moved on to the high downs of Salisbury Plain,

246

dominated the Neolithic farmers, and provided the first customers for the gold- and bronze-working metallurgists of Ireland, where a population of tomb-builders even more advanced than the Albi had settled. The native population of food-gatherers, the Hunters, probably acted as intermediaries, given their mobility and their knowledge of trails and local trade routes. The bluestones derive from Mt Prescelly, from which the Irish bronze-workers could be seen pushing off for Britain; and their erection at Stonehenge may in some way indicate Beaker emancipation from dependence on the Hunters as middlemen.

However, the Beaker folk did indeed build the double ring of bluestones on the Stonehenge site, erecting them within a circular ditch and bank laid down by the previous Neolithic inhabitants for reasons of their own.

Meanwhile, another folk movement of the third millennium emerged from southern Russia. These Neolithic peoples had been impacted by the existence of a civilization to the south, the Mesopotamian, which they nearly destroyed in the process of becoming a nomadic, copper-using, warlike pastoral people whose chosen weapon was the stone battle-axe. This stone battle-axe was modelled after a Sumerian bronze prototype. After a long journey of migration and conquest, they arrived in Britain—still attached to the old stone axe modelled after the bronze original. They were also still attached to the concept of civilization itself. Civilization—*civitas*—city. The multitudinous doors of the Yerni dun copy the city walls from some distant urban place—where great armies guard the walls, where law-codes are chiselled in stone stelai, where the markets and bazaars attract international trade. For there is nothing more imposing about the city walls of civilized lands than their great entrance-ways. And at this distance, these entrance-ways become so magnified in Yerni eyes that a city to match them—a dun—is all gates and doors. How civilized the Yerni dun! How unlike the primitive hutments of the Donbaksho and the Albi!

The Battle-axe people first arrived in central and northern

Europe around 2500 B.C., displacing the Beaker folk as the dominant warrior aristocracy. They spoke an undivided conversational Indo-European tongue which soon differentiated into Greek, Sanskrit, Celtic and a hundred others, as they moved outward from the Ukraine. They are the common ancestors of the Mycenaean Greeks and the Celtic warriors who built Stonehenge.

In archaeological literature, the Yerni are the Wessex warriors, the Battle-axe people who displaced the Beaker folk as the dominant warrior aristocracy on Salisbury Plain in about 1800 B.C. The Donbaksho are the defeated Beakers who have been assimilated to the local Neolithic farmers. The Wessex warriors enlarged the trading relationships opened up by the Beakers; thus on Salisbury Plain Irish gold and bronze from the north was exchanged for salt, bronze and Baltic amber from the continent.

Some time before the Wessex invasion, the Celts first emerged as a distinctive branch of the Indo-European peoples, an ethnically identifiable people on the margins of civilization. Descriptions of Celtic life and custom recur in Greek authors such as Atheneaus the writer of miscellanies, Strabo the geographer, and Diodorus Siculus the historian. However, most of the picture drawn by these men derives ultimately from the Greek historian and ethnographer Posidonius, who died in 51 B.C., the time of Caesar's commentaries.

The final phase of Stonehenge, the horseshoe stand of five trilithons and the uncompleted sarsen ring, is dated some 1,400 years earlier, 1470 B.C. This date is fixed by a dagger carving on the inner face of stone No. 53, a type of dagger that also occurs in the Shaft Graves of Mycenae. Indeed, while this carving points to the unique historical event that involved Mycenae in the building of Stonehenge, it does not change the fact that this unique event had to be set within the bounds of Celtic life and culture.

In the novel, that unique event is Inteb carving Ason's signature.

And Celtic culture at that time must have been very much as the Greek and Roman authors described it.

The last surviving stronghold of Celtic culture was that found by St Patrick in fifth century Ireland, a belated Indo-European culture of the Homeric and Rig-Veda type, complete with chariot-riding, cattle-lifting, war-making and loud-boasting heroes whose chief virtues were courage and violence, and with an oral literature that praised such doings. Christian monks recorded this literature, including the *Táin bó Cúalnge*, the finest and most Homeric of all the Irish Sagas.

In fact, Posidonius describes an event that is picked up a thousand years later in the Irish tale *Mac da Tho's Pig*. Posidonius writes:

The Celts sometimes engage in single combat at dinner. Assembling in arms, they engage in mock battle-drill, and mutual thrust-and-parry, but sometimes wounds are inflicted, and the irritation caused by this may even lead to the slaying of the opponent unless the bystanders hold them back. And in former times, when the hindquarters were served up the bravest hero took the thigh piece, and if another man claimed it they stood up and fought in single combat to the death [Tierney, p. 247].

In *Mac da Tho's Pig*, one warrior after another claims the right to carve the pig at a feast, and each man in turn yields to a rival after a long dialogue of boasting and abuse. Finally, the Connacht champion, Cet mac Matach, is about to carve the pig after having put several Ulstermen to shame. Then Conall Cernach enters the hall.

While he made ready with the pig and had his knife in his hand, they saw Conall the Victorious coming towards them into the house. And he sprang on to the floor of the house. The men of Ulster gave great welcome to Conall the Victorious at that time. It was then Conchobar threw his helmet from his head and shook himself in his own place. 'We are pleased,' said Conall, 'that our portion is in readiness for us. Who carves for you?' said Conall.

249

'One man of the men of Ireland has obtained by contest the carving of it, Cet mac Matach.'

'Is that true, O Cet?' said Conall. 'Art thou carving the pig?'

'It is true indeed,' said Cet....

'Get up from the pig, O Cet!' said Conall.

'What brings thee to it?' said Cet.

'It is true,' said Conall, 'I will be the challenger. I will give you competition,' said Conall, 'for I swear what my people swear, since I first took spear and weapons, I have never been a day without having slain a Connachtman, or a night without plundering, nor have I ever slept without the head of a Connachtman under my knee.'

'It is true,' said Cet, 'thou art even a better warrior than I; but if Anluan mac Matach (my brother) were in the house, he would match thee contest for contest, and it is a shame that he is not in the house to-night.'

'But he *is*,' said Conall, taking Anluan's head out of his belt and throwing it at Cet's chest, so that a gush of blood broke over his lips. After that Conall sat down by the pig, and Cet went from it [Cross and Slover, pp. 205-6].

The Irish sagas look back perhaps as far as the fourth century B.C. But the Iron Age Ireland of that time was situated on the extreme margin of the fundamental developments. These included not only iron as a cheap metal for swords, but also the riding of horses, the alphabet, money, craftsmen organized in guilds, and large-scale political organization tied together with a system of posts, as in the Persian and Roman empires. Both Conall and Cuchulain use iron swords and references to the ogham system of writing occur. But the heroes ride chariots, not horses, chariots that could have been Bronze Age weapons described by Homer for Mycenaean times. There is no empire, only small kingdoms. And craftsmen still work under the patronage of kings. Take away iron swords and the Irish tales could describe a Bronze Age kingdom. Take away chariots and kings, and what's left is barbarian Europe on the margins of Bronze Age civilization, the very position of Celtic Britain at the time Stonehenge was built.

Behind Homer and the Irish tales lies the same barbarian's militarized response to civilization.

Thus, Homer's Greece is an unlikely place for an astronomical observatory, and so is Celtic Britain.

Gerald Hawkins claims that Stonehenge was designed to compute eclipses and that Salisbury Plain is the right latitude for this. Yet not even the Babylonians, the most advanced astronomers of the time, had perfected eclipse prediction by 1470 B.C. If this be the case, what can we make of Hawkins' theory?

While we cannot doubt that Stonehenge was built with civilized guidance, stone-work with lintels does not exist anywhere in barbarian Europe. Yet Edward H. Stone—whose book is often cited but seldom read—maintains that the work of shaping the sarsen boulders was not as onerous and time-consuming as commonly assumed. He claims, as a result of petrological analysis, that the sarsen stones come from Salisbury Plain itself, not from Marlborough Downs, twenty miles to the north. The method of knocking out the uprights, observed by Stone in Hyderabad, is that used by Inteb. Sarsen boulders are split into ready-made slabs at a single stroke. And if the master-builder never completed Stonehenge, it remains, 3,500 years later, unique among the monuments of barbarian Europe.

William P. Austin, Head of the Section of Linguistics & Anthropology at Illinois Institute of Technology, died on 24 September 1971. Under the sheltering protection of his interest in this novel, not to mention his helpful suggestions and his critical reading of the final manuscript, I was able to work on it over the years without losing too many points from an academic establishment that normally expects a man to speak for truth in the form of fact, not fiction.

LEON STOVER

SELECTED READINGS

General Anthropology

Coon, Carleton S., THE STORY OF MAN, 3rd edition, New York (Alfred A. Knopf) 1969

Prehistory

Clarke, Grahme, WORLD PREHISTORY: A NEW OUTLINE, Cambridge (Cambridge University Press) 1969

Daniel, Glyn, THE MEGALITH BUILDERS OF WESTERN EUROPE, London (Penguin Books) 1962

Hawkes, Christopher and Jacquetta, PREHISTORIC BRITAIN, London (Penguin Books) 1943

Piggott, Stuart, ANCIENT EUROPE, Edinburgh (Edinburgh University Press) 1965

Powell, T. G. E., PREHISTORIC ART, London (Thames & Hudson) 1966

Atlantis

Galanopolis, A. G. and Bacon, Edward, ATLANTIS, London (Nelson) 1969

Hutchinson, R. W., PREHISTORIC CRETE, London (Penguin Books) 1962

Luce, J. V., THE END OF ATLANTIS, London (Thames & Hudson) 1969

252

Mavor, James W., Jr., VOYAGE TO ATLANTIS, London (Souvenir Press) 1969

Mycenae

McDonald, William A. PROGRESS INTO THE PAST: THE RE-DISCOVERY OF MYCENAEAN CIVILIZATION, London (Macmillan) 1967
Mylonas, George E., MYCENAE AND THE MYCENAEAN AGE, Princeton, New Jersey (Princeton University Press) 1966
Taylour, Lord William, THE MYCENAEANS, London (Thames & Hudson) 1964
Wace, A. J. B., and Stubbings, F. H., A COMPANION TO HOMER, London (Macmillan) 1962

Celts

Dillon, Myles, and Chadwick, Nora, THE CELTIC REALMS, London (Weidenfeld & Nicolson) 1967
Hencken, Hugh, INDO-EUROPEAN LANGUAGES AND ARCHAE-OLOGY, Memoir 34, American Anthropological Association, 1955
Kendrick, T. D., THE DRUIDS: A STUDY IN KELTIC PREHIS-TORY, London (Methuen) 1927
Tierney, J. J., THE CELTIC ETHNOLOGY OF POSIDONIUS, Proceedings of the Royal Irish Academy, vol. 60, no. 5, 1960, pp. 189-275

Irish Sagas

Cross, Tom Peete, and Slover, Clarke Harris (eds.), ANCIENT IRISH TALES, New York (Henry Holt) 1936
Jackson, Kenneth Hurlstone, THE OLDEST IRISH TRADITION: A WINDOW ON THE IRON AGE, Cambridge (Cambridge University Press) 1964

Joyce, P. W., A SOCIAL HISTORY OF ANCIENT IRELAND, 2 vols. London (Benjamin Blom) 1913

Kinsella, Thomas, THE TAIN, Oxford (Oxford University Press) 1970

O'Rahilly, Cecile (ed.), TÁIN BÓ CÚALNGE, Dublin Institute for Advanced Studies, 1967

Southwest Britain

Fox, Aileen, SOUTH WEST ENGLAND, London (Thames & Hudson) 1964

Hencken, Hugh, THE ARCHAEOLOGY OF CORNWALL AND SCILLY, London (Methuen) 1932

Wessex

Grinsell, L. V., THE ARCHAEOLOGY OF WESSEX, London (Methuen) 1958

Piggott, Stuart, THE EARLY BRONZE AGE IN WESSEX, The Prehistoric Society, no. 3, 1938, pp. 52-106

Stone, J. F. S., WESSEX, London (Thames & Hudson) 1958

Stonehenge

Atkinson, R. J. C., STONEHENGE, London (Penguin Books) 1960

Crampton, Patrick, STONEHENGE OF THE KINGS, London (J. Baker) 1967

Hawkins, Gerald S., STONEHENGE DECODED, London (Souvenir Press) 1966; (Fontana) 1970

Newall, R. S., STONEHENGE, 3rd edition, Official Guidebook, 1959

Stone, Edward H., THE STONES OF STONEHENGE: A FULL DESCRIPTION, London (R. Scott) 1924